One Step From The Dark

S.L. Dieruf

DiamondD Publsihing

Dedicated to Michael A. Balasa, the best PFLAG dad ever, and to you, the reader, wherever you find yourself in the journey towards your authentic self.

Contents

Chapter 1 — 1

Chapter 2 — 8

Chapter 3 — 16

Chapter 4 — 24

Chapter 5 — 32

Chapter 6 — 39

Chapter 7 — 47

Chapter 8 — 53

Chapter 9 — 61

Chapter 10 — 66

Chapter 11 — 73

Chapter 12 — 80

Chapter 13 — 86

Chapter 14 — 94

Chapter 15 — 99

Chapter 16   106

Chapter 17   111

Chapter 18   118

Chapter 19   126

Chapter 20   134

Chapter 21   143

Chapter 22   151

Chapter 23   157

Chapter 24   163

Chapter 25   170

Chapter 26   176

Chapter 27   183

Chapter 28   190

Chapter 29   199

Chapter 30   208

Chapter 31   215

Chapter 32   223

Chapter 33   231

Chapter 34   238

Chapter 35   245

Chapter 36	252
Chapter 37	261
Chapter 38	269
Chapter 39	277
Chapter 40	285
Chapter 41	294
Chapter 42	301
Chapter 43	310
Chapter 44	318
Chapter 45	327
Chapter 46	336
Chapter 47	345
Chapter 48	356
Chapter 49: Epilogue	366
Afterword	374

CHAPTER 1

Ryan Ward gripped the steering wheel tighter and looked out ahead at the green BMW swerving outside the lanes. It was 2:30 AM on a rainy night with slick road conditions. Another damn DUI. He gave his partner Fritz a knowing look. This was the third one tonight as die-hard drinkers tried to return home from the bars to their Chicago suburbs.

Switching on the siren and lights, blue and red flashed through the window as he sped up to the vehicle. "Yeah, dispatch, we've got another live one," Fritz said in his deep southern drawl. His balding head was shaved, and he had a trim white beard. It was the only thing *trim* about him. His beer belly protruded from his tight uniform. Out of shape didn't even begin to cover it. And probably why Fritz was paired with a rookie. He belched and reached for his half-eaten burrito as Ryan navigated the car to the side of the road, following the BMW to a halt.

Ryan stepped out into the misty rain. He didn't mind the night shift. He didn't even mind the DUIs, which seemed to fall to him and Fritz. But he had been in the department for over a year, and the other rookies were moving up in the ranks. But not Ryan. He had asked his sergeant about it. The answer wasn't what he wanted to hear. "You're a loner, Ward. It wouldn't hurt to get together with the guys after work. Get to know them." Of course, going out with the guys meant Howard's strip club near the airport.

The BMW had tinted windows, and Ryan cautiously approached. He looked back at the car, and Fritz wasn't even paying attention anymore. He had gotten out the paper and was reading and eating. The window rolled down slowly, and the stench of stale alcohol and cigarettes was overpowering. A man in his sixties fumbled in his glove box before red-rimmed eyes looked up, his combover barely covering his bald head. "How much have you had to drink tonight, sir?" Ryan asked.

"Not much officer. Just a few." The man twisted his wedding ring as he avoided looking at Ryan.

Same thing night after night. Like clockwork. These sad men had been out all-night drinking. And in just a few months, Ryan had seen it all, from domestic disputes to rounding up drunks on the street to go to the shelter. "Driver's License, sir," Ryan said.

The man handed him his license, now resigned. The guy knew full well what would happen next. "I need you to step out of the vehicle." Ryan barely got out of the way in time as the man opened the door and threw up on the pavement, splattering a few special bits on Ryan's shoes. A couple of cars whizzed by, tossing up water. A dreary night. Another drunk. Would going to a strip club and throwing back some beers really help his career? Probably not. Getting close to anyone seemed like a trap to him. A chance to slip up and reveal too much. He couldn't take that chance. Not now.

After the breathalyzer, he turned imploringly to Ryan, his words slurred. "Please, I'm a vet," he burped. "Cut me a teeny, tiny break."

Ryan handed the man back his license. "You need to get some help, sir," Ryan said, motioning him to the police car. "What branch were you in?"

"Air Force. Nam."

Ryan nodded. "Army. Two tours. The last one didn't work out so well."

The older man wiped his mouth with his sleeve. "Shit, I messed up." He took a few staggering steps toward the road.

"I have to take you in." Ryan took him by the shoulder and guided him towards the police car. "Promise me you'll get some help."

The man nodded as he ducked down into the back of the police car. "I promise, officer. I'll get some help." Ryan closed the door, got back in the driver's seat, and sighed deeply. This was going to be a long night.

Fritz snorted as he folded up the Chicago Tribune. "Cavorting with the drunks now, Ward? Great, just great." He sipped his coffee from the paper cup.

Ryan ignored him as he started the engine. "You buckled in back there?" Ryan called over his shoulder. There was a muffled grunt from the back seat. Fritz looked at his watch. "Crap shift's only half over." He put his burrito into the glove compartment and wrinkled his nose as he sniffed. "Damn, this drunk's ripe."

Turning the car around, Ryan headed back for the station. He turned the windshield wipers on high and listened to the rhythmic churning as they moved back and forth. Back and forth. The night in Chicago melted away, and he was back with Jack.

The Afghanistan desert where sand caught into every nook and crevice of his body. The rainy night in the Hum-V with Jack. Windshield wipers were on full as the gully washer moved over them. Other than the rain pelting the windows, it had been nighttime and quiet. Dark clouds had been moving in all day. The convoy had just left the base, and it would be a long drive to deliver the supplies.

Jack, his sergeant, had been with him that day. His sergeant was a level-headed guy with a wicked sense of humor. There had been many pranks, and Ryan had inevitably been the butt of most of them. Including the morning he woke up with a mustache drawn on his face. The ink had been permanent. It had been one of those villain mustaches from the thirties, and Jack and the others laughed and laughed over breakfast. Jack had a dark complexion, big brown eyes, and a huge heart. He said he just wanted to get all his soldiers home safely.

And that night, as they left the base and the metal gate closed behind them, Jack didn't know that he would never see his wife and son again. They all knew it could happen.

Had prepared for it, but you can never prepare for something like that. It all happened so fast. One minute, Ryan was driving, and the next, a loud whistle came from overhead. It grew louder by the second, and Ryan slammed on the brakes.

The truck in front of them exploded in a blinding light, and a boom shook the ground and caused his ears to ring. He saw Jack shouting something, but it was like being underwater. Nothing made sense. Another high-pitched whine flew overhead, and he knew they had to abandon ship. Get the fuck out of there. Ryan unstrapped and motioned to the men in the back to get out.

Jack was already motioning him to get out of there. There were only seconds as Ryan opened the door and jumped out. Jack sprinted for him. A heartbeat later, the Humvee exploded. A piece of metal struck Ryan right in the chest. He couldn't breathe. All he remembered was Jack on top of him, blood everywhere. It was in his nose and eyes, tasting salty in his mouth. "Tell Jasmine and Bo," Jack said with one breath, "I love them." It was the last thing he remembered. The last thing before waking up in the infirmary, attached to an IV and chest tube, clinging to his life. Jack hadn't made it.

Ryan turned the windshield wipers down and took a deep breath. He gripped the steering wheel of the police car and glanced back at their passenger, who had passed out. Ahead were a few people leaving a dance club, Rumors. Two young men holding hands on the curb. Then, for a moment, their lips touched. "Will you look at the damn homos?" Fritz said, letting out a snort. "Disgusting."

And how many nights in a row had Ryan sat in that same parking lot, trying to get the nerve to go into that exact bar? And he could never bring himself to take off his helmet and get off the bike.

The anonymous ad in the paper, men seeking men, had been written, deleted, and never posted. After his shift, he would see Jasmine and Bo and make sure they were okay. And after that, he promised himself he would go inside and buy a drink. He was a damn war vet. How hard was it to walk into a bar?

CHAPTER 2

The rain cleared, and the sun was still on the horizon as Ryan stepped out of the station, glad to be in his street clothes, jeans, and warm leather jacket. His motor-cycle helmet dangled from his hand as he fumbled for his keys. Ryan swore he could still smell the puke. Nothing a ride on his Harley couldn't fix.

"Hey, Ward!" someone shouted. "We're headed to Howard's. Come tip a few back with us!" Vic was a young officer hired at the same time as Ryan. He was nice enough, but they had nothing in common, whatsoever. Scantily clad women wrapped around poles? The whole thing sounded like a nightmare.

"Sorry, gotta get back," Ryan said with a forced smile. "Some other time."

"Your loss, buddy," Victor said, nudging a fellow officer in the ribs. Ryan was relieved when they walked away laughing, and it was finally just him and his Harley. His freedom. He started the engine, pulled the strap on his helmet tight, and for a moment, he just wanted to hit the road and never look back. But he had come to Chicago for a reason. He glanced at his watch. Still, a little bit of time before Jasmine and Bo woke up. He took off speeding to the on-ramp, passing cars and trucks.

Lake Michigan soon loomed before him. The large body of water always brought him back to his childhood. He smiled as he thought about reeling in his first fish, his father smiling down at him. He stopped his bike in the parking lot of Grant Park and flipped the kickstand down.

The water lapped against the shore as the rising sun turned the clouds a vivid purple and light pink. He removed his helmet and fingered the white stickers he had placed meticulously on the back: In Memory of Sergeant Jack Hayes. He hung the helmet on his bike handles and gazed at a fishing boat rocking on the horizon. A few gulls cried out from above.

One painful thought always hit him at least once a day, sometimes more, that life was too damn short. It wasn't fair that he was here and Jack wasn't. He wasn't here to see his family. He wasn't here to enjoy this sunrise. The sun moved above the horizon as Ryan took in the vast expanse.

It had been this park where he scattered his father's ashes. At eight years old, clutching the hand of a woman he didn't know, a ward of the court. She took his sticky hand and led Ryan to the water's edge. Ryan had chosen his father's secret fishing spot. The tears were difficult to hold back at that age, but he was proud he hadn't broken down. Not with the stranger there. The fine ashes slid through his fingers as he scattered them, forever a part of Lake Michigan.

Sometimes, Ryan still felt his presence in the lapping waves and the call of the shorebirds. Jogging the trails kept him sane after work. But not today. Weekends were different. He glanced again at his watch and slipped his helmet back on. Time to go see Jasmine and Bo.

Glenview was one of the nicer neighborhoods on the outskirts of Chicago. Single-story ramblers with freshly mowed lawns, zipped by one after another. He came to a stop on the curb at 111 Sycamore. The house rested on a sloping hill with a gigantic oak still with a faded yellow bow. The next-door neighbor, Mr. Cranston, came out of the house in his robe, groggy, searching for the morning paper.

Ryan got off his bike and quietly walked up the front steps. The front room was Bo's, and it was an ongoing contest to see if Ryan could sneak up on him. It was no use. The young guy always heard his bike coming. It was Saturday, which meant morning cartoons on the couch. His key was barely in the lock when the door swung open.

"Uncle Ryan!" Fresh out of bed in his Spiderman pajamas, Bo wrapped his arms tight around Ryan's legs. The little guy had his father's big brown eyes and distinguished cheekbones. When he smiled at Ryan, it was like looking at a tiny Jack replica.

Ryan ruffled his hair. "Hey, you hungry pal?" Ryan put his finger to his lips. "Let's not wake your mom."

As Ryan retrieved bread and eggs from the refrigerator, Bo climbed on a stool at the kitchen counter.

"How was your night, Uncle Ryan? Did you shoot any bad guys?"

Ryan laughed as he cracked an egg into the pan. "No bad guys. Not last night."

"Can I ride in the police car with you?"

Ryan shook his head. "You know we have to get the okay from your mom."

"She never lets me do anything! You're coming to my baseball game, right?"

Ryan held out his fist to Bo, "Wouldn't miss it, bud." Bo made a tiny fist and bumped him right back, beaming with a huge smile. They flopped together on the couch and were just in time for the start of Power Rangers.

About an hour later, after two Power Rangers episodes, Ryan heard water running in the bathroom. Jasmine was up. He fluffed Bo's hair and got up. "Time to get coffee for your mom."

Bo didn't answer, as his eyes were riveted to the screen.

Jasmine yawned as she came out wearing a flowered kimono robe. Her black braided hair scrunched up on the side, deep red creases etched in her cheek from her pillow. Ryan came to the rescue with a cup of hot, black coffee.

"You're a lifesaver, Ryan," she said, sitting at the dining room table and clutching the cup in both hands. On the wall behind her was the family picture. Ryan's eyes went up to it. A younger Jack on the right and Jasmine holding little Bo in her arms. And the draped framed flag Jasmine had gotten at his funeral hung beside it.

"Hungry?" Ryan asked.

"Starving." She yawned and glanced over as Bo bounced up and down to a commercial for Power Ranger action figures.

He set a plate of two eggs and toast in front of her as her eyes began to look more alive. "You make a mean over-easy egg, Ryan."

"What can I say?" Ryan said with a smile. Another commercial came on, and Jasmine turned in her chair with her piece of toast. It was a teaser for the news.

A woman's voice came on. "CEO and Chicago's Most Eligible Bachelor, Elias Hastings, is finally getting hitched to heiress Alicia Sandstone." The screen showed a picture of the couple, and for a moment, Ryan couldn't take his eyes off them.

Elias was in his early thirties with dark hair and riveting brown eyes. He seemed amused by all the fuss and flashing cameras. Just over six feet tall, his tailored suit accentuated his broad shoulders and muscular physique. That smile he gave to the cameras was infectious. Those dark brown eyes seemed to invite Ryan right in.

Any fantasies floating through his mind screeched to a halt when Elias's fiancé appeared beside him. She wrapped a possessive arm around his waist. Dressed to kill in a short red dress and blond hair twisted in an exquisite updo, she curtly waved at the cameras before Elias helped her into the limousine. The camera captured a close-up of Elias's face before cutting off to the next commercial.

"Man, I wouldn't mind a piece of that action," Jasmine said under her breath.

"Jazz!" Ryan said, trying not to laugh. But he couldn't agree with her more.

Jasmine glanced up at Jack's picture. "You know, Jack would understand," she said, gazing at Jack's smile. "I know he's watching over us and wants us to be happy." Her eyes twinkled as she smiled at Ryan. She was up to something. Ryan could feel it.

Jasmine held her coffee cup close to her mouth, eyes down. "My niece is coming back from college next week, and—"

"No, no, no," Ryan said, cutting her off more forcibly than he intended. "Not now."

"Ryan," she gave him a stern look. "Jack would want this for you. I know he wants you to be happy. You have no life."

"I have you and Bo."

Jasmine went silent for a moment. "You'll always have us, Ryan. But I want you to find," she paused and smiled, "love." She looked back up at Jack's picture and swirled her coffee. "I want you to have what Jack and I had."

Ryan shifted in his chair and shook his head. "Jazz, I love you and Bo, and my life is complete." But it was a lie, and even as he said it, Ryan knew the words had fallen flat. He could see it in Jasmine's knowing look. He loved both of them with all his heart. But something was missing. Something that was too terrifying to think about at the moment. And tonight, he was going to do something about it.

Chapter 3

Ryan closed his eyes as the hot water sprayed over his head. The one good thing about his cramped one-bedroom apartment was the hot water. It never failed him. Jasmine hated it, especially the bars on his windows. When he opened his computer, there was invariably a suggestion from Jasmine about other apartments for sale. However, despite its flaws, it was close to work, and the price was right. He turned the water off and leaned against the white tile wall. Tonight was the night, and he had made a promise to himself.

Steam dripped from the mirror as Ryan cleared a small circle with his palm. He could only see the big ugly scar on his chest, like a giant neon sign screaming *disfigured*. He winced as he traced the angry line from his neck to his lower stomach.

He rotated his stiff shoulder and averted his eyes. Lucky to be alive, that's what he was. But would anyone really want to be with him? He imagined the disgust and sure rejection when he took off his shirt. Just like the disgust he felt now.

Death is certain. Life is not. That one motto learned from his army days came back to him. The skull tattoo on his right arm stared back at him with its hollow sunken eyes. He ran a finger over the name Jack Hayes etched forever in black ink just below.

Those empty eyes spoke to him. Guilty, they said. You could have saved him. He squeezed his brush, letting the bristles dig into his fingers.

Ryan slicked back his long bangs and smiled. Jack would have teased him relentlessly for the longer hairstyle. The thought cheered him up and made him smile as he took out his razor.

Tonight was the night. He would go into Rumors, sit down, and order a damn drink. That was all.

He finished shaving, rinsed off the razor, and ran his hand over his smooth chin. Now, find clothes, he ordered himself. After staring at his small closet, he settled on a tan button-down shirt and jeans. He changed his mind and took out the black one. Settle down, Ward, he told himself as he slipped the black t-shirt over his head.

Bike helmet and keys waited by the front door. He paused, looking through his window past the iron bars at a row of identical apartments on the other side of the street. Low clouds threatened rain, and the street lights barely illuminated the jam-packed cars on either side of the curb. Somewhere, a dog barked, and sirens echoed in the distance. I could just stay home.

What more did he need than his TV, couch, and favorite hula girl lamp from overseas?

He looked at the picture of his regimen by the door, straightening the frame. They were all in uniform, deep in the desert, hamming it up for the photographer. It was Christmas, and they had all eaten a great meal, and many had talked to family back home. That night in the desert, as he closed his eyes on his cot, he realized no one was waiting for him at home. No one really cared if he lived or died. And later that year, nine of them had made it home, and one made it home in a coffin. He looked away from the photo, grabbed his helmet, slipped on his boots, and zipped up his leather jacket. It was time to go.

It wasn't far to Rumors, but the closer he got on his bike, the more he wished he hadn't eaten supper. The hastily eaten spaghetti was not settling well. But this time, he promised himself he was going to do it. He would open that door and enter that bar. Come hell or high water.

As he pulled into the parking lot, two young men watched him, leaning against the building, smoking cigarettes. Another car pulled up, and a group of women in their twenties got out. For a moment, laughter filled the air as they entered the building.

He rolled his bike up to the side of the two-story brick building, hiding in its shadow. He had spent many nights sitting here, watching, unable to take off his helmet. Familiar cars were parked nearby: the red Jeep and the rusty blue Chevy. Part of the bricks beside him were whitewashed, words barely visible underneath. He knew full well what those words were. It had been written on his locker in high school before the janitor mercifully washed it off.

Squeezing his eyes shut, Ryan removed his helmet. Red neon letters blinked from around the corner and hummed faintly. *Rumors*. There was nothing else to signify what it was. The constant thump of music almost made him start his engine and ride away. Almost. Returning to his apartment with a six-pack of beer seemed more frightening. He hung his helmet on the handlebars and swung his leg off the bike. He was going in.

∾

Elias Hastings had hours ago hung his coat on the chair, loosened his tie, and was now on his third glass of wine. Not that he was counting. His private suite above Rumors was leased for an outrageous sum of money. It wasn't much. Just a sparsely furnished room and a few exposed bricks. A large picture window with a peek-a-boo view of the downtown Chicago light. It reminded him of his little flat in Paris. And it served a purpose. A need.

The owner also allowed him to build an entrance to the adjoining building, which Elias owned and made for the perfect amount of privacy. He could come and go as he pleased. Most importantly, he had access to the security cameras for the bar down below. Money could buy anything. The monitor in his suite fed him images of the bar and the dance floor side by side. Any one of the men down there could be his. He loved the chase and the mystery of inviting men inside. It always led to more.

Lately, he hadn't even asked their names, and they had taken it as the unsaid that he was the infamous *Mr. Smith* that lent credence to the bar name, Rumors. He smiled. Multiple rumors were circulating about *Mr. Smith*. One was that he was a billionaire. Now, that rumor was almost true. Through his vast network and his father's inheritance, Elias was well on his way. The other was that he was a famous actor who frequented gay bars anonymously. That one just made him laugh.

Elias had been featured in several magazines. GQ in the *30 men under 30 to watch*, and several gossip magazines looking at the most eligible bachelors in the U.S. Eligible didn't even begin to describe it. It was much more complicated than that. And with his recent engagement to model Alicia Sandstone, that rumor would soon be quashed forever.

Rumors floated around Chicago about him and his father's company. Hints of dealings with the underworld and other despicable things enabled him to continue expanding his influence worldwide. He had made enemies and some good allies. But putting himself out there made it all the more essential that his dalliances were kept under wraps.

The world of high-end realty acquisitions was a good old boy network that frowned on anything that wasn't manly enough. And that was hunting and sports. Being gay was not part of the mix.

He gazed at the television screen, and for the first time, he found himself utterly bored. There were the regulars down there. The queens, the guys dressed in black into BDSM, and a few he recognized from previous encounters in his suite. The anonymous sex was good. He took another sip of his wine. Tonight would be a bust. No one at the bar or on the dance floor was the least bit interesting to him.

His right-hand man, Flynn, paced outside the suite. He insisted on coming tonight, and incessant pacing had given Elias a splitting headache.

The rugged Flynn served his father and was one of the original founding members of Hastings Enterprise. The older man seemed more at home on a ranch than in the board rooms. He had white hair in a short buzz cut, a leathery face, and intense light blue eyes. He had once served with the Irish military and never let anyone forget it.

One look and everyone fell in line, including me. He took another sip of wine.

Though it was beneath him, Flynn wanted to be the one to approach the man of Elias's choosing.

Perhaps it was his strange way of wanting to ensure his safety. But at any rate, there was little Elias could do about it other than humor him—

The most gorgeous man he had ever seen stepped through the door at Rumors. For a moment, Elias's heart stopped, and his breath caught in his throat. He zoomed the camera in. He was a biker, evident from his leather jacket replete with Sturgis patches and military insignias. But that in and of itself did not interest him much.

There was something else about him. Tight jeans that left little to the imagination hugged his long legs right down to his black boots. His slicked-back, blond hair had tumbled over his eyes and down towards his chin. He looked so out of place and vulnerable as he gazed around the bar. What was it that was so intriguing?

"Flynn," he called. "I want you to deliver a message." He smiled. Time for the mysterious *Mr. Smith* to strike again.

CHAPTER 4

Ryan's hand trembled as he grasped the door handle, nodding at the two young men smoking at the entrance. Inside, the noise was deafening. A wave of dizziness struck as the blue strobe lights flashed inside a dark interior. The floor was packed with men dancing. On a raised dais, a man in tight leather ground on a pole suggestively.

To Ryan's relief, there was an empty stool at the bar. His refuge. The perfect spot to be inconspicuous and see the entire room. Nearby, two men sat huddled in a corner booth, lips locked and hands disappearing beneath the table.

Ryan found himself staring and quickly looked away. To his left, carpeted stairs led up to a dark balcony. A lone woman, tipsy on her feet, started climbing when her friend grabbed her by the hand and brought her back down.

Behind the bar, a man in his 40s with a handlebar mustache, tight leather jeans, and a silk shirt revealing a muscular chest. "What can I get for you, handsome?" He gave Ryan a warm smile.

"Whatever's on tap," Ryan said as he flipped a fiver onto the counter.

A few minutes later, a nice cold mug was placed before him. Ryan took a sip and relaxed. He had done it. After months, he had come in and ordered a drink. His self-congratulations were interrupted when a man plunked on a stool beside him.

"Hey, stranger." A man in a pink suit, white tie, and rosy pink glasses placed a hand on his back. "I've never seen you here before."

"First time," Ryan said, taking another sip of beer to hide his trembling hand. "Nice place."

"Yeah," the man leaned in. "See the bartender? That's Hal. My husband." He pointed to a ring on his finger. The man with the black mustache looked over and winked at them. "Hal can look, but he can't touch." He laughed. "But I don't mind if you want to make him a wee bit jealous." He lowered his pink glasses and fluttered his eyes.

Ryan smiled and held out his hand. "Ryan Ward."

"Mitch Crenshaw," the man shook his hand loosely. "But on Thursday drag nights, you can call me Esmerelda. I hope you'll come to see me. I'm always looking for more groupies."

"I might just do that." For the first time, Ryan felt the discomfort ease away.

"Why don't you take off your coat and stay awhile, Ryan Ward?"

Ryan realized for the first time that he was warm. He hadn't noticed, so he unzipped his jacket and hung it over the stool next to him. Why not make himself at home? Here, he didn't have to hide. Didn't have to pretend.

"That's better. Just hang out with us for a while. There's a good bunch here." He looked around at the dance floor and waved to someone. "Have you been in Chicago long?"

"No, not long."

Hal, the bartender, was polishing a glass mug and approached them over the counter. "I see you've met my husband. He's a harmless flirt."

Mitch protested, "Hey! How do you know he's not hitting on me?"

Rolling his eyes, Hal just grinned. "Can I get you boys anything to eat?"

Ryan took another swig. "I'm good."

Hal nodded. "All right, just let me know, and keep a close eye on this one." He pointed to Mitch. "I'm watching you, hubby!"

Mitch blew kisses at him. He leaned into Ryan and whispered. "Oh, don't look now, but someone has his eyes on you."

Ryan turned his head towards the tables. "Don't look," Mitch repeated, "but to your right, the young man in the white t-shirt with the blond hair and tats. Why don't you buy him a drink, sweetie?"

Shaking his head, Ryan squeezed his eyes shut. "Oh, you're shy!" Mitch said. "Don't worry. Uncle Mitch will take care of you." He flitted to the young man's table while Ryan's face burned. Why was this so hard? In a moment, Mitch was back and dangled a little piece of paper. "See, I got you his phone number. You should call him."

Ryan raised his glass to the young man accosted by Mitch and got a smile in return. This wasn't that bad. "Thanks, Mitch," Ryan said, fingering the scrap paper.

"See you around, Ryan Ward!" With that, he took off towards the dance floor.

He watched Mitch as he started dancing with the two men, moving without any inhibition to the music. As he watched, someone tapped him on the shoulder. Ryan turned and came face to face with an older gentleman standing before him in a three-piece suit. "Excuse me," he said, with a distinct English accent, "might I have a word?"

"Of course," Ryan said, motioning to the stool Mitch had just vacated, "have a seat." The man cleared his throat, straightened his jacket, and sat down stiffly. He motioned to Hal for a drink. A scotch was poured into a glass, and the man downed it at once. For a moment, the older gentleman sat toying with his cup. "This is rather, uh, delicate." Ryan set his beer down and turned to face him.

Hal came by and poured some more scotch in his cup. The man nodded and pointed to Ryan's beer. "This gentleman's tab is on Mr. Smith," he said to Hal, who nodded and returned to another customer. Clutching the glass, the mysterious man spoke softly. "My boss would like to meet with you discreetly upstairs." He regarded Ryan and then motioned up to the dark balcony.

Ryan's gaze strayed up the dark steps and then back as the older man placed a business card on the counter and got up. "Mr. Smith will be waiting for you."

Mitch came back, also watching the older gentleman climb the steps. "Let me guess, Mr. Smith?" He wrinkled his nose.

Ryan nodded as he picked up the cream-colored paper, and in elegant writing, it said simply:

Suite #1

Nothing else. Ryan was left holding it in his hand, stunned.

Mitch gave a chuckle. "Ah, the mystery man in suite number one," he said, gazing at the card. "He never comes down. There's a way into suite one from the other building. Very few have seen him, and when someone goes up there, they never talk about it. It's infuriating! Especially for an old queen like me." He shook his head. "I have to know all the gossip here, you know?" He scoffed and motioned to his husband for another drink. "But Mr. Smith, I've heard, has broken quite a few hearts. One of those one-night stands, fuck 'em and leave 'em, if you know what I mean."

"I'm not interested," Ryan said with finality and flipped the card on the counter.

"You're smart. But I think you're just Mr. Smith's type." He glanced up towards the balcony and snickered. "Well, the mysterious Mr. Smith can have his heart broken tonight." He raised his beer to Ryan, laughed, and swished elegantly towards the dance floor.

Again, Ryan looked up the stairs towards the dark balcony. One night. He took a sip of his beer. He'd fantasized about it a million times but had never followed through. He thought about his on-again, off-again girlfriend in high school, all the time fantasizing about the boy in math class. The one-night stand he almost had in Germany before he was shipped to Afghanistan. He picked up the card and gazed at it, unsure what to do.

His mind roamed to Jasmine and Bo. He took one last look up at the balcony and then tore the card in half, tossing the pieces on the counter. He rubbed his face, then stood, motioning to Hal.

"Am I good?"

"Yup, you're all good," Hal said, wiping his hands on a towel. "Thanks for coming in." Ryan waved to Mitch, who returned it with a flourish, and then he was back out into the night. The dance beat behind him, now a low base thud as the door swung shut.

That night, after he returned to his studio, he reclined back on the couch, his ears ringing. He just couldn't get comfortable. All he could do was think about Mr. Smith. He opened the piece of paper that Mitch gave him. There was a hastily scratched phone number. And below Esmerelda, Thursday 9 PM sharp, Be There or Be Square!

Ryan closed his eyes and allowed himself a smile. He listened to the slow rush of traffic outside. His mind raced. Just who was this mysterious man, and what had he wanted? Ryan sighed. He'd never find out now. Mr. Smith was just another fantasy to play over and over in his mind. Always a fantasy, never a reality.

Chapter 5

Elias sat motionless in front of the monitor, still not believing his eyes. The offer to meet Mr. Smith in Suite #1 had never been refused before. Never. And yet, on this night, he'd have to mark it somewhere in the records of lore: He, Elias Hastings, was now officially stood up.

He let out a bitter laugh and pushed the remote to rerun the tape. The man on the screen made a face as he tore up Elias's business card and threw it on the counter. Tonight had not gone well. He smiled and poured himself some more wine. He'd been coming here for five years, and this was the first time he had been flatly refused. Usually, they come up just out of curiosity, and then it was all in Elias's hands. And he always got his man.

He rewound the tape as he sipped his wine and watched him enter the bar again. Feeling like the voyeur he admittedly was, Elias zoomed into the image. The man had beautiful blue eyes. He could get lost in those eyes. On the second viewing, Elias appreciated the way his mystery man scoped the place out, just as Elias himself would have done. Assess the people in an instant to recognize their strengths and weaknesses and move to the best place to sit and observe. Yes, those eyes showed a keen intelligence.

Flynn sheepishly opened the door. "Are you done for the evening?" he asked. "Should we head back?"

Elias shook his head and let out a deep breath, scooting his chair away from the screen. "Yes, I'm done for the night." He took the remote and switched the cameras to the parking lot. The rain had started to fall. Elias watched as the man got on his Harley and put on his helmet. In an instant, he sped away towards the south side of town. "Find out what you can on him." He rewound the tape to when the man had just entered the bar and stopped it mid-frame.

"Elias," Flynn began, "he's military." He squinted at the screen. "Military, definitely." He pointed to the man's left arm. "Special Forces tattoo." He shook his head at the frozen man on the screen. "Best leave this one alone."

Elias sighed. He trusted Flynn, for the most part, in every instant except this one. Matters of the heart were not his strength. He hadn't so much looked at another woman since his wife died of cancer ten years ago. Sig Flynn had made Hasting Enterprise his life. He had served Elias's father well and had been there when Elias truly needed him after his father died. Truthfully, he owed Sig his life.

"No, I want to meet him," Elias said. "Just once, and he'll be out of my life forever." He glanced up at Flynn, who gazed back with an inscrutable face. Of course, the older man didn't understand this. How many times had he heard, *Just be with Miss Sandstone. She's a beautiful girl*. But that was not the reality. It would never be the reality. And one-night stands, anonymous one-night stands, were his life.

Then Elias was riveted back to the screen. He could wait for this one. It filled him with an excitement he hadn't felt in some time. He felt alive. Something he couldn't have the instant he asked.

The buzz of Flynn's cell phone woke Elias from his reverie. His attention snapped back to the present. Flynn's cell phone rarely went off, and it usually meant something dire, especially at this time of night. Elias's pulse quickened as he exchanged glances with Flynn.

Flynn's face turned to stone as he answered. His eyes widened and darted to Elias. "What? When? We'll be right there." His thumb came down heavily on the cell phone as he hung it up, his face contorted by anger. "Two of our men are down. Let's go. Now."

Elias set his glass down and was up in an instant, grabbing his coat. Flynn handed him his gun. "Gretsky," Elias said out loud. It had to be Gretsky. That man had been a pain in his ass ever since he came to Chicago and tried to take over his territory. His father's territory. He slipped the gun in his side holster.

Just as they were leaving, Elias's cell rang. Alicia Sandstone's name came up across the top with her picture, smiling at him from the screen. The last thing he needed. He hit the mute button. Their engagement party was this weekend, and he still hadn't gone over the plans with her.

They left through the doorway into the adjoining building. It was a quick walk down a few flights of stairs to a black limousine waiting outside.

Flynn snapped out orders to the driver. "South Baker and 14th." The limo took off with a lurch as Elias barely jumped in.

It was a perfectly dreary night. Rain lashed at the windows, making visibility almost impossible as the windshield wipers fought to keep up. There was a tense silence in the limo, and Elias stared out at the night as the buildings and lights zipped by.

The limo came to a stop. Two figures lay motionless in the alleyway, rain soaking their clothes and bodies. Elias opened the door, oblivious to the pounding rain. One of Elias's men approached him, eyes wide and his hair plastered to his face. "I'm sorry," he said, bending over, trying to catch his breath. "I tried to get here in time. I chased them two blocks. There was a car waiting."

Elias ran over to the bodies. Even from the back of their heads, he knew who they were. Two of his most loyal men. J.J. Jones and Cam Taylor. They had been with him for ten years and his father before that. They had successfully infiltrated Gretsky's organization. Moles for the last two years. Spying and sabotaging everything they could get away with. He knelt beside each one and felt for a pulse. Taylor was gone, a bullet to the back of his head, execution-style, eyes staring blankly into oblivion. But J.J. had a faint pulse. "He's still with us," Elias said, pointing to Flynn. "Ambulance. Now."

Flynn dialed as Elias rolled J.J. over. "Stay with me." His breathing was shallow, and blood oozed from his left shoulder. Elias took off his coat and put pressure on the wound. The rain soaked the two of them. "We're going to get you home to your family," he said, "stay with me, Goddamnit, stay with me."

Already, the sirens were in the distance. Elias didn't let up the pressure. Gretsky would pay for this. He'd pay for this dearly. The medics seemed to take forever, but soon, J.J. was placed on a stretcher, and an IV slipped into the crook of his arm. He was in bad shape. He watched as the ambulance took off into the night, sirens blaring in the early morning silence.

"This won't go unanswered," Flynn said. "Just give the word."

Elias raised his hand. "Not yet. Not yet." What was Gretsky up to? He was a clever man who had been encroaching on their company for years. Slowly, deftly looking to unravel everything. All the delicate alliances, all the realty holdings. Underbidding contracts, moving in on the casinos, bars, and hotels. Unlimited funding, but from where?

His father had long ago destroyed Canyon Crest. They were ruined, defunct, and now growing again under the deft hand of Caesar Gretsky.

Elias would need time to figure out his next move. A chess game of immense proportions, and many lives were on the line. He would need to tread carefully. But at that moment, as he gazed at the lifeless form of Taylor lying in the dirty alleyway, blood mixed with water, he imagined putting a bullet straight through Gretsky's arrogant smile.

CHAPTER 6

Elias woke with a start, coming out of a dreamless sleep. Somehow, he had managed to pass out in the hospital waiting room, and he tried to rub the knot out of his neck. There was a whir of activity, beeps, and buzzes coming from behind the locked door to the ICU and overhead pages urging doctors to the OR. He rubbed his face and looked out over the sparsely furnished waiting room. The clock on the wall said 4:30 AM. A young couple rested their heads on each other, eyes closed, a well-used tissue box lying on the woman's lap.

Flynn entered through the main door, balancing two steaming Styrofoam cups in his hands.

Under the fluorescent lights, Elias could see he hadn't slept. There were heavy bags under his eyes, his expression tight and guarded. Cam Taylor hadn't made it. He was a personal friend of Flynn's, and he had died like an animal in that alley last night. Shot in the back of the head execution style. The other man, J.J., was just beyond the locked door in intensive care on a ventilator and chest tube. The bastards had missed his heart, but a bullet made its mark deep inside his left lung.

Elias took a sip of the strong black coffee and grimaced. Damn Gretsky to hell. If this was supposed to be a message, it was heard loud and clear. And there would be repercussions. Gretsky would know this.

Flynn sat down beside Elias, his posture rigid. He stared at a picture of a snowy mountain peak on the wall, the sunrise just coming over the hills. Flynn sipped his black coffee and spoke without emotion. "Gretsky found out we infiltrated him. Made an example of our men."

Elias knew this. He knew this the moment he stepped into that alley. The plan to infiltrate Gretsky's organization had failed on many levels. Families had been notified and would be here soon. All the men and women who worked for Elias knew the risks coming in. The risks and the great benefits. They were all richly compensated for the work they did. But nothing could compensate the families right now. The money would be a cold comfort. But he would try. No expense was spared for those who risked their lives for him.

"We are ready on your word," Flynn said. "Our people are prepared."

The main door opened, and several cops in uniform barged in, eyes concentrated solely on Elias and Flynn. Trailing behind them, in a brown off-the-rack suit, was a small, compact man with a shaved head and trim beard. He sauntered leisurely, wearing a smug grin.

Elias knew him on sight: Detective Lorenzo Chavez, another thorn in his side.

"It looks like you've had a long night, Elias." Chavez walked over and leaned against the closest chair. Flynn glared daggers at him.

"Yes, it's been a long night, detective," Elias said, not bothering to look up.

Detective Chavez brought the chair over and positioned it directly in front of Elias, uninvited. He sat down, leaning forward. "So, Elias, who did this?"

Elias frowned down into his coffee cup. "I'm leaving that in your very capable hands."

The detective smiled at him. "I'd like you to come down to the precinct just to chat, of course."

Elias returned a smile. "As much as I enjoy your company, detective, I'd rather stay here until the families arrive."

"Some other time then." Detective Chavez rose and motioned to the officers. Standing at the main door, he turned to face Elias. "If anything happens to Caesar Gretsky or any of his people," he paused, "I'm coming for you, Elias. That's a promise."

Elias sat stone-faced, staring straight ahead. "Enough bloodshed for the night, detective."

With that, they left, and Elias drew in a deep breath. Now was not the time for revenge. Revenge would come later. Gretsky liked getting his hands dirty, but Elias was more reluctant.

This reluctance had cost Elias both Los Angeles and Seoul, but that was in the past. He wasn't going to lose his hometown of Chicago. He took the last few drops of coffee and threw the cup in the trash. As soon as Flynn got more intel, whoever did this at Gretsky's orders would be very sorry. But the greatest revenge would be for Gretsky. Elias vowed to destroy the man and his company utterly and completely.

A nurse came out of the ICU, her brown hair in a messy bun, eyes tired, and a stethoscope around her neck. "Elias Hastings?" she asked.

"Yes?" Elias stood up.

"Mr. Jones would like to speak to you."

"He's awake?" Elias turned to Flynn. "I'll be right back."

The nurse looked down at her clipboard. "We were able to extubate him. It may not hold for long." She pressed a button to open the door and motioned for him to follow.

Within the ICU, little glass cubicles were aligned in a row across from the nurse's stations.

Monitors everywhere had heart rhythms and vital signs. A whiteboard had the names of the patients and assigned staff. In the corner, he saw Jones. A retired cop who appreciated the higher corporate pay and the finer things in life. Liked to travel overseas with his wife. His usually manicured appearance was now a disheveled wreck. His skin looked unbelievably pale. Several bags of blood hung on an IV pole. Elias paused before entering the room.

"Eli," he said, his voice barely a whisper.

Elias sat down by his side and grasped his hand. "Who did this to you?"

"It was Gretsky's men. The leader is a man named Benton." He let out a weak cough.

"A thug Gretsky hired from a nasty cartel down south. What happened to Cam?" His voice trailed off and his eyes closed tight. He knew.

"I'm sorry, J.J. I'm truly sorry. This Benton will pay, and so will Gretsky."

J.J. tried to raise his head, then fell back on the pillow. "They know what we've been doing. I think they'll come after you next, Elias. They want to take down everything, everyone." His eyes rested on Elias and slowly became heavier. After a minute, he closed his eyes, and breathing became more rhythmic.

The nurse stepped back in. "We need to let him rest. His family will be here shortly."

Elias nodded and stood. Benton would be taken care of before morning. He would make sure of it. And then he would get down to business. The business of destroying Gretsky's company once and for all.

He filled Flynn in. By nightfall, Benton would find himself in a shallow, unmarked grave.

His phone buzzed. A cryptic text came through:

Tuscans 7 PM CG

CG was Caesar Gretsky. The bastard had the nerve to demand a meeting. He showed the screen to Flynn, who said something inaudible. Of course, he would want to meet. But Caesar and himself had a complicated history. Something Caesar always capitalized on.

It had been a weekend in Rome, and Elias had just inherited his father's company. Caesar was a good-looking man, albeit ten years older. A distinguished-looking man of Russian descent. He was conversant in several languages, and his knowledge of art and architecture was unrivaled.

And that weekend, his only preoccupation had been Elias. Elias didn't regret anything, only the person he had done it with. If he knew then what he did now, he would have run the other way. One unfortunate aspect was that Caesar had gained insight into his psyche and passions. It had cost Elias dearly in several business ventures. He tossed the phone in his pocket. Oh yes, he'd meet up with Caesar. But this time, he knew who he was up against. Elias would not make the same mistake twice.

Chapter 7

Elias sipped his espresso on the veranda overlooking the infinity pool that appeared to pour over the edge into the garden below. The sprawling brick mansion he inherited from his father absorbed the full light of the noon sun, exposing various colors of red, deep burgundy, and chestnut. The mature trees and shrubs provided the privacy that Elias needed. Privacy from the media and privacy from his enemies. And he knew much of the money he'd acquired had been delivered through blood. How many lives had been lost to gain such wealth, he didn't know. But he had a good idea.

And more blood had been shed last night. Taylor had died, and J.J. barely pulled through the night. The butcher who had done this to them was dead. He had gotten the call from Flynn this morning. And Flynn did not provide merciful deaths.

The screen door behind him opened, and Flynn walked through. He had showered and wore his usually impeccable button-down shirt and slacks, but his face was drawn. The man had barely slept. "It's done," Flynn said, collapsing on the deck chair next to Elias.

"Any further responses from Gretsky?" Elias asked.

"I don't believe he knows yet. But," Flynn added with a dark smile, "he will. The message will be loud and clear."

"Excellent," Elias said. "Gretsky asked for a meeting tonight. 7 PM at Tuscans."

Flynn nodded. "Perhaps we can bring this all to a close at last." The older man's phone buzzed, and he glanced at it. "The intel you asked for has come through. It will be on your desk shortly."

Elias hid a smile. That *intel* was on the man he had seen in the bar last night. This was a welcome distraction.

There was movement down towards the pool. Elias watched Alicia Sandstone come out in a silk-flowered half robe and bikini. She glanced up at them and waved, gathering the robe around her as she walked to the veranda. Flynn averted his eyes. She had the body of a goddess. Blond hair was tousled up in a bun. Alas, it did nothing for Elias. His life would be much easier, much simpler if it did.

"My two favorite men," Alicia said, giving Flynn a kiss on the top of his head. "And where were you two last night?

Elias frowned. "Business, Alicia, you know that." He took another sip of his espresso. Of course, he had forgotten about their engagement planning. He didn't really want anything to do with it.

"You promised me," she scolded. "No one is going to believe this charade if you don't participate." She leaned against the railing, gesturing out towards the city. "No one, Elias. Are you even listening to me?"

Elias realized he was thinking about the information on his desk. "Yes," he gazed directly at her. "Yes. Tomorrow night. I'll be there at the planners. We'll get everything done."

"You promised to take me to the Caribbean afterward." Those hazel eyes glared at him, unblinking. Elias let out a sigh. He did owe her for what she was doing for him. The rumors had been nipped in the bud since they publicly announced their marriage. He could not afford the rumors to continue. "I can arrange a trip for you and a person of your choice," Elias said with a wave. "Just tell me when."

"And what will the media say if I take a trip without you?" Suddenly, her face softened, and the anger melted away. Her hand came down on his shoulder. "I want to go with you, Elias." She took a deep breath. "I don't want to go with someone else."

Elias sighed and set the cup down, reaching up for her hand. "Soon, Alicia. I need you to be patient. It will happen soon."

She looked about to say something, then her lips tightened. She nodded and walked down the steps towards the pool. Elias watched her dive gracefully into the water. Elias shook his head. Alicia knew what she was getting into when she signed up for this. Why she had to be so unpleasant about everything, Elias didn't know. But if Alicia wanted anything more than financial compensation, she wasn't going to get it.

Flynn stood and stretched. "I'm going to get some rest. Tuscan's tonight?" he asked.

"7 PM."

"Excellent." With that, Flynn strode back to the house, glancing toward the pool once more before retiring.

The one thing, the only thing that was on Elias's mind right now was the information about the man in the bar. He got up and slid open the glass door to his office. His large oak desk was waiting for him. A picture window looked out at the cityscape of Chicago. It was a private room that once belonged to his father.

On the top of his desk was the information he was waiting for. He put on his reading glasses and picked up the two-page dossier. The mystery man's name was Ryan Ward. Nice ring to it. His eyes narrowed when he saw that he was a cop. Well, they could work around that. Ex-military, just as Flynn had predicted. He was an orphan moving between foster homes across the country. He flicked the paper with his hand. Nothing interesting. But what was interesting was the lack of information from his early years. It was as if this man's life started at age 10. Nothing before that. He looked on the back of the sheets. Nothing. Elias frowned. This was odd. He would have his men look into that further.

Under habits was a morning jog in Seward Park after his night shift. Elias could work with that. He smiled, glancing at the photo of Ryan jogging. Baggy gray sweatpants and black t-shirt drenched in sweat couldn't hide his chiseled, slender physique. Elias traced a finger down the photo.

Ryan was exquisite, and very soon, Elias would seduce him just for one night. He took off the glasses and gazed out the window. It had been so long since he had plotted any type of seduction. How many years? He folded his hands and savored the thought. But for the moment, he had other matters to attend to. Business called. First, he would deal with Caesar, and then he could concentrate on this more interesting matter. He glanced again at Ryan's picture, then placed the dossier in the bottom drawer, locking it firmly in place.

Soon, he thought with a smile.

Chapter 8

Elias gazed out the tinted window in the limo's back seat as they pulled up to Tuscan's, the high-end restaurant Gretsky and his crew frequented. This was enemy territory.

White Roman pillars stood out in front, and a large sign lit up in red above the packed parking lot. He glanced at his wristwatch. It was 6:30, and the dinner rush was in full swing. It was no secret that the place was owned by Gretsky. But with a full house, Elias had his own people inside, disguised as customers, should anything go awry. Flynn was in the back seat, fiddling with his cufflinks. Gretsky would be ready, but so was Elias.

Flynn leaned down and picked up a briefcase from the carpeted floor. He unsnapped it and took out a couple of sheets of paper. "Before we go in, Elias, we need to talk."

Elias was about to open the door and stopped. "What is it, Flynn?"

"This Ryan Ward," Flynn paused and threw the paperwork over on the seat.

The name snapped Elias out of his concentration. "What about him?"

Flynn cleared his throat and put on his reading glasses. "The whole thing doesn't smell right." He glanced up at Elias. "For one, he's a cop," he adjusted his glasses as he continued down the page, "and other discrepancies." He set the papers down and took off his glasses. "Nothing on the subject's early life. Nothing." He leaned against the door, not taking his gaze off Elias. "You've always trusted my judgment, as did your father." Flynn was silent for a moment. "Let this one go."

Elias let out a steady breath. This was the last thing he needed right now. Flynn was the one who had to let this go. "I trust you and," he paused, "I'll take your thoughts under advisement."

Flynn shook his head and muttered something unintelligible under his breath.

Elias grimaced as his gaze lingered on the front entrance, his hand resting on the latch. Caesar Gretsky was waiting for him inside. "Let's go. Keep everyone at the ready."

He stepped out onto the freshly mowed grass. Several customers were seated at the edge of a mosaic-tiled fountain. Elias had once made a wish in that fountain so long ago before Gretsky made his life a living hell.

Flynn pointed to the entrance. Several of Gretsky's well-known associates, or thugs, were waiting there, trying to be inconspicuous in their stiff suits and recently polished shoes. Elias passed them without a glance.

Flynn opened the door for him, and an overwhelming smell of crusty garlic bread wafted from the back kitchen. The host, a young man in his 20s with a trim beard and glasses, nodded to them.

Behind the young man was a large framed picture that had very recently been placed. It hadn't been there the last time Elias had come in.

And as Elias gazed at it, his skin began to prickle. The picture showed the exact damn spot where he had stayed with Caesar way back when. The same bed and breakfast overlooking the fountain and square at Piazza Navona. Those exquisite marble statues and the morning walks along the cobblestone streets. It was as if he was there again. Caesar had put this picture up with the sole purpose of flustering him. A hand came down on his shoulder, and Flynn patted him. "You, okay?"

"Fine, fine," Elias said.

Caesar had aged well, now in his mid-40s, with flecks of gray in his dark hair and a familiar scar on his forehead from a boxing incident. His nose had been broken at one time. It only added to his rugged good looks. The immaculate Italian suit smoothed out the rough edges.

Caesar stood facing him with a welcoming smile. "Elias," Caesar said, arms open for an embrace, "so good to see you."

Elias took his hand, and Caesar held on, lingering as he gazed at Elias's fingers. He was so damn charismatic, and there was a reason he had risen to the top of Canyon Crest. And behind that smile was the mind of a ruthless killer. Elias extricated his hand, not returning the smile. They both sat, and Caesar motioned to the waiter.

A waiter dressed head to toe in black poured Elias a glass of red wine and set down a basket with lightly oiled fresh breadsticks.

Gretsky waved his hand towards the tables, candles flickering as the clank of silverware and muted conversations surrounded them. He whispered, "I love this place, don't you, Elias?"

"You've done well, Caesar," Elias acknowledged, nodding appreciatively as he sipped the robust wine.

"That was some nasty business," Caesar continued, shaking his head as he gave Elias a reproving glance. "What your men did to poor Benton this morning."

Elias ignored him as he picked up the menu and flipped through the entrees. The cheapest was $50. Figured. "What did you really want to talk about, Caesar?"

Caesar swirled his glass and took a long sip of his wine. Again, he smiled with that cold, unnerving grin. "It's time to end the animosity between us, Elias." He paused for a moment. "It was very foolish sending your men to infiltrate our organization. Very foolish indeed."

Elias slipped the red cloth napkin onto his lap and gripped it into a fist. He wasn't going to lose it. Not here.

Caesar leaned forward on the table. "I have a proposal for you, Elias. I hope you will listen." Light blue eyes regarded Elias.

"I'm listening."

"Chicago is my home. I'm not leaving. This vendetta needs to end." He raised his glass to Elias. "Think of what we could do together, Elias. You and me. We forget the past and start a new future, here and now."

"You want me to join with you?" Elias repeated, glancing back again at Flynn. Flynn had taken a table nearby and appeared to be reading the menu.

"I would hate to see more bloodshed, wouldn't you? And that is the path we are headed for, Elias. More bloodshed. More lives lost. If we combine our companies, think of what we could do." There was a silence between them, and Caesar continued. "You are to be married soon. Ms. Sandstone is a lovely lady and very lucky." He smiled. "If you had less on your plate, you could devote more time to her." He tilted his head to the side. "You would still have power, Elias, but I would be the head of the organization, with the ultimate responsibility, the long hours, and the grind. And you would be with me, at my side."

Elias was quiet as he absorbed the words. "Is this what you wanted to tell me?" He tossed his napkin on the table and motioned for the waiter. "Because that will never happen. The only option for you is to pack up and leave Chicago."

Caesar nodded his head, frowning. "I'm sorry to hear you say that, Elias. I truly am. Because that way means more bloodshed. Is that what you want, Elias? You are starting a new family, and I can't imagine that you would want to put them in that kind of jeopardy."

Elias stood. "Is this a threat, Caesar?"

That infuriating smile came back to Caesar's lips. "I'm just bringing you back to reality, Elias. Chicago is mine now. You either leave or take my generous offer." Caesar also stood and moved closer, his tone softening. "I don't regret anything that happened between us, Elias. If anything, it will make us more formidable partners. I just ask that you think about it."

"You knew full well what you were doing in Rome." He gazed at the older man and tossed a twenty down on the table. "We're done here." He stood and motioned to Flynn.

"You're making a big mistake, Elias," Caesar said, smoothing out his jacket and sitting back down. "I don't want anything to happen to you, but if you force my hand," he paused and picked up his fork, "I can't guarantee your safety."

"We're done here."

"You leave, and the offer is off the table." Caesar leisurely sipped his wine.

Elias gazed at him a moment longer. As he turned to walk out, he felt Caesar's eyes burning a hole in his back.

Chapter 9

Ryan paused his jog for a moment, leaning on his knees to catch his breath. The paved trail stretched ahead, following the curve of Lake Michigan. At this early hour, there were only a few people, and that was preferable.

After a night of drunks and defiant speeders, being alone with his thoughts and steady breath was a welcome refuge. The sun was rising over Lake Michigan, showing deep purple clouds on the horizon with a hint of gold at the water's edge. The birds were waking up and warbling to each other in the trees.

Ryan took a deep breath and started his jog again. He wanted to get to the water's edge and watch the sunrise, and he had the perfect place to do it.

As he passed a wooden bench with a memorial plaque, he thought about his visit to Jack's grave this past week. It was the second anniversary of his death, and seeing his name on the rounded white tombstone was heart-wrenching, especially with Jasmine and Bo at his side.

What could he have done to prevent Jack's death? He knew the thoughts were not productive and went down a dark path, but he couldn't help thinking if he had only seen the warning signs and re-read the intel report.

Standing beside Jack's grave also made him realize where his priorities lay. And it was not going to gay bars and dating. He owed his life to Jack, and he would take care of his family. That was his main priority and his reason for living.

And yet, as he slept on his couch, the longings only grew stronger. Each time, he pushed them away. Somewhere they might disappear forever. Concentrate on work, he told himself, and most importantly, concentrate on Jasmine and Bo.

When his mind wandered late at night it was difficult not to think of Mr. Smith. In his dreams, he actually went up those steps to the balcony. There was Suite #1, and he paused, imagining what was behind that door. But his feet wouldn't move. The door handle was just a foot away.

Behind that door, someone was waiting, no, anticipating his arrival.

All he had to do was open it. But each time in his dream, the door moved farther and farther from his reach. And each time he had that dream, he woke up restless and unsatisfied. A one-night stand with a stranger was not what he wanted, he kept telling himself. Though his body seemed to delight in rebelling.

He slowed his jogging as he came to a little dirt path off the main paved trail. It might look like a little rabbit trail through the brush to anyone just walking by. But it held much more importance to Ryan. It had been the spot where his father took him fishing early on Sunday mornings. It was their time alone together, and his father never answered his phone, which most days rang constantly.

They often just sat in silence and cast their lures into the water. They arrived by flashlight in the cold of the early morning, a cup of hot cocoa with marshmallows for Ryan and his father with his black coffee. The steam rose from the cups as they gazed at the lake and waited for the sun to rise.

This was the place where he scattered his father's ashes. Ryan followed the trail around a large oak to a grassy cliff overlooking the lake. The perfect place to watch the sunrise and think about his father and what might have been.

But when he pushed through the brush, Ryan abruptly stopped when he saw someone sitting there. A man dressed in black shorts and a gray t-shirt sat on the grassy cliff, gazing at the horizon. Ryan backed away, tripping on a branch when the man turned his head and smiled at him.

And that smile came from one of the most handsome men Ryan had ever seen. He had a chiseled face, strong jaw, and dark riveting eyes. Ryan caught himself staring and stammered, "I'll just be going."

The man's smile broadened as he stood and brushed himself off. "No need. Please stay." That face looked oddly familiar, and Ryan scanned his memory for where he had seen him before. The stranger brushed his hair off his forehead and squinted his eyes toward the horizon. "In fact, I was just leaving. It's a beautiful sunrise."

Ryan stood in place, his feet feeling like stone. The stranger stood and was a head taller than Ryan, broader in the shoulders, and had an infectious smile. "Elias Hastings," the man said, extending his hand. Ryan paused for a moment and then took it. The grip was strong, and a stir of electricity coursed through his body at the touch.

Ryan let go of the stranger's hand, stepped back, and finally found his voice. "Ryan Ward." The man nodded and gazed at the water, gently lapping at the beach.

"Well, it's good to meet you, Ryan Ward." He motioned to the horizon. "It's nice to get away from everything for just a few minutes before the day begins."

"Or ends," Ryan added with a smile. "Night shift."

"Oh?" Elias said, raising his brow. "And what do you do?"

"Police officer," Ryan explained. "I just started on the force a year ago.."

"You must see some interesting things on the night shift," Elias said. Ryan suppressed a smile. Nothing was interesting about the three drunks they arrested last night. Every night the same routine, and every night, the same crap from his partner Fritz.

Elias motioned back to the main trail with his head, "I'm headed to the coffee shop down the block. Care to join me?" Again, that irresistible smile.

And why not? Ryan thought. Why the hell not?

Chapter 10

Ryan watched Elias out of the corner of his eye as they strolled together down the sidewalk. The man's steps were effortless and graceful. The postal service drop box unexpectedly came up in his path, and Ryan jumped off the curb to avoid running into it. Mercifully, Elias didn't seem to notice. He chided himself. Was he in high school again? Ryan took a few deep breaths and tried to center himself.

For the life of him, Ryan couldn't think of anything worthwhile to say. Ryan was horrible at small talk, and after speaking about the weather and the sunrise, he couldn't think of anything else. So they talked about how much rain they had been getting recently. Ryan shook his head and almost let out a bitter laugh. Yes, the damn weather. There were a few points about jogging, but that was it. Then there was an uncomfortable silence, which Elias filled by talking a little about his work as a real estate developer and investor.

The guy was just so damn good-looking; it seemed to put Ryan's brain into some kind of mush soup. It was a relief to make it to the coffee shop. A little bell on the door tinkled as Elias opened the door for him. The Sip of Heaven Café was located on a busy corner of State Street. The morning rush was just starting as cars with frustrated drivers began piling up at the red light. Bikes and pedestrians in work clothes and tennis shoes trying to beat the morning rush.

The steamer's whoosh and freshly ground coffee aroma woke Ryan from his stupor. One sip of his plain black coffee helped clear his mind. Elias had recited a list of things he wanted for his latté. Light jazz played from the speakers, drowning out the low murmur of customers.

They found a cozy table in the corner. Elias was gazing out the window at the traffic as Ryan took another sip of his coffee and shook his head. "I'm sorry I suck at small talk."

Letting out a chuckle, Elias said, "With all the gregarious people I work with, this is actually quite a relief. I never get a moment of silence at work." Even as he spoke, his cell phone pinged. He looked at it and shoved it back in his pocket.

Ryan swirled his coffee. One thought turned around and around in his mind. Just how do you find out if the person you are talking to is gay? Do you ask? Was there some kind of code that he knew nothing about? The lingering handshake came to mind, but he shook it off. Even if Elias did lean that way, Ryan wasn't sure if he wanted to go there.

"So, Ryan, what brought you to Chicago?" Once again, those eyes held Ryan's. They were absorbing, curious, and strangely beckoning.

Clearing his throat, Ryan said, "Long story. Boring, really." He inclined his head, and Elias appeared to be hanging on his every word. "I lost my buddy in the war. His wife and son are here, up in Glenview." He gazed down at the table. "I just wanted to be close to them."

"Fate does give us some nasty turns," Elias said.

"So true," Ryan said with a wistful smile. "And how about you, Elias? What brought you to the city?"

"I grew up here," Elias motioned towards the window. "This is my home. Even with the good and the bad, I wouldn't change it for anything."

Ryan nodded, thinking about the time when he felt the same way. The time before his father passed.

"Listen," Elias said, "I need to tell you that our meeting was not quite a coincidence. And I understand if you walk out of here after what I tell you, and we never see each other again." His voice grew softer. "I am taking a risk. A huge risk."

Ryan set his coffee down. What was he saying? Elias continued. "I saw you at Rumors the other day. Forgive my being presumptuous..." His words trailed off.

Oh shit, Rumors. Ryan felt his face turn warm, and he glanced over his shoulder. "That was a mistake," Ryan began and watched as Elias's face fell. "No," he shook his head, "not in that way. I just wasn't ready."

"I understand," Elias said, inclining his head with a nod. "Most of the people I deal with in my business have no idea that I'm gay." Ryan marveled at how comfortable he was saying those words. "In fact, it would be disastrous for my line of work if it came out. I'm a bit of a public figure here in Chicago," he glanced around the small café, "and I have to be discreet."

Ryan let out a breath he didn't know he was holding. "Yes, I understand. Completely." He paused, not wanting to say anything more.

Ryan watched as Elias reached his hand over and touched the top of his hand. A gentle, warm touch. A pulse of electricity, a spark, glided over where Elias had touched. He looked down at their hands touching on the table, and then back up to Elias's eyes. Deep brown eyes were beckoning him with a language only his body understood. Did Elias feel it, too? He shook himself out of the spell. This guy was way out of his league. Big time.

Elias ran his finger lightly over Ryan's hand and brought it back to his coffee cup, eyes cast downward. "I would very much like it if you would join me for dinner." He glanced back up at Ryan. "Just as friends. I'd like to get to know you better. Someplace more private than this, where we can talk freely."

Ryan's heart was pounding in his chest, and his mind seemed to freeze. "I'm sorry." His tongue felt thick. "With Jasmine and Bo, I just can't do anything like that. Not now."

Elias nodded, frowned, and dabbed his mouth with a napkin. "I understand. I'm disappointed, but I understand."

He reached into his pocket and pulled out a cream-colored business card. "I'll be at Toulon's this evening at nine. I hope you'll come."

Ryan fingered the card, gazing down at the fine lettering written in calligraphy: Hastings Realty Development and Investment. He remembered seeing Toulons deep in the heart of the town. It was in one of the original buildings from the turn of the century. He turned the card over and saw that it had a cell phone number. Elias's private number. Ryan shook his head. "Toulons is a bit pricey on my salary."

Elias grinned. "I'm part owner, and I get a great deal. If you change your mind. I'll be there tonight. If not, I'm glad I got to meet you, regardless." Elias stood and extended a hand again to Ryan. Ryan paused, then took it, and for a moment, he didn't want to let go.

As Elias left, Ryan watched as he got out his cell phone and walked down the sidewalk back toward the park. There was no way he would go to Toulons tonight. But as he watched Elias walk away, he wished things were different. His life and his past just didn't allow for such things. He pocketed the business card and then, after another moment, brought it out again. Toulons. What would it hurt to have dinner? It was nothing. Nothing at all.

CHAPTER 11

E lias stood on the corner of the parking lot, his hands in his pockets, a baseball cap now shading his eyes. One person had recognized him during his impromptu visit to the coffee shop with another man. The black Lincoln was still creeping slowly as Elias opened the door and slid into the back seat. "Take us home, Bradley," he said to the driver. The older man nodded and accelerated toward the freeway.

It had all been so exhilarating, and Elias noticed for the first time that he was out of breath and felt giddy. He could still smell Ryan's aftershave and felt the touch of his hand. The skull tattoo on his forearm piqued his interest. Was there more? He wanted to trace each tattoo on that slender body. Undress Ryan right there in that damn café and take him on the table. That would make quite the headlines, he chuckled to himself.

It had been a wonderful distraction, and that's what he told himself. Coming back to reality as they drove past the familiar streets towards home was a letdown. The life and death games that Gretsky played had truthfully made him second guess his life. How many people would die for these little games? The adrenaline rush left him, and he slid against the back seat, exhausted. His father seemed to enjoy it all: the high stakes, the danger, and, most of all, holding other people's lives in his hands. How the hell did he do it?

He straightened his back and removed the baseball cap as they pulled into the driveway. His people counted on him. Hundreds in his company depended on him for their livelihood. And just across the threshold, Alicia would be furious at him. She had called twice this morning while he was meeting Ryan. He closed his eyes. Everything was happening too fast. They were supposed to be married next month.

And then his mind turned to Ryan Ward as the possibilities washed over him. Elias made a mental note to book a private dining room at Toulons tonight. Would Ryan come? He was the first to stand him up since he'd inherited his father's business. But even if Ryan didn't show up, this was far from over. The pursuit had begun, and it felt exciting and new to Elias. So different from the dark rooms above Rumors. He hadn't even bothered to get anyone's name, and they didn't want to know his. No, this was different. And to be truthful, a bit scary.

The iron gates opened as the car pulled into the driveway of his stately home. They closed behind with a loud clang as the vehicle continued up the winding drive. The house was hidden as his father intended: behind a mature growth of trees and shrubs, all manicured to perfection. Attention to detail had been the lesson his father had drilled into him. This attention was something that Alicia wished he had in more abundance.

And there, standing at the end of the drive, Alicia waited for them, glaring. Her white minidress and high heels stood in contrast to the red brick driveway and house. The windows were tinted, but Elias could swear she was staring him down. Before the car could come to a complete stop, she banged her fist against the side door, then opened the door and hopped in. "Where the hell have you been?" she asked, shoving Elias in the shoulder. "Once again, we're late to meet our wedding planner, Elias. Humiliating." She let out a frustrated scream. "Humiliating," she said again through her teeth.

She slumped down in the plush seat as her unsettling blue eyes narrowed on him. "I put it on your calendar. I called you twice—no three times, and you ignored me." She sat back in the seat, closed her eyes, and crossed her arms tight across her chest. "You know, maybe we should just call this whole thing off." She sat quietly now, staring straight ahead at the back of the front seat.

"Alicia," Elias started speaking, then paused. He took a deep breath. "I'm sorry I missed the appointment."

She gazed down at his shorts and scowled. "You can't go out like that. Damn you, Elias. I'll have to reschedule."

"We'll reschedule, and I will be there, Alicia."

She was quiet in her seat as she glared out the window. "If you're not there next time, Elias, I'm calling this off." She turned her narrowed gaze onto him. "Publicly, calling this off."

"Alicia," Elias sighed. "Please, I'm sorry."

She sat silent and fuming for a moment. Finally, she spoke, almost in a whisper. "After all we've been through togeth-er, I thought you would at least treat me with respect." Her words cut through him like acid.

Elias let out a deep breath and gazed down at his hands. "I'm sorry. Truly sorry. I'll make it up to you." He faced her squarely. "I truly appreciate what you're doing." She had been there when he had been at his lowest point: Overseas, heartbroken, and penniless. That foolish time, he tried to get away from his father.

Her blue eyes brightened. "I made us a dinner reservation tonight at the Cashmere Club. I thought we could just talk and have a good time. I'm getting calls every day for photo ops and interviews. I think if we could just have a night out, it'll be all over the papers and magazines."

Elias looked down at his hands. "I can't tonight. I'm so sorry. I've already made plans. What about tomorrow?"

"No, tomorrow doesn't work at all, Elias! It's hard to get reservations there." Her eyes narrowed. "You know that." With that, she opened the car door and slammed it, walking back up to the house without a glance behind.

Bradley was gazing back at him in the mirror. "Shall I proceed up the drive, sir?"

Elias nodded. He had to make time for this, or the rumors would start all over again, probably with more of a vengeance than before. If he was wise, he would just cancel everything, meet with the planner, and go to the club with Alicia. Elias shook his head. He was going to Toulon's tonight, and that was that. Even if Ryan didn't show up, it would still be worth it. Because if he did show up. He allowed himself a smile. Well, that would be a night to remember.

Before Elias could leave the car, Flynn jogged up to him. "Sir," he said, trying to catch his breath, "we've received word of a viable threat on your life."

Elias nodded, tempted to roll his eyes. "Of course, Gretsky would spread that rumor. I've been expecting it, Flynn. Up the security and keep an extra eye on Alicia."

Flynn nodded and rubbed his neck. "And this Ryan Ward?"

Elias looked up as the name at the forefront of his mind was spoken. "What of him?"

"This is the worst possible time to meet someone like that, Elias. I think you should call it off."

Elias paused. "I'm not worried, Flynn."

"I hope you're right, Sir," Flynn muttered. "I'll get on that security detail."

Gretsky had made empty threats before. Elias was prepared. But that would wait for a later date. Tonight was all about Ryan Ward.

Chapter 12

Ryan stepped out of the shower and grabbed a towel off the rack. It was getting close to the time Elias would be at Toulons. Gazing at his reflection, he took a slow breath and released it. He had done a quick search on the computer for Elias Hastings and wasn't sure what to make of the results. Elias was engaged to a woman, Alicia Sandstone, something or other. That had made him hesitate. There was a picture of them running on the beach barefoot, hand in hand, both smiling. It felt as if someone poured ice water over his head.

So, Elias was engaged. Did that mean anything? Elias was high profile in the news, and the photographers loved him. All the economic bigwigs lauded his realty purchases and successful investments. If Ryan wanted to stay under the radar, this was really a stupid move meeting this, Elias. Really stupid. He rubbed his chin and got out his razor. And yet here he was showering and had already picked out a suit. Toulons was not a place he would have chosen. Beer and hot wings would have been just fine. He wondered what Jasmine would think if she knew he was gay. He winced as he nicked himself with the razor.

Even though this was perhaps the stupidest thing he had ever done, Ryan kept going through the motions. After-shave, button-up shirt that's not too wrinkled—check and check. He glanced at the time. He could still make it.

His only transportation was the Harley, and Ryan was thankful it wasn't raining. Walking into Toulons with muddy dress pants was not how he wanted to present himself. Shit, he didn't want to walk into Toulons, period. Ryan didn't belong in a place like that. For a moment, he thought about unbuttoning the shirt, throwing on jeans and a t-shirt, and just nursing a beer in front of the television. Forget about Elias entirely. He stopped as he went to put on his pants. This was the moment. Stop what he was doing and just not go. He thought about Elias's hand touching his on the table. And with that memory lingering, he slipped the pants on and zipped them up.

The framed picture of Jasmine and Bo sat on the table by the door, and he gazed at it as he grabbed his leather jacket and helmet. Jasmine had said he should find someone to love and experience what she and Jack shared. He switched off the light, and his apartment fell into darkness behind him. A darkness he didn't want to face again. With this thought, he grabbed the keys and headed for his Harley.

Toulons was in the heart of town and had valet parking. The man at the front regarded him as he pulled up on his bike. Motorcycles were not the norm here, and Ryan was surrounded by BMWs and shiny red and black Porches. "Mr. Ward?" the man asked formally as Ryan flipped up the front of his helmet.

"Yes," Ryan said, idling the engine.

"You're expected, sir." He pointed to a spot next to a large planter. "There's room for your bike on the sidewalk here. Mr. Hastings has arranged to keep it safe."

Ryan paused. How the hell did he know about his motorcycle? Ryan's life was not a very open book, and the fact that Elias knew as much as he obviously did made him hesitant. Just how much did Elias really know about him? He suddenly wished he had done more research as well. Found out more about Elias Hastings than a few headlines. But he remembered that enticing smile, the touch, and kept going forward despite his new misgivings. Drawn enough to park his damn bike on the sidewalk and follow the gangly young man who didn't look old enough to drive.

He hesitated, then stepped through and into a small parlor. Large multi-paned glass windows looked out onto the main dining room floor. "Hello, Sir," a hostess stood behind a small wooden lectern. She smoothed her black dress and regarded her clipboard. "Reservation?" She took one look at his leather jacket, and her eyes narrowed. The valet whispered something in her ear, and she nodded, her facial features relaxing.

"Follow me," she said without enthusiasm. The hostess opened the glass doors to the dining area as gentle piano music greeted him, mixed with low conversations and clinking glasses. The place was packed with men and women dressed to the hilt in suits and elegant evening gowns. Ryan resisted the urge to find the main exit. More than a few people glanced his way, conversations halting as he passed in his leather jacket.

The hostess led him up a curving oak stairway leading to a balcony overlooking the main floor. A wrought-iron elevator stood waiting at the top, and the woman opened the gate and motioned him in. "You're going to the 10th floor," she said, without a hint of warmth, as she pushed several buttons and pulled a lever.

Did the elevator even work? Ryan stepped down on the grated floor and felt it sway. He peered up at the pulley system overhead. At least the ropes did not look frayed. "10th floor," she repeated as she left and made her way back down the stairs. He watched her for a moment and then stepped farther inside. The iron doors clanged shut, and the box began moving upward. Gears grinding from somewhere far above, Ryan hung on and was grateful when the whole thing came to a shuddering stop. A light indicated the 10th floor, and the iron doors opened.

As he stepped out, glass windows extended from the floor to the ceiling, revealing Chicago's night lights and skyline. He could see O'Hare airport and a plane taxied on the runway, taking off into the night sky. Below, tiny cars moved slowly on the freeway with row after row of red taillights.

"Ryan, you made it," a pleased and now familiar voice called to him from behind.

Ryan turned and saw Elias for what felt like the first time. Gone were the wrinkled t-shirt and shorts. This was the Elias he had seen online—clean-shaven, in a tailored black jacket and button-down shirt. Ryan was at a loss for words.

He was beside him, extending a smooth hand, and Ryan took it. His own hands felt calloused and rough in that firm grip.

For a moment, Ryan didn't want to let go. Let this moment linger. Elias swung an arm casually over his shoulder. "Come on, let me show you around."

As Elias led him to the double doors at the end of the hall, Ryan smiled. At this moment, close to Elias, there was no other place he'd rather be.

CHAPTER 13

Ryan sat back on the couch in the small room surrounded by tall windows, looking down at the Chicago skyline. Blue and red flames danced in a large gas-powered fireplace. Uncovered brick lined the walls with pictures of various snow-covered peaks. Ryan had already peeled off his jacket and finished a glass of the most delicious red wine he'd ever tasted.

Elias chopped onions and peppers in a makeshift kitchen with a hot plate and mini fridge as he talked about a recent trek to the Andes and his intense hatred of insects that bite.

Ryan caught himself laughing several times as Elias described trying to sleep with a small net around him and waking up to millions of bugs swarming him. Fresh crusty bread rested on a table, so warm it melted in Ryan's mouth.

"Quite a place you have here, Elias."

"Thank you," he said, handing Ryan a plate of stir fry. "My father was an original investor, and I've kept it. I love the view up here." Elias grinned and raised a toast. "To overpriced, over-dressed food joints."

Laughing, Ryan got up and clinked Elias's glass before downing the rest. Their eyes met momentarily, and Ryan noticed Elias's hand trembling. Was he affected, too? Ryan moved closer, his hand sliding up the back of Elias's hair, and pressed his lips gently against his. Those dark eyes bore hungrily into his. For a moment, the electricity moving between them was too much to handle. Elias's arms moved around him and brought him close for a deep, long kiss. Elias broke it off and smiled down at him, taking his hand. "Come on, I want you to try my stir-fry." He led Ryan back to a couch looking out the window, and he sat down.

The stir fry was delicious, and Ryan sat back on the couch, watching as Elias made himself comfortable, sitting cross-legged. "This is excellent, Elias."

Elias beamed. "I learned from the best. There was this cook at the boarding school in England. I helped him out, and in exchange, he taught me." He shrugged. "I've just kept cooking."

"I looked up your company," Ryan said between bites. "You own a lot of properties around here."

Elias smiled over his cup. "Yes, Hastings Enterprise is worldwide. But my roots are here in Chicago, and I wouldn't change it for the world."

"Congratulations on your engagement," Ryan said, watching him.

Elias's face flushed, and he struggled to swallow his last bite. "Yes," he said softly, "I should have known you'd see that. The whole town knows about it." He gazed out the window. "My arrangement with Ms. Sandstone benefits us both, but it's business and nothing else. Will that be a problem?" He watched Ryan.

"No, not a problem, Elias. It just surprised me."

"Rumors were starting to get out of hand, affecting business. But that's all it is: business."

Ryan allowed himself a slow smile. "And how does she feel about that?"

Elias brought his napkin to his mouth, still looking down at his plate. "Her modeling and acting career has taken off with the publicity. It's benefited us both." He glanced up at Ryan, "But that's all it is. I need to be discreet, and I understand if that's a non-starter for you." He winced, putting his fork down. "In fact," he paused, "I completely understand."

"I prefer discreet."

Elias's face instantly relaxed, and he smiled. "Okay, enough about me and my boring life. I'd like to know more about you, Ryan. Did you grow up here?"

Ryan thought about this, mopping up some of the sauce on his plate. "Yes, as a matter of fact, I spent my early years here."

"Your parents are from here?" Elias prodded.

"My mother was from here but died when I was young."

"Oh, I'm sorry, Ryan." Elias sat back thoughtfully. "I didn't know."

Ryan shook his head. "No, it's okay." He looked out the window at the city that had been less than kind.

"And your father?"

Ryan shook his head. "Also died when I was young. An unfortunate accident." His mouth felt dry. "Life goes on."

"Indeed," Elias said. "I lost my father as well when I was young. It takes a toll on you. A huge toll. Fortunately, I had Flynn, who raised me like a son. But I know others aren't as fortunate."

Ryan shrugged. "I was fortunate. I found some good homes, went into the system, and got bounced around, but had some good families."

"You know," Elias said with a smile, "I always thought I'd have kids of my own someday."

"I could see you as a father, Elias," Ryan grinned at the thought. "I've kind of adopted my buddy's son, Bo. He's a great kid. He's nine years old, and I'm sure he'll be a famous first baseman someday."

"You're lucky, Ryan. I just can't allow anyone to get that close. I've gotten burned so many times." He motioned around them. "And I have these clandestine meetings in dark back rooms." Elias grimaced, then looked back hopefully at Ryan.

Ryan responded by moving closer to him on the couch.

Elias grabbed his hand. "Come on, let me show you the rooftop."

He grabbed his leather jacket and followed Elias down the windowed corridor to a large metal door with a *No Entry* sign. Elias punched in a code, and the door clicked open. He swung the door, revealing worn wooden stairs that led up to a smaller wooden door. Elias punched in another keypad lock, and the door to the outside opened. The cold air hit them as they got to the top of the building. And in the distance, the skyline of Chicago stretched before them. Ryan reached the edge and gazed out. The nighttime lights were beautiful and extended as far as the eye could see. The moon was a crescent, and dim stars were faded by the bright city lights. Ryan thought he saw movement on the rooftop across the street. He looked again. Nothing.

"It's beautiful, Elias," Ryan leaned over to gaze down at the street below.

Elias came up beside him on the edge and turned to face him. A hand came under his leather jacket and around his waist. Ryan moved closer, nuzzling into Elias's neck, lips brushing against his cheek.

It was a gentle, exploratory kiss, and Elias was content to follow his lead. But when Ryan moved his tongue between Elias's lips, he no longer followed Ryan's pace. Elias moved in hungrily, a deep kiss, cupping his hands under Ryan's chin, and drawing him in close. His hands ran down under Ryan's shirt, and he undid his belt. They moved back farther into the shadows of the brick wall. Elias came up for air, tracing his lips down Ryan's neck, the leather jacket falling to the ground. Elias lowered Ryan onto the ground, his mouth fully pressed against his, fumbling with his shirt buttons.

The sound of a scrape on the roof was faint, but it was enough for them both to stop momentarily. On the roof, not far from them, was a shadow. It hadn't been there before. Ryan instinctively reached for a gun that wasn't there. A man in a black jacket and black ski mask was on the roof edge. A weapon with a silencer leveled at the two of them.

"Keep your hands where I can see them," the man said, motioning them apart. His voice had the raspy twang of a lifelong smoker. "Stay on your knees. Any sudden movements and I shoot." Cold eyes under that mask regarded Elias. "I bring one last message from Gretsky." Ryan raised his hands, wishing he had his gun, chastising himself. The intruder wasn't a large man. Ryan knew he could take him. But as soon as he thought it, a crack came down on his skull. Lightning flashed before his closed eyes, sudden and swift. Ryan fell to the ground, an excruciating pain turning everything black.

CHAPTER 14

Ryan's head exploded with pain as he woke up and couldn't remember where he was. His ears rang, and he felt a surge of panic. The cold cement of the rooftop had scraped his hands and cheek where he fell. It hurt to move his arm, but he could do it. Without opening his eyes, he carefully moved his fingers and flexed his toes. The ringing slowed, and he started to make out words.

Someone was speaking, but it wasn't Elias. He opened one eye, just a slit, and saw that malevolent figure dressed in black, and his mind started to clear. It took an effort to keep his breathing slow and even. Instinctively, Ryan reached for his gun, but again, it wasn't there. Only an unbuttoned shirt. He swore under his breath. What he wouldn't do for his gun right now.

The words became clearer, and the man was speaking to Elias. Words filled with bitter hatred. "Gretsky wanted this to be as painless as possible. I don't work that way." Ryan saw the man put his Ruger up to Elias's temple, pushing the barrel hard into his skin. "You had Tommy killed." He took off the safety. "I'm going to fuckin enjoy this."

"Get it over with," Elias said, voice calm and steady.

The man let out a cruel laugh. "Let me savor the moment. Do you think Flynn will miss you? He'll come work for us. No one will miss you, Elias. No one." He pushed the gun harder against Elias's head, forcing him to twist his neck to the side.

"Tommy deserved to die," Elias said through clenched teeth. "He was a low-life prostitute who did anything for the highest bidder."

"You son of a bitch." He struck Elias across the face with a sickening crunch of bone.

Elias fell to the ground, moaning and holding his nose, then became very still. The attacker brought his gun down towards Elias's head. "Eat this, you little prick."

Without thinking, Ryan got up and lunged from behind. He wrapped his arm around the man's neck, placing him in a chokehold.

"What the hell?" the man said, his voice muffled as he squirmed under Ryan's arm. He brought his gun up, and it went off with a deafening crack. The brick wall behind him was hit inches from Ryan's head.

The sound of the gun had frozen Ryan, and the man elbowed him hard in the gut. As Ryan doubled over in pain, the attacker gave him a swift kick in the upper thigh that burned and brought Ryan down hard on the cement. The gun went off once more, and Ryan felt a wave of deep pain in his shoulder that made his breath stop. He had been hit. A frantic knocking and rattling came from the rooftop door down to the main building.

For a moment, his vision faded, and Ryan was back in Afghanistan. The taste of blood and sand on his tongue, the Humvee hit by an IED, his ears ringing from the explosion. The shrapnel had burrowed deep into his chest, but Ryan kept breathing. As long as he had breath, he would fight. Ryan shook his head. He was not in Afghanistan. He was here, and he was in danger.

Adrenalin surged through Ryan, and he managed to stand. He brought his arm down hard against the attacker's gun arm, trying to gain control. But the man had it in an iron grip, and they locked arms. A loud gunshot burst went off behind them, and the rooftop door came crashing in.

The man turned just for an instant, and it was enough. Ryan twisted the gun barrel towards the attacker and nudged the trigger, and it went off with a deafening boom. For a moment, the man was still as fearful eyes regarded Ryan out of the slits of the black mask. The gun clattered to the ground as his hands went up to his neck. Blood oozed around his fingers and onto his jacket as he fell forward, collapsing on the ground.

His head was twisted into an unnatural position as his chest heaved unevenly. Blood spilled out onto the white cement. His breath was now an audible gurgle and then nothing. A horrible silence. Ryan was frozen in place and then kicked the gun away from his grasp. But he knew. The man had died from the gunshot. His gunshot.

He knelt, feeling for a pulse. The attacker was still under that black mask, a tongue protruding from the mouth hole. *Oh shit, oh shit, oh shit.* Ryan reached for a cell phone that wasn't there. Only then did he turn his head and see Elias lying lifeless on the ground.

"Elias!" he shouted. He took several uneven steps and collapsed beside him. "Elias," he said as he felt for a pulse.

Relief flooded through him when he found it, and Elias moaned. Voices started shouting behind them. The pain in his shoulder became excruciating, and Ryan longed for oblivion as he wrapped his arm around Elias.

"Ryan Ward," he heard a familiar voice from above them. Several men Ryan didn't recognize began moving him away from Elias. They had a medical kit, and Ryan caught a whiff of the familiar odor of smelling salts. He heard Elias begin to cough. "He's out cold," a voice said.

"Ryan Ward," a voice said, this time more urgently. The familiar lilt of an English accent made Ryan remember. He turned to see the older man with a white crew cut and light blue eyes. It hit him now. It was the older gentleman from Rumors. "Come, let's get you off the roof and get you some help."

Ryan didn't move. "No, I'm staying right here with Elias." Ryan gazed up at the older man as ice-cold eyes met his.

"You're coming with us," the older man repeated, motioning to two other men. They both grabbed Ryan roughly by the arms. This time, he didn't resist as they hauled him away.

Chapter 15

Pain surged down Ryan's shoulder as the two men, dressed in blue shirts and caps with the Toulon's restaurant logo, eased him onto the floor, a throw blanket for a makeshift pillow. His shoulder was oozing blood slowly where he had been shot. They stripped him of his shirt and applied a pressure bandage.

The bullet had just grazed his shoulder, and one of the men gave him the infuriating nickname *Lucky Boy*. If Ryan heard it one more time, he was going to punch him. And now he lay down alone, gazing out the window. The same room, what seemed like minutes before he had eaten with Elias. But at first, where Ryan had seen the beauty of the city skyline at night, it now took on a more sinister glow.

Somewhere out there were people who wanted Elias killed. And why? As for his part, killing a man, even in self-defense as an off-duty officer, was something that needed to be reported and investigated as soon as possible. Where was his damn phone? Why wasn't an ambulance here yet? All these questions flooded his mind as an older, compact man crouched beside him.

"Hello, Ryan," he said with that distinct English accent. Ryan turned to the familiar icy blue eyes with distinguished wrinkles at the edges and trim crew cut. "We've met before under very different circumstances," he said slowly. "Do you remember me?"

The night he first stepped into the gay bar flooded Ryan's mind: the business card that said Suite #1 and Mr. Smith. "Yes," he said through dry lips, "I remember."

"My name is Flynn, and I work for Elias."

The entire night started to snap into place. "Where's Elias?" Ryan raised his head, searching the room. Dizziness and nausea swept over him. "Is he okay?"

"He'll be fine. Lay down and rest." He gently pushed Ryan back down onto the floor. "I'd take it easy for a few more minutes. You've had a nasty concussion. How's your shoulder?"

His bandage was starting to seep with blood, and the dull ache only seemed to increase in intensity. "I'll be all right," Ryan said. "What happened to Elias?"

Flynn's gaze traveled to the floor. "He's had a bad concussion and a broken nose. He'll be all right. But you won't be seeing him." He leveled his gaze again at Ryan. "In fact, it would be for the best if the two of you never crossed paths again."

"No." Ryan groaned as he sat up. "I need to see him." This time, the dizziness eased. "Where is he?"

"You think you're special?" Flynn flipped a familiar card in his lap.

Suite #1

Ryan's face flushed.   A growing realization settled over him as he realized he'd been played. Had it all been a lie? The meeting at the park? He'd been blinded by a longing to open up. Never again. The flags had been there, but he'd been too eager to see them.

"Now you get it. Mr. Smith chews through guys like you.. You're not special. Elias does this all the time. Tomorrow he'll be on to someone new."

Ryan glanced around the room, seeing only strangers. And as his mind cleared further, he realized the shooting had never been reported. What the hell? There were no sirens in the distance. The men in this room were not police or medics. His cell phone was in his jacket, which was nowhere to be seen. "Where's my coat?"

Flynn glanced towards the door and at the men who had assisted Ryan. "We didn't see a coat." It was a lie, Ryan knew. An outright lie.

Ryan reached up to the table to help himself stand. He squeezed his eyes shut as a wave of pain shot down his arm. "I need to report this. Can someone find me a phone?" His voice rose in volume as he addressed the men in the room. "Can someone get me a damn phone?"

Flynn put his finger to his lips. "Shhh. Calm down. You aren't helping anyone." His hand touched Ryan's back, his voice lowered. "It would be better for all involved if this didn't get reported."

"What?" Ryan didn't think he heard correctly.

Flynn nodded with a frown as he lowered his voice. "You heard me," he motioned to the rooftop. "We've already cleaned up the body and the evidence. And we will deny any of this happened, as will Elias."

"They'll believe me," Ryan replied, leaning against the wall and pointing to his bandage. "I have a gunshot wound to prove it."

"You need to think, Ryan. Really think. What will happen to you if you report this? What will happen to your career?" He paused, then glanced at Ryan, his face unreadable. "You've just killed a man. And if you hadn't, Elias would be dead, and so would you." He took a breath in through clenched teeth. "I'm grateful for what you've done. You've done everyone a favor. But, if this goes through the police, it will get very messy."

Ryan let out a slow, steady breath. This was not a battle he could win. It was best to wait until he got home to do anything. This Flynn had a dangerous edge to him. Ryan had seen it in his eyes. It was best not to say anything further.

Flynn motioned to the men nearby. "These two will get you fixed up and take you home. What you do after that is up to you." The two men with blue uniforms crowded to either side of Ryan, grabbing an arm. Ryan pushed him away.

"Easy there, Lucky Boy," one man said, "go easy on that right shoulder."

Ryan nodded, avoiding Flynn's gaze. They had brought him a button-down Toulon uniform and helped him slip it on.

As he was being escorted out, Ryan had one more question for Flynn. "Who was that up there? He mentioned someone named Gretsky?"

Flynn held him in a steady gaze, then shook his head. "Hmm? Never heard that name."

Once again, Ryan held Flynn's gaze. The lie was obvious. Ryan knew what he heard up there on the rooftop. He would never forget those lifeless brown eyes or that protruding tongue out of the mask.

"We'll deal with this ourselves," Flynn said. "I promise you. Whoever's responsible will be brought to justice."

Ryan nodded. The man had said the name Gretsky more than once. He would find out himself.

"Come on," Flynn said. "We've arranged your transport home." Flynn nodded to the men. "We'll keep your bike safe until you can come to pick it up."

The men moved to either side of Ryan and took him by the arms. As he left the door, he looked back again at Flynn. "This isn't over," Ryan said to him.

"That's your choice," Flynn replied with a shrug. He gazed at his fingernails. "But if you choose that path, I promise you..." Those blue eyes regarded him with an unspoken menace. "Your life will become a living hell. That much I can promise."

It was far from over. Ryan craned his neck, looking for Elias as he was guided firmly down the hall. He wanted to speak to him, if only for a moment. How much did Elias know? He had ties to this Gretsky, and the man on the roof had accused Elias of killing someone. These thoughts swirled around his mind as the men led him out of the back loading dock. A black car was waiting for him, with the engine running.

CHAPTER 16

The only light in the apartment was the red glow from the clock that read 3:10 AM and the shadows cast by the outside streetlights. Ryan hadn't bothered to turn the lights on as he flopped on the couch with his blood-stained shirt.

He lay on his back, staring up at the ceiling. The men had shoved him out of the back seat and deposited him on his doorstep. "Guys like you are a dime a dozen to Elias," one of the men said with a cruel smile.

"Remember that for next time. *Lucky Boy*." The man tossed his lost cell phone at him. They had kept it from him all this time. The bastards. The car sped off into the night as Ryan fumbled with his keys.

Ryan couldn't close his eyes. When he did, all he saw was blood pooling on that roof and lifeless eyes staring at him from beneath a black mask. The body was out there, somewhere in Chicago, rotting away. And he had done it. The blood was on his hands.

He held his cell phone in his hands, staring at the picture of Jasmine and Bo, wearing White Sox baseball caps and smiling at him. The right thing was to call the police.

All of this could come back to bite him. Hard. What would keep Flynn and his buddies from framing him? Somehow, he didn't think that would be the case. They wanted this kept quiet. From Flynn's expression, he wouldn't mind if Ryan's body ended up as fish food at the bottom of Lake Michigan.

Outside, a dog barked, and a car drove slowly past his apartment. Ryan tensed as the headlights briefly flashed inside his apartment and then disappeared down the road.

Loneliness washed over him. He was alone. Truly alone, with no one to call in the wee hours of the morning when he needed to talk. Jasmine had to work at the hospital at the crack of dawn. He would never forgive himself for waking her up.

He tossed the cell phone on the coffee table and sank helplessly back on the couch. In dark times, memories of his father washed over him. He thought about their last fishing trip together.

Sitting side by side on a grassy bank, lines loose as Lake Michigan lapped onto the rocks. "Son," he said as he reeled in his line, "some people are evil. You need to know that." He patted Ryan on the back and gave him a half-smile. There was an urgency in his father's voice that morning. "Some men deserve to die, Ryan. In this world, it's kill or be killed."

Ryan had watched his father's face, memorized it as his gaze turned back toward the horizon. He would never forget that day. It was the last time he would ever see him. And that advice, to kill or be killed, had served him well. Had kept him alive in his tours overseas. And tonight was no different. That man had deserved to die. If he hadn't shot him, both he and Elias would be dead. It was a good kill. A *clean kill,* as his commanding officer used to say.

He cradled the bandage on his shoulder, which had started to throb. The attacker on the roof had said the name Gretsky. He remembered it clearly. It was a familiar name, like a far-away dream he couldn't quite grasp. "You have to forget about your past," his caseworker explained when he was 8 years old. "You have a new name now." They had flown him from Chicago to Gainesville, and he had gone into a home with other girls and boys. Gretsky. That name meant something.

He got up, poured himself some water, and found the old ibuprofen bottle to remove the pain. *A dime a dozen.* That's all he was to someone like Elias. Nothing more. Time to focus on what mattered the most, and that was protecting Jasmine and Bo. His promise to Jack. He had no business doing anything else and wouldn't make the same mistake twice.

Ryan grabbed a cold beer from the fridge and shuffled down to the hall closet, pausing as he stared down at his safe. He turned the combination, and it opened with a click. Inside was his personal 9 MM, which he had bought after serving in Afghanistan.

He hadn't wanted to touch a weapon off duty and was reluctant even now. Keep work at work, he told himself. But now, he would need to carry again. To protect himself. Protect Jasmine and Bo. Protect Elias? His stomach felt a lurch at the thought. He felt the heft of the gun, the familiar grooves on the grip, and the smooth trigger. He checked the magazine. He wouldn't be without it now. A necessary evil.

As he closed the closet door and returned to the living room, he thought about his promise to devote his life to Jasmine and Bo. The truth was, his mind betrayed him. Despite all the subterfuge, all he wanted to do was be with Elias. The physical memory of him invaded his senses. A hint of his aftershave was still present even now. There was a connection when he was with Elias. Something he couldn't put his finger on. A familiarity as if he knew him inside and out and still longed to discover more. To experience life at his side, to look into those dark eyes and get lost in them. Just being in his presence was intoxicating.

He sat back on the couch, popped open his beer, and took a long swig, letting the cold, bitter taste wash down his throat. He longed for something stronger. Just an hour ago, he had killed a man.

Ryan was alone in this world. Just as it was always meant to be. But as he lay in the darkness beside his gun, all he could think about was Elias. Where was he right now? Was he all right? More than anything, Ryan wanted to be beside him, take him in his arms, and tell him everything would be all right.

Chapter 17

Elias awoke in his bed, feet twisted in the sheets, sunlight streaming through the curtains. A cool breeze filtered in from the open window, feeling good on his aching body. Birds chirped from the old oak outside. The light hurt his eyes. He squinted at the clock, and it was already mid-afternoon.

Memory fragments began to return to his mind. He smiled as he remembered his mouth on Ryan's, feeling his skin and his passionate reaction to his touch. He reached for Ryan but came down on the empty sheets beside him. The bed was empty. His eyes widened when he saw a bloodstain on his pillowcase, reached up, and felt steri-strips across his nose and cheek.

Where was Ryan? Memories of the attack crashed back. What the hell? He tried to get up, but his head began to pound and he collapsed back down on the pillow. He remembered the masked man on the roof, the gun digging into his head.

He looked again at the splatter of dried blood soaked into the white pillowcase. His blood? Where was Ryan? Adrenaline struck through the pain. As he tried to get up, a wave of nausea struck him, and once again, he fell back on the bed. Near the door, Flynn slumped in the recliner, his eyes closed and breathing even. He was still in his wrinkled evening clothes, unshaven.

More gingerly, Elias raised sat up. The movement caused Flynn to awaken.

"Elias," he muttered, raising his hand. "Don't get up. You need to rest."

Elias managed to remain upright, his head clearing. "What happened, Flynn?" His throat was dry, and his voice raspy. He frowned as he tasted blood on his lip. "How did I get back home? What the hell happened?"

Flynn shook his head, not looking up. "I've been over it a thousand times, Elias. I don't know." He finally looked up at Elias with those cold blue eyes. "I promise you I'll find out. Whoever's responsible will pay."

"And Ryan?" Elias swung his legs over the bed as a deep ache hit his thighs. He rubbed his face with his hands and felt his tender, swollen nose. Breathing itself was painful. He had to clear his mind, to think.

Flynn sat up, more awake now. "Please don't get up, Elias. Ryan is all right. He's fine."

Memories swirled in Elias's mind. The gun. The blood. It just didn't add up. "The truth, Flynn."

Again that damning silence, and then Flynn let out a long sigh. "He's alive. A bullet grazed his shoulder. He'll be fine."

Elias's chest tightened. "And the attacker?"

"Shot dead. It's all taken care of. No need to concern yourself."

Elias's eyes narrowed. "How exactly did he die, Flynn?" He was hiding something. "Tell me the truth."

Flynn's expression was grim. "Ryan killed the attacker. Shot him in the neck."

Elias ran his hand through his hair and wanted to punch something. Anything. His worst nightmare had come to pass. He had gotten Ryan mixed up in this. The reason why he never got involved with anyone. He had broken his own rule, and now everyone would pay. He squeezed his eyes shut. "How could this happen, Flynn? How did Gretsky know we'd be up there?"

"I'm looking into that," Flynn hesitated, "and there's another matter that we need to discuss."

How could things get any worse? Elias shook his head. It had only taken a few moments for everything to fall apart.

Flynn regarded Elias with a steady gaze. "We have a mole."

A mole? It took Elias a moment to comprehend. The thought was like a punch to the gut, but it had to be. How else would Gretsky have known his whereabouts? All the employees in his company were carefully vetted. Loyalty and integrity were of the utmost importance. Had Gretsky managed to plant someone close to him? Only a few knew about his rendezvous last night.

Flynn stood and smoothed out the wrinkles in his jacket. "As for this Ryan Ward, we will deny any knowledge of him. I warned him not to call the police, but," he paused, "he may have already."

Elias usually kept his cell phone by his bedside, but for the first time, he noticed it wasn't there. "Where's my phone, Flynn?"

Flynn regarded him suspiciously. "Why? Why do you need a phone right now?"

"I'm calling Ryan."

Flynn did not break eye contact. His voice was even and steady. "That's a bad idea, Elias. A really bad idea. You need to think. Your father trusted me with his life, and so should you. Do not contact him."

Elias shook his head. "You'll have to trust me, Flynn. Just once, and I'll ensure he's out of our lives."

Flynn was silent, got up, and walked to the window, peering through the curtains. "I could have lost you last night." His voice softened. "Gretsky came too close to taking the one thing in this world that means the most to me."

"I know Flynn. But I'm alive. I'm here. And Gretsky will pay."

"If your cop hadn't been there..." Flynn trailed off.

"Have someone check on Ryan, Flynn. Those are my direct orders. Make sure he's all right." When Flynn hesitated, Elias continued. "And we'll make Gretsky pay. That's a promise."

Flynn looked like he was about to say something but changed his mind. He nodded with a bitter expression, fishing Elias's cell phone out of his pocket and dropping it on the dresser. "I'll send someone over to check on Ryan Ward," Flynn said with a clipped voice. He took one last look at Elias before closing the door firmly behind him.

Elias fell back on the bed and stared up at the ceiling. He could have been killed last night. Ryan could have died. This mess was of his own making. Ryan had saved his life. Flynn was right. The best thing to do was forget him. Deny knowing him. And still, he longed to get in touch with him. Speak to him and make sure he was all right. There was just something about him. Something that made him not want just a one-night stand. He wasn't like the others.

He closed his eyes, and the image of Ryan came unbidden to his mind. Imagined him at his bedside. Elias gazed into those troubled blue eyes, wanting to feel the warmth of his skin, explore every inch of that body with his tongue, and trace every tattoo. He tried to stop the fantasy, but his mind did not cooperate. He turned to his side, the pain obliterating the image.

He pulled the blanket over his head to block the light streaming from the window. Despite everything, he felt a connection—a longing that he hadn't felt in some time. He couldn't endanger Ryan again, and he vowed never to put him in harm's way again. But for now, his head ached, and as he closed his eyes, oblivion soon came over him.

CHAPTER 18

T he street lights flickered outside Ryan's first-floor apartment, casting shadows on the street. Strong coffee percolated in the kitchen.

A piece of toast lay half-eaten on the counter and hadn't settled on his stomach. One hour until his shift started. He was not looking forward to walking into the department.

Ryan slipped on his black uniform pants and fastened his belt. The shirt he'd leave for last.

The bandage on his shoulder still seeped. Anything against his skin was painful. Even reaching up to the cupboard for his coffee cup had been excruciating.

Three low raps banged against his front door. Ryan reached for a gun that wasn't there. Three more knocks, now louder. He peered out the curtain. A nondescript black sedan had parked outside by the curb.

His phone lay untouched on the kitchen counter, and he glanced at it guiltily. He still hadn't called in the shooting. "Ryan Ward?" A voice called from outside, followed by two more insistent raps.

"Coming," Ryan called and slipped on his shirt, only bothering with a few buttons. He peered through the spy hole and saw a man on the other side he didn't recognize.

He was a head shorter than Ryan but compact. He sported a shaved head and had light brown skin. Stubble from a 5:00 shadow was on his chin, and a grin revealed straight white teeth. The man glanced back at the street and then smiled at the keyhole. "Chicago PD, just want to ask a few questions," he called through the door.

Ryan opened the door part-way, and the man flashed a badge. "Detective Lorenzo Chavez, are you Ryan Ward?"

"Yes, I am." Ryan didn't budge from the doorway.

Brown world-weary eyes met his own. The detective flashed a disarming smile. "Can I come in?"

The detective slipped by him as Ryan continued buttoning his shirt. The detective eyed the gun holster on the couch, then glanced back at Ryan. "Quite a place you have here." He picked up a picture on the table beside the door. "This your regimen?"

"Yeah, Afghanistan, 2 tours." Ryan grimaced. "Look, I can't talk right now. I'm getting ready for work."

Chavez tapped the picture. "I've done a check on you, Ryan Ward. Military honors. The first year on the force," he glanced up. "Stuck on DUI patrol." His eyes locked on Ryan's. "So what were you doing with the likes of Elias Hastings last night?"

Ryan went to the kitchen and poured himself some coffee, his hand shaking. "Just dinner."

"What did you discuss?"

Ryan clutched his coffee cup, his mind reeling. "Nothing much. We met during a jog at the park. That's it."

Chavez nodded his head, glancing down. "I see. And I'll ask again, what did you discuss?"

"Real estate," Ryan shrugged. "It wasn't a big deal."

Chavez raised a brow. "Trying to find a better place?"

"Something like that," Ryan said, plopping back on the couch. He was done standing, his shoulder stabbed at him.

Frowning, Chavez looked around and lowered his voice. "Listen, I've been investigating Hastings Enterprise for years now." He reached into his jacket and took out a picture. It was an older man talking to Elias. "Did you see this man last night?"

Ryan glanced at the picture. A handsome man with gray teasing the edge of his temples sat across a table from Elias. The two were locked in an intense conversation. Who was that? "No, I've never seen him before," Ryan said, shaking his head.

"Caesar Gretsky," the detective said, placing the picture back in his inner pocket. "Did Elias mention his name last night?"

The name Gretsky coming up once again. The man on the roof had said that name. Something nagged at the back of his mind. "No, nothing."

The detective handed him a small white card. "If you re-member anything, call me. It's important."

Detective Lorenzo Chavez was written in tiny print, with a phone number at the bottom. He turned before leav-ing. "Listen, from one cop to another. Elias Hastings is bad news. Stay away." He took one last glance around the apartment and left without a word.

Ryan locked the door and drew in a long breath. He threw the card on the side table. What the hell was that all about? Did the police know about the shooting and were testing him? He pulled the curtains aside and glanced out the window. The sedan had already driven away.

There were decisions he needed to make—life-altering decisions. He glanced at his cell. Elias's number was on the screen, just waiting for him to push the button to dial.

He thought of his father, tousling his hair before work. He had always known when something was bothering him. "You can tell me anything, son. Anything."

A thought hit him, and he went to the hallway closet. Cardboard boxes were stacked neatly inside and labeled in black marker. He scanned the contents: books, shoes, and a box labeled *pictures* on the bottom of the stack. His last remnants from childhood were all stuffed into an 8x8 box. He slid it out and ripped open the packaging tape.

Loose pictures, ticket stubs to baseball games, and a few GI Joe action figures were all mixed in a heap, one on top of the other. He reached to the bottom and pulled out the older pictures.

He had managed to grab a few things before they were confiscated. "Forget the past," his social worker said. "Forget everything." As a boy, he hadn't understood. But he hung on to what he could.

One picture was stuck on the bottom and had gotten wet, and an orange blob had overtaken part of the photo. It was of Ryan's father and his four business partners, and behind them, a white granite high-rise building with large windows. They stood beneath a tree with red blossoms. Right next to his father was an older man with a full head of white hair and striking high cheekbones, arms around each other's backs.

He flipped over the picture, and on the back, in cursive writing, were the men's names. There, clear as day, was the name Alexis Gretsky. He knew he had seen that name before.

Ryan turned the picture back over and looked at his father again. He was so happy, and that smile on his face was genuine. Handsome, even in his business suit, he looked like he would be more at home on a cattle ranch. Brown hair slicked back from his forehead, he had the same athletic build as Ryan.

His father was charismatic, and that quick wit drew everyone into his sphere. Ryan suddenly wished he was with him again, fishing, just side by side for the morning and afternoon. During those moments, he didn't have to share his father with anyone else.

Forget the past, echoed in his mind again. He glanced at his father again before stuffing the picture into his shirt pocket.

He fingered the numbers on his cell phone and thought about Elias. The pain in his shoulder throbbed, so he gulped down a couple more Ibuprofen and finished fastening his tie.

His reflection looked pale and gaunt. He could go to work and reveal everything. And then what?

He heard tires rolling on the pavement outside, and Ryan peered out through the curtains. There was another vehicle outside that he didn't recognize. A black SUV had parked nearby. Dark windows illuminated by the streetlight. He adjusted the holster under his jacket, gripping the handle of his 9MM reassuringly.   Outside, the SUV disappeared.

Focus, he told himself. *Focus through the pain.* He took a large swig of coffee from his cup and reached up to the hook for his bike keys. They weren't there. He cursed under his breath. He had forgotten. His bike was still at Toulon's. He'd have to take the damn bus to work.

Chapter 19

Ryan walked at a brisk pace through the streets of Chicago. Streetlights casting shadows down the alley ways.

He still had a good half hour before his shift started. A couple of blocks down, a horn honked behind him. He looked back and saw a familiar red Jeep with the Ass, Cash or Grass, No One Rides For Free sticker on the bumper. The first part of the sticker was scraped off and mostly unreadable. Ryan smiled. That had happened when Bo started learning to read.

Jasmine pulled up and rolled the window down. "Ryan!" she called out.

"I've been worried sick about you. Get in."

Ryan gave her a huge smile. "Thank you, Jazz."

Jasmine scooped the 70s rock CDs aside as Ryan hopped in. Her long black hair was pulled up in a bun, and she was in her jeans and flowered t-shirt. "Why didn't you answer my calls? I thought something had happened to you. I even called down to the station."

"I'm so sorry, Jazz. I got caught up in some things."

She came to a stoplight and raised a brow. "Really? Have you met someone?" She slipped into a half-smile. "Someone I should know about?"

Ryan felt his face redden. "No, nothing like that."

The light turned green, and she turned away. "Yeah, you wouldn't look like shit if you had met someone. Honestly, Ryan, you look like you belong in a morgue."

"Thanks, Jazz."

"Why are you walking to work? Where's your bike?"

Ryan paused. He hated lying to her. "It's in the shop," he said finally. "I should get it back shortly. But for now, I have to hit the pavement."

"Not when you've got me, you don't! I'll take you to work and pick you up."

"No need, Jasmine. You've got enough on your plate." In the rearview mirror, he saw a black SUV briefly illuminated by a streetlight. His chest tightened.

Then the SUV turned down a side street, and he kept his eyes trained on the mirror.

"You are wound tight, Ryan. What the hell?"

Ryan took two calming breaths and sank back in the seat. "I'm sorry, Jazz. It'll be okay."

"Well, shake yourself out of it. Bo's game is this weekend, and he doesn't want you to miss it."

Ryan glanced out the window. He had forgotten about his big game. He was going to be playing 2nd base. "I'll be there. I promise."

"You better, mister."

She drove up to the entrance of the police station and put on the brakes. "We should have a date night out. Just the two of us. You know my niece extended her stay by a few days. Maybe she could join us?"

Ryan smiled. "Thanks. I'll pass."

She raised a brow. "Your loss!"

Ryan hopped out and leaned into the window. "Thanks for the ride, Jazz. I'll see you and Bo at the game."

Jasmine smiled. "Luv ya!" she called out as she sped off into the night.

Ryan walked through the main doors of the Chicago Police Department. The sturdy three-story brick building built in the 1870s had survived fires, riots, and a few homemade bombs.

Inside, pictures of all the fallen officers lined the walls. A solemn row of men and women in uniform, all captured in still life at the prime of their careers. Last night, Ryan came close to joining them.

As he entered the lobby, security glanced up at him. Officers and well-dressed lawyers were walking out like they were on a mission. Phones rang nonstop inside the control center.

"Look who the cat dragged in." The voice came from behind, and Ryan turned to his partner, Fritz. A coffee cup in his hand. "You look like shit, Ward." His little desk was next to Fritz below a coveted window. He hung his backpack over the chair.

Over by the break room, several officers gathered around the little television mounted on the wall. The sound was muted, but scrolling along the bottom were the words:

Body Washed up at Riverside Park.

Fritz guzzled his coffee. "You haven't heard? This is the second body to wash up at Riverside Park recently." He shook his head. "What's the city coming to anyway? They need more cops like us. That's what they need."

"Have they identified the body?" Ryan asked, feigning disinterest.

"Not yet," Fritz said,

"Have you heard anything else?" Ryan couldn't take his eyes off the television screen. Could this be the man he killed? The TV briefly flashed to a long black body bag being hoisted onto a stretcher.

"Maybe you and I will get the killers tonight," Fritz chortled. "In between drunks, that is. Come on, Ward. We've got to get going."

"Give me just a minute," Ryan said.

"I'll meet you in the parking lot. We'll stop by Chesters for some hot dogs?"

Ryan nodded. "I'll be right there."

Ryan fished in his shirt pocket, where he stashed the picture of his father and the four other men. He looked again at the words: Alexis Gretsky.

Gretsky, he thought again. Caesar Gretsky. Part of him wanted to let it go, but he couldn't. That man had almost caused Elias's death. And his own.

He glanced over his shoulder as he typed Caesar Gretsky into his computer. A list of holdings that popped up immediately. One company downtown caught his eye:

Canyon Crest

Ryan couldn't stop now. He punched in Canyon Crest, and the smiling countenance of Caesar Gretsky popped up. Caesar was a handsome, rugged man with short-cropped graying hair, striking features including deep blue eyes, and a square chin. He was posing by a desk, with a framed degree in the background—Harvard.

Ryan scanned the page. Canyon Crest was an international business involving real estate holdings, estates, and hotels. Lots of money exchanged hands in this business. He typed in the name Alexis Gretsky, and it turned out that he was one of the founders of Canyon Crest. How had Alexis Gretsky known his father?

The phone rang at his desk, and Ryan jumped. "Ryan Ward," he said into the phone.

"Ward, this is security. Why is your motorcycle parked in the emergency zone?"

"What?" Ryan asked, wondering if he heard right. "Are you sure it's my bike?"

"It's registered to you. Now get your ass down here and move it."

Had Elias and his men brought his bike over? This was another means of ridding themselves of him.

"Be right there."

He hoped that Flynn wasn't so careless when he dumped the body. He'd know soon enough if that body at River-side Park was any indication. Ryan just hoped this would blow over soon and prayed his silence wouldn't come back to haunt him.

Outside, his bike sat alongside the red paint of the Emer-gency Vehicles Only section in front of the station. The security guard gave him a once-over. "Did you catch a glimpse of who parked it here?" Ryan asked.

"Yeah, someone drove it in and then ran into the station. I thought it was you." Again, that glare.

"No, it wasn't me. Someone stole it and parked it here."

"Well, listen, buddy, whoever put it here, the bike needs to move now."

Ryan got on his bike, raised the kickstand, and started the motor. At least Flynn had returned his bike as promised.

As he rode to the parking garage, the little hairs on the back of his neck stood on end. He was sure he was being watched.

Chapter 20

E arly mornings were always the calm before the storm. Elias knew this and treasured the few moments of silence. He sat on the deck outside his bedroom and sipped his hot coffee.

The sun was starting to rise, tinting the clouds a faint peach across the eastern horizon. He had been in and out of consciousness all day, and parts of it he didn't even remember.

Even with the concussion, he would never forget being with Ryan. But what had happened between them had been a mistake on his part. The first rule was never, ever get attached.

But try as he might, Elias couldn't stop thinking about him. Somewhere out there, Ryan was finishing his shift. He wanted to see him, speak to him, and just make sure he was all right.

He glanced at his phone and felt like a schoolboy again. There were other much more pressing matters, and here he was thinking about Ryan.

For what felt like the hundredth time, he picked up his phone, dialed, and promptly hung up.

More resolutely, he picked up the phone and texted:

Park 7 AM?

Elias drew in a deep breath and hit *send*.

He imagined Ryan getting it at work. Would he text back? After a while, he gave up and set the phone on his nightstand. Of course, Ryan would want nothing to do with him and his world.

It hadn't been fair to bring him in. Things were getting heated up with Gretsky. He could approach Ryan again when Gretsky was out of the picture.

Waiting was not his strong suit, he admitted to himself. And a part of him could not let it go. His phone chimed, and he picked it up greedily. It was from Ryan. It said simply:

Ok

His heart raced as he gazed at that simple word. 7 AM could not come soon enough.

Elias tried not to make a sound as he snuck out of his house. He didn't want to be talked out of this, so he fumbled to find the keys to the little black Lexus.

It felt good to slide into the driver's seat and grip the steering wheel. For the last year, he had been driven everywhere. He glanced over his shoulder. No one was up yet. He turned over the engine and rolled slowly out of the drive.

The park was still quiet this early in the morning. A single jogger went by without a glance. The sun was now above the horizon, and several fishing boats were headed back to a nearby dock.

Elias sat on the edge of the grass and watched as the water lapped gently against the rocks below. Several ducks swam by, hoping for a treat. He tossed a stone into the water and watched the ripples filter out.

Would Ryan come? He glanced at his phone. It was past 7 AM now, and his heart grew heavy. Maybe Ryan had changed his mind.

A rustle came from behind him, and he turned to see one of the most gorgeous men he had ever known. Whenever he saw him, he felt a flutter in his chest and an absolute lack of control.

Dirty blond hair slicked away from his face, a stubbly shadow on his chin. There were dark circles under his eyes. He gave Elias a wary smile.

"Hello, Elias," he said, shifting from foot to foot. He looked like a little lost puppy, and Elias wanted to take him in his arms right then and there.

"Hello, Ryan." Elias patted the grass beside him. "Have a seat?"

Ryan settled beside him and looked out at the horizon. They sat for a moment together in silence. He was so close, and Elias could feel his warmth and longed to have him in his arms.

"I'm sorry, Ryan. I'm truly sorry. About Mr. Smith. About everything. I should have told you." He wanted to say more but lapsed again into silence.

"That meeting in the park?"

Elias shook his head. "I planned it. I wanted to meet you."

Ryan was silent, looking off into the distance, and Elias felt his chest crush. He'd lost him, and after everything, he didn't deserve someone like Ryan.

Ryan turned to face him, showing off those expressive blue eyes that Elias wanted to get lost in. "Promise me no more secrets."

Elias nodded, releasing his held breath. "I promise. No more secrets."

Ryan considered, and all Elias wanted to do was erase the pain he saw on his face. "What happened?" Ryan asked. "Who was that up there on the roof?"

"I have my theories." Elias got up and brushed off his coat. He didn't want to say too much and squeezed his eyes shut. His tongue felt thick in his mouth. Ryan got up as well, and he was close, so damn close. "I'm sorry I got you into this, Ryan. It was the last thing I wanted."

"You could come in with me," Ryan started, "to the precinct and report it. The police could protect you."

Elias shook his head. "I have to handle this my way. No police."

"I was approached yesterday by a detective," Ryan said softly.

Elias's eyes narrowed. "What did he want?"

"He showed me a picture of you, Elias, and a man named Gretsky."

"What did you tell him?" Elias tried to hide the growing panic washing over him.

Ryan was silent for a moment. "I told him I didn't know anything."

Elias let out a long, slow breath. Ryan had stayed silent. "Thank you, Ryan. Thank you," Elias said at last. "This is a messy situation. I need to handle it myself." Elias gazed at Ryan. Could he understand this?

Ryan nodded, face unreadable as he searched Elias's face. "Tell me who Gretsky is."

Elias broke Ryan's gaze. He never wanted to hear that name again, and the words felt bitter in his mouth. "Gretsky is the CEO of an old company called Canyon Crest." Elias stopped, hoping that was enough. Ryan's expression told him he needed more.

Elias grimaced, "He's ruthless, and when Gretsky wants something, he gets it—no matter the cost or how dirty his hands get."

Ryan appeared to take this in, still looking out over the water. "I can't get involved in this, Elias." He shook his head. "I need to look out for Jasmine and Bo. They're my priority right now." He turned to face Elias. "But I wanted a chance to say goodbye."

Elias felt a stab of pain at the words, closed his eyes, and gave a slow nod. It wasn't what he wanted, damn it all. Not at all what he wanted. Elias opened his eyes and took in Ryan's face. He wanted to remember every detail.

But before he could finish talking, Ryan touched Elias's shoulder and gently pressed his lips against his.

Elias pulled him in closer, deepening the kiss. Wanting so much more. He didn't want this moment to end as he ran his hands down Ryan's back. But as his hands moved up to the shoulder, he felt Ryan flinch.

Ryan broke off, wincing, and Elias leaned back. Had he hurt him? "I'm sorry, Ryan." He gazed at Ryan's chest. "I forgot."

Ryan cradled his right shoulder with his hand. Elias saw the outline of a bandage underneath. He wanted to strangle Gretsky right now with his bare hands.

"It's still sore," Ryan said, rotating his shoulder. "It'll be okay."

Elias tensed and resisted the urge to touch Ryan once more. Gretsky would pay for this.

"I should go," Ryan said, starting to get up.

Elias reached in for one last kiss. Their lips met, but it was for the briefest of moments. "Goodbye, Ryan," he whispered.

Still inches from Elias, Ryan finally said, "Goodbye, Elias."
Ryan hesitated and glanced at Elias before turning and
heading back through the brush.

Elias rubbed his hand over his face as he watched the
spot where Ryan had just disappeared. This was not what
he wanted. But it had to be. It was for the best. Still, it
wouldn't hurt to make sure Ryan got home safely.

Pausing momentarily, Elias left the parking lot with a new
resolve. He owed Ryan one last thing.

Chapter 21

Ryan swung his leg over the Harley and peered back at the trail. If Elias came after him, Ryan wasn't sure he could resist. Their first meeting had not been a coincidence.

Running a hand through his hair, Ryan put his helmet on. He let out a slow, deep breath as he fastened the strap under his chin. The sun was blinding above the horizon. Impatient drivers honked in the line of cars out on the main strip.A relationship with Elias was doomed from the start, he reminded himself. No more nightclubs. No more dating.

Ryan vowed to keep the promise he had made over Jack's grave. His only priority was Jasmine and Bo. Nothing else. He flipped the kickstand with his heel and started the engine. Glancing back at the trail, he resolutely pulled his helmet visor down and hit the throttle.

A little sleep and a little beer, and everything would become clear again. Ryan wove his bike through the parking lot and into the thick Chicago morning traffic. As the car in front of him slowed, Ryan glanced in his rear-view mirror. A large SUV with dark windows rolled up to his rear tire. Too close for comfort.

He adjusted his mirror to look at the plates. There were no plates on the front. Odd. Still, Chicago had a million SUVs just like it. The traffic started back up, and he weaved between the cars, getting a good distance away. A few miles later, he lost the SUV in the traffic.

Ryan relaxed his shoulders and drew in a deep breath.

He parked his bike two blocks from his apartment complex and walked the rest of the way. He placed his hand reassuringly on his gun holster, the 9 MM snug beneath his leather jacket. He glanced over his shoulder and fished his keys out of his pocket. When he went to insert them, the door pushed open.

It was unlocked.

Ryan looked back again at the sunlit street behind him. Had he forgotten to lock it? Taking his gun out of the holster, he opened the door and flipped on the light switch. No lights came on.

Frowning, he paused in the doorway, waiting for his eyes to adjust to the dark. He took one step in, gun drawn, as he cleared the room. "Hello?" he called out. Silence.

A faint footstep echoed from the back. "Who's there?" Ryan called out again.

No one answered. Gun raised, Ryan made his way to the bathroom. He opened the door. Sunlight filtered in through a tiny opaque window.

The shower curtain tightly encircled the tub edge. Had Ryan left it that way? He took the edge in his hand and opened it. He released a breath. It was empty.

The complex had lost power before. The electricity from the 1950s building was still not up to date.

He lowered his gun and leaned against the counter, staring at himself in the dark mirror. "Get it together, Ryan," he said to himself. He ran his hand through his dirty blond hair and grimaced at his reflection.

Keeping the gun in his hand, he stepped into his bedroom. Heavy curtains kept the light from getting in. He peered into the room. There was no movement.

A partially opened closet door caught his attention. He held up his gun as he opened the door, the hinges creaking in the silence.

Nothing was there but his clothes and a few uniforms. He pushed the clothes aside on the rack. Nothing.

A creak came from behind him. As soon as he whirled around, something tight slipped around his throat. A gentle constriction at first and then tugged tight. He gagged.

The scream never made it past his lips. A powerful blow sent his gun clattering to the floor.

Ryan lifted his hands to his neck, prying at the tight wire. An icy voice whispered in his ear. "This is for Colt, motherfucker."

The wire tightened again, and Ryan's vision faded. His lungs burned as he tried to gasp for air. Any air. In a last-ditch effort, Ryan brought his elbow down hard into the attacker's groin.

The man let out a grunt of pain and shoved Ryan onto his knees. "You little faggot," the man whispered. "I'm going to enjoy slicing you up into little bits and feeding you to the sharks."

The pain crushed his chest. No air would come through the constriction. Two sharp bursts rang in his ears, and everything faded to black.

A familiar voice called out to him through the darkness. "Ryan? Ryan, can you hear me?" He wondered where he was, and it all came back to him.

Ryan opened his eyes and flinched. Directly beside him was the face of a dead man. Wide, unblinking eyes stared into oblivion. The mouth was gaping as if he tried to say something as he died.

One arm flung unnaturally to his side, the gun just a few inches away as deep red blood pooled on the carpet.

A warm hand touched his shoulder, and Ryan saw Elias crouched above him. Concern flooded his face as he tucked his gun with a silencer under his jacket.

"Elias?" Ryan whispered. His hands went up to his raw throat. Elias reached his arms around him and helped him to sit up.

"It's okay," Elias whispered. "You're okay."

With his vision blurring again, Ryan saw the bleak land-scape of Afghanistan. The oppressive sun beat down through his uniform, leaving him no respite.

Sand and heat made his mouth gritty. The pack on his back got heavier by the minute. Behind enemy lines and vulner-able, he crouched behind a crumbling stone foundation.

"Ryan," a steady voice said through the fog. "Ryan, are you okay?"

The vision cleared, and Ryan coughed. "I'm sorry," he said in a rasp. He was here, on his bedroom floor, safe with Elias.

"Is there somewhere I can take you?" Elias asked. "Maybe out of town?"

Ryan shook his head.

"Come on." Elias stood, taking Ryan's arm. "You're coming with me."

He didn't resist as Elias helped him to his feet. The lifeless body kept him rooted in place, unable to tear his eyes away.

"We need to get out of here." Elias tugged him away from the grotesque scene, grasping his hand. "We can't leave out the front. Come on."

The back door led out into the shared courtyard. Late in the morning, the neighbors were at work and school. Ryan glanced over his shoulder as he followed Elias, scanning the windows for any signs of movement.

"I'm taking you home," Elias said firmly, reaching for his car keys. "You'll be safe until I figure this out. Flynn will clean this up."

Clean up. Ryan thought of the man back there. He was in way over his head. Elias motioned to him, and finally, Ryan followed.

They walked a short distance, and Elias opened the passenger door to his Lexus. As they sped away, Ryan glanced back at his complex. He had entered the deep end with no going back.

He closed his eyes. A brief stay with Elias. What could the harm be?

Chapter 22

Ryan stretched his legs out as he sat back in the passenger seat of the black Lexus. Elias navigated the last of the morning commute, swerving around a truck and hitting the accelerator.

Lucky for Elias, Ryan wasn't on patrol right now. He hid a smile. Oh yes, he'd pull Elias's Lexus speeding-ass over in a heartbeat. He drove too fast, too recklessly. Thankfully, he was always in control, his reflexes lightning quick.

Ryan rested his head and tried to relax. He hated being a passenger. Glancing beside him, Elias seemed lost in his own world, keeping one eye on the rear-view mirror. Ryan patted his jacket. His gun? What happened to his gun? He swallowed a rising panic.

The city receded as they drove past the suburbs and into a gated community with a guard who let Elias in with no questions asked. This part of Chicago is where the rich flaunt their money with abandon.

Towering estates lined both sides of the street, one after another. Elias slowed and turned into a drive lined with mature trees and a massive iron gate barring the way. He reached up to the visor and pushed a button. A gate opened to reveal a winding lane with a canopy of oaks.

"This is it," Elias said, gripping the wheel. They entered the drive as the iron gate shut with a clang behind them. Ryan gazed back a moment at the locked gate. He'd been warned not to see Elias again. Hand clutching the armrest, Ryan sucked in a deep breath.

Elias flashed him a reassuring smile, but it wasn't convincing. Around the bend, a circular drive led up to a three-story burnt brick mansion. Ivy vines wound their way up the walls, and a beautifully rounded turret looked out over the trees towards the skyline. As Ryan's eyes wandered up the brick-stone steps, the front door opened.

Out stepped an older man who gazed down at them with a scowl. Short, yet compact with silver-white cropped hair and the regal bearing of a General. Ryan recognized Flynn immediately. The man he wished he had never met that horrible night. The one who threatened him. He thought about asking Elias to turn around. All the while, Flynn stalked down the steps towards them, eyes narrowed.

"He's pissed," Elias said as he gripped the steering wheel and brought the car to an abrupt stop. "I neglected to tell Flynn I was leaving, " he muttered. "Stay here."

Ryan didn't argue as Elias opened the car door and met Flynn halfway. Flynn's eyes locked on Ryan through the front car window. Slouching down in the seat, if it was possible to disappear, he would right now.

Through the closed windows, Ryan couldn't hear the exact words. Flynn shouted at Elias, his face contorted in anger. Flynn gazed over at the car, giving Ryan the evil eye before storming off.

Elias came back to the car, face flushed. "I'm sorry, Ryan. Flynn's taking care of our problem." Ryan watched a moment longer as Flynn disappeared inside the garage. He drew a deep breath and wondered if he was making a huge mistake.

"Let's go inside." Elias came around and opened Ryan's door. Ryan hesitated and glanced up at Elias. Those dark eyes were pleading and sincere.

Ryan swung his legs to the ground, and Elias extended his hand to help him up. "I'm sorry, Ryan. Sorry for all of this."

Taking Elias's hand, Ryan got out and stretched. He hadn't slept in over 24 hours, and his adrenaline was waning. "If you hadn't been there," Ryan began, then trailed off, shaking his head. He would be dead right now.

Another casualty recorded as a routine home break-in turned sour. And another dead cop with his picture hanging in the outer hall of the station. Something sinister was happening here. Something out of control. And if they had been following him.

A horrible thought entered his mind. He rode with Jasmine yesterday. Did they know about her as well?

"Elias," Ryan said, letting go of his hand. "I can't stay here. I need to go to the police. What if they know about Jasmine and Bo?"

Elias chewed on his cheek for a moment and then took out his phone. He turned and whispered into the receiver, then hung up abruptly. "My men are on their way to her house. They will make sure she's okay and watch over them. Discreetly, of course."

Ryan wanted to ask how Elias knew where Jasmine lived and bit his tongue. Elias placed his hands on Ryan's shoulders and faced him straight on. "You have my word, Ryan. I'm going to make this right. Gretsky has deep ties to the police. You need to know that. Going to the police will accomplish nothing without tangible proof."

Hesitating, Ryan nodded. Elias had a point. He thought about calling Jasmine and warning her. Would it make things worse? He took his cell phone out of his pocket and glanced at it. It was now past high noon. She would still be asleep after working the night shift.

Elias appeared thoughtful as Ryan turned back towards him. "I will do everything in my power to make sure Jasmine and Bo are safe. Everything."

Ryan nodded, and Elias visibly relaxed.

"I promise you right now," Elias said in a soft voice. "By tomorrow, the problem with Gretsky will disappear. Please give me that chance, and then you can go to the police. Please give me 24 hours." Those eyes pleaded with Ryan, and he relented.

"24 hours, that's it," Ryan said at last.

He gazed out at the lush grass and gardens with manicured bushes and flowers just starting to grow. Nearby, a bird chirped at them in a tall willow tree. Beyond that peaceful garden and secure iron gate, the world outside spun helplessly out of control.

An arm draped around Ryan's shoulders, and Elias pulled him in close.

The chaos outside seemed to vanish in Elias's arms. Ryan leaned his head into his shoulder. "Come inside," Elias murmured softly, his lips against Ryan's hair. "Let's get something to drink. I'll show you around."

His chance to turn back had already passed. Ryan was in the deep end. The absolute deep end. He held on to Elias's hand as he led him up the stone steps. As they approached the front door together, Ryan knew one thing with absolute certainty. His life was about to become much more complicated.

CHAPTER 23

Ryan followed Elias inside and found himself in a spacious foyer. A vaulted ceiling stretched up to three stories high. Behind him, above the door, a circular stained-glass window with the family crest cast natural light on the black and white tile floors.

"Nice place you have here, Elias," Ryan said, his voice echoing.

Elias gave him a shy smile. "If you like ostentatious. Sure."

Ryan returned the smile as he walked over to the curved marble staircase. Life-size Romanesque statues posed within lighted alcoves. On the walls, replicas of Renaissance paintings hung in heavy oak frames.

"This house was passed down to me through several generations. Nothing has changed much." He waved his hand around the foyer at the artwork. "More museum than a house, if you ask me."

Ryan sat down on the white marble steps, feeling the weight of the last few hours. He rubbed his temples as a headache began to pound.

"Where are my manners?" Elias shook his head. "I forgot you haven't slept. Let's go upstairs and find you a place to lie down."

All adrenaline left Ryan's body, leaving him sluggish. His body ached to lie down and rest. A confrontation with Flynn was the last thing he needed.

"Flynn," Ryan began and then stopped. "Flynn doesn't want me here." The older man had promised to make his life a living hell.

Elias shook his head. "Don't worry about Flynn. His bark is much worse than his bite." Elias drew nearer. "You won't even know he's around. One night, and I'll make sure your paths never cross."

Ryan gazed at him. What could one night hurt? And the thought of waiting an hour for a cab sounded like pure hell. "All right," he said, relenting. "One night, Elias. That's all."

Elias inclined his head and gave a slight smile. "That's all I ask."

Starting up the staircase, Elias motioned for Ryan to follow. Floor-to-ceiling windows on the back of the house revealed an infinity pool flowing out back and a beautiful garden. Elias caught him looking and let out a chuckle. "Believe it or not, Flynn likes to garden."

Ryan raised his brow. Gardening wouldn't have been his first guess. At the top of the landing, he followed Elias down a narrow hall. They stopped before a door with a *Keep Out* sign taped to the front. Below was a lame attempt at drawing a skull and crossbones. Elias glanced back at Ryan, pausing. "My old room."

As the bedroom door opened, dust particles floated up. It was musty inside, and Elias went over and opened the back window. There was a double bed and an attached bathroom. A fine layer of dust was on every surface, and cobwebs lined the upper corners of the walls. There were several trophies on a shelf. Ryan picked one up. A statue of a young man kicking a soccer ball and a second-place regional plaque attached to the front. On the wall above the bed, men on the Barcelona Soccer team smiled down at them.

"A brief moment in my life," Elias said, admiring the poster with a grin. "My father sent me off to boarding school when I turned eleven." The grin faded as he turned to Ryan. "I hope you'll feel comfortable here."

"Thank you, Elias." Without thinking, Ryan stepped closer to Elias and put his hand up to his cheek. Arms came around his shoulders, drawing Ryan in for a gentle, lingering kiss on the lips. There was longing in those eyes and something more. Ryan pulled him in even closer as his mouth parted, and that kiss turned into something deeper, more primal.

Ryan almost didn't hear the door opening behind him. "Elias?" a woman's voice called out. "What the hell?"

Ryan turned to see a young woman in her late 20s. Platinum blond hair lay loose around her shoulders, and a long wrap-around skirt enveloped her curves and exposed a trim midriff. A low tube top left little to the imagination.

"What the hell is he doing here, Elias?" She looked between the two of them as Ryan backed away.

Elias regarded her with a frown. "Can't you knock, Alicia?"

She placed a hand on her hip and looked between them. "You said you wouldn't bring your boy toys home." She scowled, looking Ryan up and down. "What the hell is this?"

"Alicia," Elias's eyes narrowed, "that's no way to talk to our guest." He composed himself and motioned to his side. "Let me introduce Ryan Ward. Ryan, Alicia Sandstone."

Alicia's mouth formed into a smile that didn't reach her eyes. "His fiancé." She sniffed, then took Elias's arm. "Elias is late for lunch. Aren't you Elias?"

Elias closed his eyes briefly, then extricated himself from her grip. "Yes, of course, I promised you lunch. Give me a moment, and I'll meet you down there."

Alicia gave Ryan one last glare, turned, and left without a word.

Elias drew in a breath and took both of Ryan's hands. "I'm sorry. It's complicated," he said, glancing back at the door. "I promised her lunch." He squeezed his hands and led him to the bed. "Get some sleep. We'll talk again soon." He looked longingly at Ryan's face, then brought his hand up to his cheek. He came in for one last brief kiss.

Then he released Ryan's hands, his face pained, as he headed out the door.

Collapsing on the bed, Ryan stared up at the ceiling. He kicked off his boots and nestled under the silk sheets. His tired body sank into the plush mattress. Just one night. And after that? His eyes grew heavy. He thought about Gretsky, and anger surged briefly through the fatigue. He needed to bring him down. Get his life back. But as his mind wandered, memories of Elias soon prevailed. He imagined him beside him, intertwined on the bed. The warmth of his body beside him and the touch of his lips on his own. Soon, Ryan was fast asleep.

CHAPTER 24

Elias squinted in the sunlight as he closed the slider behind him and stepped onto the back patio. Alicia sat at the patio table, wearing oversized, rounded sunglasses lined with faux diamonds.

She laid a plate full of sushi on her lap and held her chopsticks ready. Sushi Garden boxes lay at the center of the table beside a porcelain tea kettle. She turned and smiled at him, patting the seat beside her.

"I got the spring rolls. Your favorite." She dished a few out of the container onto a plate and poured a steaming cup of tea.

Elias slipped on his sunglasses and sat on the chair. A slight breeze ruffled his hair, and he sipped the jasmine tea. Just a few feet away, Ryan's presence was like a magnet, tugging at him. He gave Alisha a sheepish smile.

"So, who is this guy?" she asked, her eyes searching his face.

"No one, not really," he said, clearing his throat. Words were not coming easily.

Alicia propped her feet up on a chair and narrowed her eyes. "I thought we agreed you wouldn't bring your little indiscretions into our house." She watched him, unflinching, waiting for his response.

Elias nodded. "Just trust me on this one. He'll be out of our lives soon."

"Uh, huh," she said, raising her eyebrows. "And I was going to ask you about the extra security guards you've placed on me?"

"Just a precaution," Elias mumbled between bites.

"Make it up to me." She gave him a warm smile and leaned forward. "Come with me to the art gallery this Friday. Two of my photos are on display."

Elias shook his head and dabbed his mouth with a napkin. "I can't make it. I have some business to attend to."

Alicia shoved her plate away and glared at him. "I didn't sign up for this, Eli. You promised me we'd do things together." She held up her ring finger where a shiny diamond glittered in the sun. "We're getting married soon. Things will be different." She pointed up at the third floor, where Ryan slept. "That won't happen again."

"Of course, Alicia," he said. The wedding would come soon, and the thought of it made his stomach tighten. In two months, they would be married, Mr. and Mrs. Hastings. A ring on his finger and an end to the whispers and speculation. He sighed. "I'll make an appearance at your event," he said. "I can't promise you I'll be able to stay long."

A smile spread across her face as she kissed his cheek. "Thank you, Elias. Thank you. I'm so excited. Curators are coming from all over. With you there," she sat back with a satisfied grin, "media exposure will be out of this world."

Elias picked at his food.

"Don't look so glum, Elias," she said. "You're going to have fun. I promise."

Elias knew Ryan would leave soon, and Alicia was all he would have left. As it had always been. And always would be. Alicia and Flynn had been by his side since he inherited his father's legacy. But letting Ryan go was like having a tooth pulled without Novocain. There was only one way now to keep Ryan safe: Let him go.

Alicia continued to talk as Elias's mind wandered to Ryan. Caesar's thug had come so close to killing him. He had gotten Ryan into this mess, and Gretsky wouldn't stop until he had his revenge.

Glancing at his watch, Elias threw his napkin on the table. "Thanks for lunch, Alicia. I have to get going."

"Can't it wait? I'm going on a road trip," she said, smiling. "Come with me."

"Some other time," he said and stretched. "Thanks again, Alicia." She was already on the phone with her publicist as he left her, talking excitedly. She didn't seem to notice as Elias slipped back into the foyer.

The empty hall reminded him of his childhood. Lonely and sterile. His footsteps echoed on the spotless tile.

Elias glanced at his cell phone and hesitated. Long ago, Caesar Gretsky gave him his cell number. Beyond all understanding, he had kept it. He had swallowed Caesar's scam hook, line, and sinker. Seduced him before Elias knew his true identity.

Those days after his 21st birthday, Elias was on top of the world just before inheriting everything. He should have known then—he should have bloody known.

Elias drew in a deep breath. Caesar was cruel and manipulative, and right now, he held all the cards.

Elias couldn't get his fingers to type in the numbers. His chest tight, he sat down on the stairs and tried to center himself. Then, he typed in the number on his cell phone. It rang twice before a familiar voice picked up.

"Elias Hastings, what a pleasant surprise."

"Cut the bull, Caesar. I need to talk to you."

Silence greeted him on the other end of the line. "Of course, Elias. You know I'm always here for you. I've just been waiting for you to come to your senses."

Elias clenched his teeth and resisted the urge to hang up. That would get him nowhere. He needed to figure out how to extricate Ryan from this. "We need to meet in person."

Silence hung on the line, and Caesar let out a satisfied sigh. "I've waited so long for you to say those words, Elias."

Elias glanced out the window. Flynn hadn't returned yet. If Flynn knew he was talking to Caesar, there would be hell to pay. Elias closed his eyes. "Where can we meet?"

"I have a luxury suite at the Pendry. Meet me there at 8 PM tonight. Don't be late, Elias." There was a heavy silence between them.

His mind screamed at this. A luxury suite? He shook his head. This had mind-fuck written all over it. "All right," Elias said, the hastily eaten lunch threatening to come back up.

"Don't tell Flynn. This is between us."

Elias wanted to say something snarky but bit his tongue. "Right."

Silence hung between them, and finally, Caesar spoke, pleasure radiating from his voice. "Elias, I'm so looking forward to seeing you again."

Grimacing, Elias glanced up the steps towards Ryan, reminding himself of his purpose. "8 PM, Caesar." The words were bitter on his tongue.

"I'll text you the room number," Caesar said, "closer to the time."

Elias hung up without saying another word. He couldn't listen to that silky voice any longer. Soon, Ryan would be free. But freedom came at a significant cost.

Elias took several steps on the grand staircase. There was a magnetic pull that was difficult to resist. Just a quick peek in on Ryan, he told himself. Make sure he was sleeping.

What could the harm be? He stopped, clinging to the banister and looking down at the foyer. He shouldn't do this. Even as his mind rebelled, his feet took him up the stairs toward Ryan's room.

CHAPTER 25

R yan awoke with a start, unsure at first where he was. After briefly passing out, it had been a dreamless sleep. The blanket had fallen off the bed, his legs tangled in the cool, silk sheets. He smiled, thinking of Elias here as a boy. The handsome men from the Barcelona Soccer team poster watched over him above the headboard.

Light streamed through the curtains, and he glanced at his phone. It was still mid-afternoon. He rubbed his face as memories flooded his mind. The wire wrapped around his neck, choking him out, escaping with Elias. Too many complications. Ryan needed to be strong tomorrow, leave, and never return. A wave of depression washed over him, and he collapsed on his back.

He stared at the wood ceiling, watching a cobweb float in the corner. Three quiet raps came from the bedroom door. He sat up, reaching for his shirt. "Who is it?" he called out.

There was a long pause. "It's Elias. Can I come in?"

The voice was barely a whisper. Ryan's pulse quickened. He ran his hand through his hair, sweeping it off his face.

"Just a sec," Ryan said as he slipped back into his jeans. "Come in," he called out.

Elias leaned against the door frame and gave Ryan a sheepish smile. His button-down shirt was partially open and untucked. He looked exhausted, his face drawn and dark circles under his eyes. "Hope I didn't wake you."

Ryan sat up on the side of the bed and stretched his arms. "No, I was up. I actually got a little sleep."

Elias leaned his head back against the wall. "I wanted to make sure you were okay. Do you work tonight?"

Ryan shook his head. "No, not tonight."

"Good." Elias let out a deep breath. "Listen, Ryan, I'm meeting with Gretsky tonight."

Ryan was about to tell him no, but Elias raised his hand. "It's the only way to end this. I promised to protect your friend and her son, and I will."

"What are you going to do?" Ryan asked, panic rising in his chest. "You can't just walk in there alone."

Elias frowned, looking down at his hands. "Caesar and I have a," he paused, "past." He glanced up at Ryan. "I don't think he'll hurt me. Not in the physical sense, anyway. I have too much he wants, and if he thinks he can get it, he won't harm me."

Ryan shook his head. "There has to be another way. I can come with you. Talk to him."

"There is no other way," Elias said, walking over to the window and parting the curtains. "This has gone on too long. It started many years ago with my father, and it will end tonight." He kept his back to Ryan. "You're the only one who knows about this. And I want you to know, in case I don't return."

Before he could finish, Ryan approached him, wrapping one arm around his chest. Elias grasped onto his hand, and they gazed out the window together toward the city skyline.

"Don't go, Elias," Ryan whispered in his ear. "Talk to Flynn. Don't do this alone."

Elias turned to face him, inches apart. "Ryan, I want to end this." A hand caressed Ryan's hair and came down to his back. Elias whispered in his ear. "I don't want to lose you."

Elias came in for a kiss, passionate and intense. Ryan wrapped his arms around him and drew him close, feeling every inch of his body pressed against his own.

A hand came down to unbutton Ryan's jeans. When Ryan hesitated, Elias stopped and whispered. "It's okay if you don't want to do this. I understand."

In response, Ryan stepped out of his jeans and let them fall to the floor. "No, I want this." Ryan drew him in for another deep kiss.

Elias smiled as he backed Ryan towards the bed, nibbling on his neck. "I wanted this the first time I laid eyes on you," he murmured. He unbuttoned his shirt as Ryan watched, entranced. He was muscular and toned. Ryan brought his hands up and caressed his chest, fumbling with the zipper on Elias's pants.

As Elias reached down to help him out of his shirt, fear overtook Ryan. The scars. For a brief moment, he had forgotten about them. Elias noticed his discomfort and kissed him gently as he helped him out of his shirt. Frowning,

Elias traced the scars on his chest with his finger, then kissed them, his tongue lightly tracing them.

"They're ugly," Ryan whispered, shaking his head.

Elias put a finger up to his mouth. "You are absolutely gorgeous, every inch of you," Elias said.

Ryan relaxed into his embrace, skin against skin. "I don't have what I need for what I really want to do with you," Elias said with a low growl, frustration in his eyes. He straddled Ryan and started kissing him on the chest and working his way down to his midsection, pausing at his stomach before going down farther. Ryan felt him hard against him. His body aching and responding to every single caress and touch.

Elias took him in his mouth, warm and moist. Tantalizing him with his tongue and lips. Ryan was already hard, but now the intensity was almost too much. He groaned under Elias, wanting more and wanting it faster. Just when he didn't think he could ever get enough, everything exploded, and his body cascaded into ecstasy. "I can't get enough of you," Elias murmured, now coming up and kissing Ryan on the mouth. "I don't think I could ever get enough of you."

Elias moved against him, soon coming on top of Ryan. "I'm sorry, I'm sorry," he said.

This time, Ryan rolled him over and got on top of him. Their lips met, and Ryan didn't want to let him go. Bodies intertwined on the bed. Ryan had never felt so complete, so whole.

Then he heard the bedroom door click shut. Ryan jumped and looked towards the door. "What was that?"

They both glanced up. The door was now closed. Elias opened it, checking down the hall. "Shit, it was Alicia."

"Come on," Elias said, stretching out his hand with a sly smile. "Let's take a shower."

Ryan frowned, but as he took Elias's hand, everything else melted away. A shower with Elias was just what he needed.

CHAPTER 26

Alicia slid the door to Elias's bedroom shut. It made a soft click, and she stood frozen in the hallway. Did they hear? There was no movement behind her, and she relaxed. The floor creaked under her bare feet, and she cringed.

Blood rising to her cheeks, she dug her nails into her palm and closed her eyes. Elias promised he wouldn't bring his one-night stands home—ever. He promised the trysts meant nothing to him. All these promises were thick, syrupy, and everything she wanted to hear.

She twisted the ring around on her finger. Yes, it was all a sham, but when he was home, Elias was hers, dammit. All she wanted was his heart and full attention.

And someday, she knew, he would come around. What was going on in that room was a slap in the face. She put her fist into her mouth and bit down on her knuckles. Elias was going to pay for this. Dearly.

She stayed momentarily on the top floor hall, peering down at the foyer. Elias couldn't call the wedding off. If he did that, everything she worked hard for would go to hell.

And just who was Ryan? A cop, no less. She shook her head. Sometimes, Elias just was not that bright. That's why he needed her.

She glanced at the front door. Where was Flynn? He was usually home by now. She glanced out the window to the front and frowned. Flynn had been the one constant for her all these years, the protective father she'd never had, and she'd come to care for him. Couldn't imagine her life without him. His absence this afternoon was baffling. She suspected something big was going down. As always, she was in the dark about everything. She heard the shower starting in the bathroom and let out a frustrated sigh. Something needed to be done. And she was the one to do it.

Elias's office door loomed at the end of the hall. She glanced over her shoulder and walked softly to the office. Slipping a hairpin from her bun, she placed it in her mouth as she examined the lock. She hadn't been in Elias's office snooping for some time. Not since Elias was drafting the prenup.

After their wedding, half of what he owned would be hers. Proof he cared. And now, Elias needed her help. He was about to make a huge mistake.

Glancing over her shoulder, she moved the hairpin into the lock and closed her eyes as she explored the inside. A soft click let her know it worked. With a satisfied smile, she opened the door and slid inside.

Elias's office was one of the larger rooms in the house. It had once belonged to his father, and Elias had done little to change it. Except for a picture of Alicia, nothing reflected Elias's personality. His father's Harvard degree and framed clippings of yellowed and faded news articles hung on the walls.

She sat at the desk facing the door and ran her hand over the smooth, dark oak. Two locked drawers on the left side caught her attention. "What are you hiding, Elias?" she said softly. "Let's find out."

Slipping the pin out of her hair again, she jiggled it in the lock. It opened with ease. Folders with different realty holdings were in perfect alphabetical order. She frowned as she leafed through them.

Nothing she didn't already know. Boring contracts, one after another, on properties in Chicago. Reaching into the back, she stopped. Loose papers were in the very back. Eureka. She plucked them out and placed them on the desk. Scribbled on the top were the words Ryan Ward.

She spread them out in front of her. The top page had a picture of Ryan jogging in the park. Removing the paperclip, she picked up the Polaroid and held it. Did Ryan know about this stalking?

Alicia leaned back in the leather chair. "Just who are you, Ryan?" He was a handsome man with blond hair swept back off his face and exquisite yet haunted eyes. He was lean and fit, muscular but not bulky.

She clipped the picture back on the front and flipped through the pages. Military discharged with honors. Graduated near the top of the police academy, but his career stalled for some reason. Reports state he was prone to melancholy and was a loner, orphaned at an early age. She glanced through the following pages. There was nothing about his family. Absolutely nothing.

Her eyes narrowed. And why would that be? Elias would have found something, especially if he was this interested. She peered up at the ceiling. They were still together, and it made her blood boil. There was no way Ryan Ward was this squeaky clean.

She placed the papers where she found them and closed the drawer. Swiveling around in the chair, she gazed out at the gardens below. Spring was her favorite time of year when everything was blossoming. New possibilities were always around the corner.

It was spring five years ago in Rome when her life changed forever. Her life became intertwined with two powerful and incredibly sexy men. Caesar Gretsky had noticed her during a fashion shoot, and since then, her life had been swept up in success after success. She went from a nobody to a top-rated fashion model in a matter of months.

Later, Caesar pointed out Elias Hastings sitting by himself at an outside café. He was sipping a cappuccino, and dark sunglasses hid most of his face. "His heart has been broken, Alicia. Why don't you mend it?"

She sat down across from him at the café and was mesmerized. Elias seemed pleased to have company as they watched the crowd of tourists walking down the cobblestone streets. An ancient stone statue of a woman holding a gourd flowed with water nearby. Elias's eyes were so damn seductive.

That captivating smile melted her right there and then. They chatted about Rome and his business ventures. She was sure he was coming back to her flat that afternoon, but it never happened. Elias didn't have an eye for women. Patience, she told herself. Someday, Elias would be hers.

They spent many nights together lying on the deck of the yacht Old Mission. Feeling the ebb and flow of the waves against their backs. Foghorns blew lazily in the distance. A million stars shone above them in the sky. Sometimes, they would hold hands and watch the night unfold above them, silent and comfortable.

Back then, they were inseparable, and he told her everything. Not anymore. This past year, they had grown apart. Try as she might, their connection was breaking, and she had to repair it. Too much was at stake.

Her reflection stared back at her in the window. Her eyes looked tired, and she reached up to her cheek. The cover-girl beauty she prided herself on was slipping away before her very eyes.

She would not lose Elias to some low-class piece of ass. Pushing up from the chair, she left the office and locked it behind her.

Alisha took her cell phone from her pocket and gazed at it momentarily. Her fingers typed in the numbers she had memorized so long ago. A familiar voice greeted her. "Caesar," she whispered, "we need to talk."

Chapter 27

Elias tucked the red bellboy uniform into his waistband and adjusted the black cap. The round window to the supply room reflected his fake mustache and thick black glasses.

He looked ridiculous but had eluded Caesar's thugs at the Hotel. His hand went down to his gun, fastened securely in his belt. He wasn't about to meet Caesar without a backup plan.

The basement of the Pendry Hotel was the underbelly of everything. Sewer and water lines, electronics, and the damn buzzing fluorescent lights. He waited for the text from Caesar.

No question that meeting Caesar alone was a bad idea. For one, no backup and, most importantly, a disastrous plan B. Flynn would say no one person was worth the risk.

Everything for the damn company. But when it came to Ryan, it was worth it.

The memory of Ryan's touch flooded his senses for a moment, and he closed his eyes. Focus. The dreaded moment was coming: Giving Caesar something in exchange for Ryan's safety.

Elias sat on a bench and glanced at his phone. There had been no word from Caesar. Above him, the Pendry was a flurry of activity, with a constant parade of taxis and weary travelers dragging their suitcases to the front desk. And he had counted seven of Gretsky's men up there. They weren't hard to spot.

The cell phone buzzed with a text.

3701. Come alone. Don't be late.

Pulse quickening as he read it, he knew this was it—a do-or-die moment. The stairwell lock was easy to pick, and he let the chain and lock dangle as he opened the door and gazed up at the endless row of stairs before him. It would be a long hike, but worth it to evade the thugs waiting to snatch him in the lobby.

He opened the emergency exit and glanced both ways down the hall. Room 3701 was on the right.

A chain clattered, a lock clicked, and the door opened. Caesar leaned against the doorway; his light gray eyes flickered with recognition, and a smile spread across his face. "I trust you came alone?" He glanced outside the hall, then motioned Elias in.

Caesar had aged little since those days in Rome. He was just as fit. The gray tinge in his hair and new wrinkles around his eyes made him all the more distinguished.

He was unusually casual, with a five o'clock shadow and shirt unbuttoned at the top. Elias was transported back to Rome. The memory of lovers sharing everything. All ending with betrayal and pain.

Caesar Gretsky was not the man he pretended to be.

Elias walked to the gas fireplace, holding his hands to its warmth. The apartment was dark inside, save for the flames and the lights shining from nearby buildings.

Caesar went over to the bar to pour himself a drink. "What can I get you?" he asked.

"I'm good." Elias peered out the window towards the surrounding skyscrapers. His eyes roamed around the suite to several rooms, including the plush living room with floor-to-ceiling windows and a kitchenette.

Caesar helped himself to the bar and let out a chuckle. "How did you get away from Flynn? He always keeps you under a tight leash."

Elias took in a breath and didn't rise to the bait. "I came alone, as promised."

"Clever getting around my men. No need for all the subterfuge, Elias," he chided. "My men were only there to bring you here safely. I always keep my word." Caesar brought his drink over to the chairs by the fire and motioned Elias to sit.

Elias watched the flames, mesmerized. "This isn't easy, Caesar. But I need you to lay off Ryan Ward. He's innocent in all this."

Caesar sipped his bourbon. "If I remember right, he has killed two of my men."

"Self-defense," Elias said. "Wrong place at the wrong time."

Caesar nodded thoughtfully, swirling the ice in his glass. "You must know I would never kill you. I only wanted to teach you a lesson."

Elias remained silent.

"And you know you ask a lot. My men want revenge."

Mouth suddenly dry, Elias cleared his throat. The next words were difficult to say. "I need a favor, Caesar."

A grin spread across Caesar's face as he leaned back into the chair, legs crossed. "A favor," he said slowly, savoring the words, and pointed to Elias. "I've been thinking about our time together all those years ago. It was beautiful, and it meant something to me. It ended with a huge misunderstanding. I was going to tell you about my ties to your father."

Elias shook his head. "Please, don't." The lies were painful, even now. His words came out sharper than he intended. "Will you leave Ryan alone or not?"

Inclining his head, Caesar said, "Nothing is ever that simple, is it? You started this when you put spies in my company."

Elias gritted his teeth. "What do you want?"

Caesar set his snifter down. "You will owe me a favor, Elias. A big favor. And I will collect it at a time of my choosing."

Elias closed his eyes for a moment and gave a resigned nod.

Caesar extended his hand, and Elias glanced at it, hesitating. "We have a deal then?" Caesar prodded, barely containing his smile.

Elias reached out and took his hand. A smooth and firm grip met his own. Caesar's grasp lingered, and he spoke softly, "We could re-write the Rome fiasco. The two of us. We were good together."

He tenderly raised his hand to caress Elias's cheek and gazed into his eyes. "I'm the only one who can accept you as you are. You know it's true. Will that cop stay with you?" He shook his head sadly and snapped his fingers. "He'll be gone just like that when he sees the real you."

Elias stood abruptly, brushing Caesar's hand away. "This meeting is over."

Caesar let out a wry chuckle. "You'll be back, Elias, mark my words. They'll all leave you. Your cop will leave, and

Alisha too. And when everyone abandons you," he let out a satisfied sigh, "I'll be right here, waiting for you."

Walking to the door, Elias's hand rested shakily on the doorknob. "Do we have a deal or not? You'll leave Ryan alone?"

Caesar let out a scoff and nodded. "Yes, you have my word."

Elias glanced back and left the suite, closing the door behind him. He stood in the hall, squeezing his eyes shut. They'll all leave you. Caesar's words echoed through his mind as he entered the stairwell and started the long trek down to the first floor.

Chapter 28

It was eleven at night, and the wind rattled the upper-story window of Hastings' Mansion. Ryan watched from the dark upper room as rain pelted the glass. Elias's headlights should come down the drive any minute. It had been two hours since he left. His cell phone was silent in his hand. No texts or calls.

The movement came from the iron gates, a fleeting shadow, then nothing. Ryan's pulse quickened. A single headlight moved down the drive.

It was a motorcycle. The single streetlight illuminated a rider with a black helmet. He squinted. Was that an army sticker on it? As the bike rolled in closer, Ryan realized it was his bike. His bike. Adrenaline hit him hard as he rushed down the stairs.

Wind and rain blew against him as he opened the front door. As he removed the helmet, Ryan saw Flynn's face in the porch lights.

Racing up the steps, Flynn brushed Ryan aside, helmet in hand. He placed his riding gloves on the side table and grinned. "Well, if it isn't the Cop of the Year."

Placing his hands behind his back, Ryan resisted the urge to punch the man. He took a step closer to Flynn. "That's my bike. What the hell are you doing?"

"Come off it," Flynn said, sizing him up. "I just spent five hours saving your sorry ass."

They stood toe to toe, eyeing each other. Ryan readied himself in case Flynn made the first move. Those steady, controlled eyes and features made apparent this man had seen death, doled it out, and would readily accept his own.

Ryan took a step back.

"Good man," Flynn said, brushing him aside and walking towards the kitchen. "Elias wanted me to bring your bike." He raised a brow. "I'm surprised he didn't tell you. You're welcome."

Standing frozen in the foyer, Ryan gritted his teeth, his fist balled into a fist.

Flynn called out to him. "Oh, and you're also welcome for disposing of the body. Not bloody easy, let me tell you. Also, careless to let that thug get your gun." He let out a quiet "tsk, tsk" and smiled. "Don't worry, I locked it in your pathetic safe."

Ryan said nothing wanting to wipe that smug look off of his face.

"Oh, cut the innocent act." Flynn shook his head as his eyes narrowed. "Where is Elias?" He craned his head around the corner to the living room.

"He's not here," Ryan said, glancing towards the drive. "He'll be back shortly."

Flynn had an unguarded moment as surprise washed over his features. His voice was stern as he stepped closer to Ryan. "What? He's gone? Where is he?"

Ryan remained silent.

"I've been a patient man," Flynn said, taking a few steps forward, the gun under his jacket now exposed. Flynn ran his hand over the stone railing. "I made a promise to you that first night you met Elias. I promised I'd make your life hell if you returned." He patted the gun under his jacket. "Your bike is right there." He inclined his head towards the door. "Best get going."

The sound of tires on gravel came down the drive. Flynn parted the curtain and glanced out the window. "It's Elias," he said, turning back to Ryan. "Be a good lad, give him an excuse, and get going." There was a warning glance as his eyes motioned Ryan towards the door.

Elias parked crooked, headlights still shining at the front door. He was halfway up the front steps when Flynn rushed down to greet him. The two men huddled together in the rain, talking in hushed voices that Ryan strained to hear.

The cell buzzed in his pocket. Ryan fished it out and looked at the caller. Jasmine's bright smile flashed on his screen. A moment of panic hit him as he fumbled to answer. "Jasmine, hello. Is everything alright?"

She let out a sharp laugh. "Ryan, yes. Fine. You didn't get my message?"

Ryan glanced at his phone and realized he had missed two calls from her. "I'm sorry, Jazz. You're sure everything is okay?"

"We're fine, Ryan. But I hadn't heard from you, and Bo's ballgame is tomorrow morning."

Shit, shit, shit. He had forgotten. Ryan rubbed his eyes. "I'll be there. You tell Bo. I'll see him early to practice."

Jasmine let out a relieved sigh. "I'm glad I got hold of you. Bo's been looking forward to seeing you all week."

"I wouldn't miss it for the world," Ryan said. Below, Flynn and Elias were arguing, their voices raised. With hair plastered by the rain, Flynn gestured towards the house, then stormed off.

Elias came through the door. His eyes were bloodshot, his shirt untucked and wrinkled, and he looked ready to collapse. Managing a smile when he saw Ryan, Elias took him into a soggy embrace.

"How'd it go?" Ryan whispered.

Elias shook his head. "Let's just say I've made things right. For now."

"Flynn wants me to go," Ryan said, gesturing at the helmet on the table.

Elias reached and grabbed his arm. "Stay."

Those words reverberated around Ryan's mind as he turned towards Elias. "Are you sure?" he whispered.

"Stay," Elias said again, as his hand caressed his arm, eyes locked on Ryan. Those dark eyes. Those dangerous eyes.

"Come on," Elias said, extending his hand. "Let's go upstairs."

Ryan hesitated and took his hand, following Elias to the third-floor landing. Elias gripped Ryan's hand tighter, leading him to a different section of the house. Elias opened the door and beckoned Ryan inside. This was the master suite. A jacuzzi tub overlooked the gardens below, while a gas fireplace ignited as Elias flipped the switch. Warmth radiated through the room. The rain and cold outside were now a distant memory.

Warning bells rang in Ryan's mind as Elias pulled him closer, nibbling on his neck, as a warm hand moved under his shirt, caressing his chest.

Shivers went down Ryan's body, pulse-quickening as Ryan unbuttoned Elias's shirt. Too many clothes. Everything else in his life was forgotten.

They moved closer to the bed, and Ryan reached, pulling Elias down on top of him. They were intertwined in warmth and heat as one kiss deepened into something more. One desire pushed everything else out of Ryan's mind. Elias reached up under his pillow and grabbed a tube and condom. "Trust me?"

"Yes, anything," Ryan whispered as a smile spread over Elias's face. One cool, moist finger entered him so gently that Ryan's body exploded in need.

"You're so beautiful," Elias murmured in his ear. "So beautiful."

Elias entered him, smooth and gentle, and Ryan felt at that moment like they were one. No boundaries existed between them. There was no world outside. No danger. Just a steady rhythm that grew in intensity until Ryan didn't think he could handle it anymore.

Then release, as everything came cascading down, and a peace settled over him, a belonging as Elias wrapped his arms around him and they closed their eyes, intertwined together on the bed. There was no one else in the world but Elias beside him.

"I don't want to lose you." Elias propped his head up on one arm and caressed Ryan's chest.

Ryan reached up and brought Elias in for a deep kiss. This was where he wanted to be, right in Elias's arms.

They fell back together on the pillows, silent. Elias wrapped his arms tight around him as if he were terrified that Ryan might disappear at any moment. "I have to leave early in the morning," Ryan whispered.

"Where?" Elias said sleepily.

"Bo has a ball game early in the morning. I promised I'd be there."

Up against Elias's chest, he could hear his heart rate quicken. "Are you sure? Can you wait?"

Ryan positioned himself up on an elbow, facing Elias. "You don't think it's safe?"

Elias nodded. "Yes," his eyes tightened. "I'll send Flynn with you just to make sure."

"No," Ryan said, shaking his head. "Not Flynn. He's the last thing I need."

"You won't even notice he's there. You have my word. Please, Ryan." Elias nibbled on his ear and swung on top of him, putting a finger on Ryan's lips. "Just think about it, please." Elias came in for another deep kiss, making his way down slowly to his neck, chest, and farther down still.

All thoughts abandoned, Ryan closed his eyes. Morning would come soon enough.

Chapter 29

Ryan woke up in the dark, warm beside Elias, an arm wrapped around his chest. Elias let out a soft moan as Ryan extricated himself and placed his feet on the cold floor.

Running his hand through his hair, he leaned over and kissed Elias gently on the shoulder. A soft moan escaped Elias's lips. It was all he could do not to crawl back under the covers and feel his skin warm against his own.

With a sigh, he grabbed his jeans from the floor and slipped them on. He pulled back the curtains and gazed out at the early morning sky. The rain had stopped, and a faint hint of dark peach was on the horizon. There was plenty of time to get to Bo's baseball game.

He left the room, and the door closed with a gentle click. The house was dark as he descended the stairs, hoping he wouldn't run into either Flynn or Alicia.

The cold morning air hit him as he left the mansion. The bike was parked in the circular drive where Flynn had left it. Ryan got on, grasped the handlebars, and revved the engine. One quick look back, and he left the mansion grounds, Elias's sleepy neighborhood flying by him.

As he merged onto the freeway, he glanced in his rear-view mirror. A dark truck had been behind him for several miles. He swerved into the passing lane, barely missing a white sedan. His heart rate quickened, and he accelerated and broke away from the pack.

He knew paranoia was not his friend. Still, he needed his gun from the apartment where Flynn had stashed it. He couldn't afford to be without it.

Altering course, Ryan headed for his apartment. The gun was right where Flynn left it, locked in the safe. He fastened his shoulder holster and slid the gun under his jacket. If there was any threat to Jasmine and Bo, he was ready.

Just a little late, Ryan pulled into the parking lot at the baseball field and stopped alongside Jasmine's red jeep. Bo ran up beside him, engulfing his legs in a bear hug.

"Ryan!" Bo glanced up at him with a smile. "You made it!" He was all decked out in his Badger uniform, baseball cap backward, his mitt dangling under his arm.

"Wouldn't miss it, buddy." Ryan hugged him back. God, it was good to see him. His father would be so proud of the young man he was becoming.

Jasmine walked up to them leisurely, a steaming coffee cup in her hands.

"We've both missed you, Ryan," she said. Jasmine also sported a Badger hat, dark curly hair escaping the edges. That smile of hers could melt any heart.

"Missed you too, Jazz." Ryan averted his gaze as he stared down at the pavement. He wanted to tell her everything. He started to speak, then stopped, unable to continue.

He felt a tug on his jacket, and Bo motioned to the field. "Come on, Ryan. You promised we'd practice."

"All right, Buddy." Ryan nodded. "Be right there." Bo ran to home plate, where his teammates tossed the ball to each other. Those little guys had wicked arms, and a dull thud came from their mitts as the baseball flew from hand to hand.

"It's so good to see you, Ryan. I was worried when you didn't answer your phone right away."

"I'm sorry," Ryan said. "It won't happen again."

Jasmine punched him in the arm. "It better not, mister." Her smile returned. "There's a certain guy who's expecting you." She pointed to Bo, who now held a bat over his shoulder.

Ryan hugged her, then jogged over to the batter's cage. Bo took two practice swings as the pitcher lowered the brim of his hat, poised to pitch. The catcher crouched behind Bo, making hand signals as the pitcher nodded.

In the last two games, Bo could not hit anything. A big zero. Jack, his dad, could have helped him. If only Bo's dad could be here to guide him. Ryan watched, knowing what was coming next.

Bo swung wildly at a slider, the ball landing neatly in the catcher's mitt. Two more pitches whizzed by his bat as he tried in vain to chase them outside. "You're out, Bo!" the pitcher called from the mound. Bo flung his bat on the ground and walked with his head down to the dugout.

"Hey buddy," Ryan said, picking up the bat and jogging after him, "how's it going?"

"I can't hit anything." Bo threw his baseball hat off and slumped on the bench. "Why do I even bother?"

Ryan squeezed his shoulder, then motioned him over to the surrounding grass. "Let's do a little practice, just you and me."

"Okay." Bo grabbed his bat and ran to the grass. Ryan picked up a ball and started pitching to him. Bo swung erratically, missing the ball, and collapsed in a heap on the ground.

A voice called out to them just as Ryan walked up to Bo. "No, no, no." The hairs on the back of Ryan's neck prickled. The Irish brogue was unmistakable. Flynn now stood near them, scooping up Bo's bat. "You're doing it all wrong," he knelt and whispered in Bo's ear.

Ryan grabbed him by the shoulder, turning him away from Bo. "A word, Flynn?"

Flynn glanced between him and Bo, eyes unreadable.

Ryan took him by the arm. "What the hell are you doing here?"

Jasmine jogged up to both of them and tapped Ryan on the shoulder.

"Who's this?" Jasmine asked, nodding to Flynn.

"No one. He was just leaving." Ryan narrowed his eyes in warning.

"Actually, I have the morning off," Flynn replied with a grin, avoiding Ryan's gaze. "Let's try a few tricks to see if we can get your swing back on track?"

Jasmine glared at Ryan and punched him in the arm. "Well, aren't you going to introduce us?"

Ryan gave Flynn a warning glance. "Certainly," he said between gritted teeth. "Jasmine, this is Flynn."

Jasmine extended her hand. "Good to meet you, Mr. Flynn. Ryan never introduces us to his friends."

Sig gave her a genuine smile and took her hand. Ryan had never seen him smile like that before. "Please, call me Sig."

Flynn gave Bo the bat and motioned to try a different stance. Bo imitated the moves as Ryan watched, trying to keep his anger in check. Flynn had no right to be here. No right at all.

"Try pitching to me, Ryan!" Bo called out. "Let's try it!"

Ryan glared at Flynn as he took some steps away and started pitching to Bo. CRACK. The little guy hit it, and the ball flew toward the street.

"Whoo-hoo!" Bo yelled, jumping up and down, a grin spreading across his face. He readied the bat. "Pitch again, Ryan!"

Flynn helped him adjust his stance and whispered as Ryan prepared to pitch. The little guy was ecstatic. Curveballs were his downfall, and Ryan motioned to Bo to keep an eye on them. Ryan threw the ball, and once again, CRACK, the ball flew overhead.

Jasmine sidled up to Flynn, sipping her coffee. "Do you know Ryan from work?"

"You could say that," Flynn grinned at Jasmine.

"Come join us," Jasmine said with a smile. "The Badgers are gathering."

The coach called all the kids to the pitcher's mound. "Thanks, mister!" Bo said, grinning up at Flynn. "I hope you'll stay for the game."

"Wouldn't miss it," Flynn said. "Don't forget what I told you. And the secret sauce, don't forget the secret sauce." Flynn tapped his chest right above the heart.

Bo tapped his chest, still smiling from ear to ear. He ran off to meet with the other kids gathered around a tall man with a thick beard who herded all the Badgers into a circle.

Jasmine and Flynn were talking amongst themselves. "So you work at Hastings Enterprise?" Jasmine asked as they found a seat on the bleachers. "I've seen your boss on TV."

"Oh yeah," Flynn said, "the media hound him constantly. It's a lot of rubbish."

Ryan rubbed his temples, and a nasty headache came on. "Hey, Jazz," he called out. "Flynn is a busy man. We should let him go."

Jasmine glared at Ryan and then turned back to Flynn. "Oh, I like to garden too."

Ryan listened and drew a sharp breath. They were both deep in a conversation about tending roses. Ryan buried his face in his hands. What the hell? He needed to get them apart. Jack had to be rolling in his grave right now.

After two hours of sitting on the cold bleachers, the Badgers pulled out a narrow win. Flynn and Jasmine chatted non-stop, then walked down to the field together, leaving Ryan behind on the bleachers.

"It worked! Thank you, Mr. Flynn!" Bo reached over and hugged him.

Flynn crouched down to his height. "Just don't forget what I taught you."

Bo smiled as one of his teammates patted him on the back. "Good game, Bo."

"Can Mr. Flynn come with us for pizza?" Bo looked between his mom and Ryan.

"Of course," Jasmine said and gave Ryan a sharp grin. As Ryan trailed Jasmine and Flynn to the parking lot, he wondered if he'd entered his own personal nightmare.

Chapter 30

Ryan had just covered the day shift for a co-worker and was now stuck in bumper-to-bumper traffic on his Harley. The day shift had its advantages, including more time with Elias. Still, instead of clear sailing on the freeways in the early morning, the evening commute was a congested mess.

As he threaded his bike between the cars, frustrated drivers gave him the occasional honk or finger. But spending a few extra hours with Elias was all worth it.

Spending the night with Elias has become routine the past few nights. Elias has even cleared a space for his clothes in the closet. How long could they keep their relationship under wraps?

But going back to his apartment was too painful. He couldn't stand being in the bedroom where his nameless attacker had died. That dead man's eyes still haunted his nightmares.

They stared up at him, lifeless and accusing. Flynn had disposed of the body and cleaned the place up. He weaved between more cars, letting the sheer speed and adrenalin clear his mind.

He thought of Elias and smiled, reducing his speed as he approached the gate. Spending time at Elias's house had its definite bonuses. And then some. He just hoped there would be no Flynn or Alicia around.

Flynn was a piece of work. Ryan tried to keep his distance since that encounter at the ball game.

He warned Jasmine to do the same. "He's bad news. Trust me." And Flynn dared to tell her Ryan was working for him, pulling extra security shifts. Working for him. Wiping that smug grin off Flynn's face would be a pleasure.

Pizza after Saturday's game was the last of it, he was sure. After all, Flynn was at least ten years her senior. She couldn't possibly be interested in him, he assured himself. She had just been polite to invite him.

Slowing the Harley, he brought his bike to a stop. Ryan let out a slow, pained breath when he saw Jasmine's jeep parked by the front door.

Nearby in the garden, Flynn was showing Jasmine one of his plants. Bo was behind them, tossing a baseball to himself. He turned when he heard Ryan's engine, his expression breaking into a huge grin.

Ryan took off his helmet as Bo ran over to him. "You should see this place, Ryan. It's huge!" He reached down and took Bo in an embrace. What the hell were they doing here?

Jasmine glanced over her shoulder and walked over to them. Flynn watched from behind, his face unreadable.

"I thought I told you to stay away from Flynn?" Ryan muttered under his breath, stealing a glance at Flynn. Ryan had to admit she looked like a million bucks, wearing a black dress that showed off her figure, hair flowing loosely down her shoulders. Sweats or scrubs were her usual attire, and she was stunning tonight. He took her by both shoulders and faced her square on. "What are you doing here?"

She punched Ryan on the shoulder and broke his hold. "Stop being so over-protective. Sig invited us for dinner, that's all. Seeing you is just a bonus!" She smiled and motioned over to Flynn. "Let me check with your boss and see if you can join us."

Ryan watched helplessly as Flynn approached, an evil grin spreading over his face. "Yeah, he can join us," Flynn said flippantly, "if he minds his manners. Maybe I'll consider giving him a raise." He kept his eyes on Ryan as he threw his arm around Jasmine. "Shall we go in for dinner?"

Ryan could do nothing but follow them in. Bo was by his side, talking non-stop about how cool Flynn was and how his mom and Flynn had taken him to the downtown zoo.

Ryan plastered a smile on his face. "That's great, buddy." Great, just great.

Jasmine stepped inside and looked up at the vaulted ceilings, an expression of awe spreading over her face. Elias stepped out to greet them. "Welcome to my humble abode," he said, extending a hand to Jasmine. "I'm Elias Hastings." He wore his *Kiss The Cook* apron and wiped flour on his jeans. Ryan's pulse quickened at the sight of him. Elias gave him a subtle nod as he welcomed his new guests.

Eyes wide, Jasmine said, "I know who you are. I'm a bit tongue-tied. Sig has told me so much about you."

Elias took her hand and smiled. "Flynn talks about you non-stop," he said, giving Ryan a guilty grin.

Flynn was not amused. "He exaggerates," he grumbled, throwing a scowl at Elias.

"Come on," Elias said, still grinning. Dinner will be ready soon." Jasmine blushed as she followed Elias into the kitchen. She circled around, admiring the spacious marble countertops with dual ovens. Fresh sliced bread lay on the counter, still piping hot.

Jasmine ran her hand over the smooth counter, heading for the stools, Bo close behind her. Ryan looked away as Flynn helped her onto the bar stool.

Ryan motioned to the pair with his eyes and mouthed, 'What the hell?'

Elias shrugged.

"This smells amazing," Jasmine continued. Melting cheese, sauteed onions, garlic, and fresh bread wafted from the ovens.

Bo spoke up. "I've seen you on TV, Mr. Hastings."

"Yeah, that's pretty embarrassing," Elias said, leaning down and offering his hand. "I'm glad you and your mom could make it. Help yourself to some bread while you're waiting." He glanced apologetically at Ryan.

Flynn and Jasmine sat next to each other at the counter, heads together, whispering. Ryan strained to hear.

Elias tapped Ryan on the shoulder. "Bo, I need to steal Ryan for just a moment. We'll be right back. Security matters," he said, raising his voice for the last part so Jasmine and Flynn could hear him.

Ryan nodded. "Be right back, buddy, and we'll set the table."

"Okay." Bo hopped on a barstool and helped himself to a slice of bread.

Once outside the kitchen, Elias pushed Ryan up against the foyer wall and kissed him deeply. "I've missed you," Elias whispered, coming up for air. "How was work?"

"Same old, same old," Ryan said, coming in for another kiss.

Elias pulled away. "Can you stay the night?"

Ryan smiled. "I have to work tomorrow, but yes, absolutely."

Elias took his hand and led him back to the kitchen door. "Now, are you okay with the story?" He reached down and caressed Ryan's back, going lower still. I look forward to discussing the terms of your employment tonight." Elias smiled, then leaned in to nibble on his neck.

The door started opening, and Ryan disentangled himself from Elias's grasp. Jasmine glanced between them. "I'm sorry. I was looking for the bathroom."

"Just over there," Elias said, motioning to the sitting room. "First door on the right."

"Thanks," Jasmine muttered again and disappeared out of sight.

"I don't think she saw anything," Elias whispered. "Are you ready for this?"

Ryan took in a deep breath and nodded. What could possibly go wrong?

CHAPTER 31

As Ryan took the last few lasagna bites in his mouth, he savored the melted cheese, zucchini, and ricotta and smiled. Elias was a man of many talents. Sitting at the head of the table, wine in hand, Elias seemed to enjoy watching everyone devour his lasagna and homemade bread.

Flynn and Jasmine were seated much too close on one side of the table while Ryan and Bo took the other. Flynn remained silent, but occasionally, his eyes flickered to Ryan's, and they would glare at each other before Ryan inevitably looked away. He would deal with Flynn later—not now.

Ryan was still reeling from the surprise of the evening and tried to remain composed. The formal attire everyone sported, in contrast to his faded jeans and T-shirt, made him self-conscious. Why hadn't Elias warned him? Even Bo wore a white button-down shirt and slacks.

Ryan took another long sip of his wine. The alcohol began to take effect, making him forget his unease. He listened to Elias and Jasmine converse about boating. Jasmine recalled getting seasick when she and Jack had gone out overnight on Lake Michigan.

Watching her talk, he couldn't help but wonder if Jasmine suspected him and Elias? That had been a close call back in the foyer. Bo tugged on his shirt. "Bathroom?" he whispered.

Ryan pointed him in the right direction. "So, how did you find Ryan?" Jasmine turned to Flynn and then Elias.

Now, that was a pointed question. Silence followed, and Elias's eyes sparkled as he met Ryan's. "We were fortunate," he said, avoiding the answer. "Very fortunate," Flynn grunted, something sounding like an agreement.

Jasmine shrugged and looked at Ryan, mouthing the word, WOW. Smiling in return, Ryan wiped his mouth with the napkin and raised his wine glass to Jasmine.

Bo returned from the bathroom and sat down at the table. "Thank you for dinner, Mr. Hastings," Bo said as his mom gave him a proud smile.

"You are welcome, Bo," Elias said, swirling the wine in his glass. "I learned to cook when I was your age."

Bo's eyes got wide. "Really?" He looked between Elias and his mom. "All I can make is toast."

"But it's a mean piece of toast," Ryan said, nudging the little guy in the arm.

Elias smiled at Bo. "Don't feel bad. I learned out of pure self-preservation. The boarding school I went to wasn't exactly a friendly place. The cook took me under his wing and taught me everything I know."

"Well, it was wonderful, Elias," Jasmine said. "Thank you for having us over."

Elias inclined his head. "Any friend of Ryan and Flynn is a friend of mine."

Jasmine raised her brows and looked at Ryan, who gave her a sheepish smile.

"I had no idea that Ryan was moonlighting." She glared at Ryan. "I'm always the last to know everything."

Ryan decided it was best to remain quiet and took his last bite of dinner.

"A toast," Elias said, raising his glass to everyone. "To new friendships."

Just as Ryan raised his glass, the side door opened with a bang, causing him to turn in his seat. In stepped Alicia Sandstone.

Holding several large shopping bags from Bloomingdale and Saks, she paused as she regarded everyone around the table, her eyes finally resting on Ryan. Her faux fur coat hung over her red, low-cut dress, and her blond hair was worn down her shoulders. She looked beautiful and formidable as they all stared at her, standing perfectly framed in the doorway.

"I'm sorry I'm late," she said, dropping her bags on the floor and coming over to wrap an arm around Elias's chest. "And who are these lovely people, Elias?" She looked pointedly at Jasmine and Bo.

"I'm sorry, everyone," Elias said absently. "This is Alicia Sandstone." He motioned across the table. "These are our guests, Jasmine and her son Bo."

"His fiancée," she added, holding her hand over the table, revealing her engagement ring. A beautiful diamond centered among two smaller blue gems glimmered in the low crystal chandelier.

"It's gorgeous," Jasmine said with a smile.

Alicia turned to Ryan. "Could you be a dear and park my car?" She dangled the keys in her hand.

Ryan glanced at Elias, frozen and looking for some guidance. What should he do? His face flushing, he pushed his chair out and stood, taking the keys now shoved into his hand. Alicia removed her coat and shoved it into Ryan's arms. "Hang this for me."

Ryan took the coat and draped it over an arm as a sickeningly sweet perfume invaded his senses.

Elias got up from the table and stood between them. "Alicia," he said, wiping his mouth with a napkin. "Can't this wait?" He punctuated the words with a glare that Alicia chose to ignore.

"Absolutely not. There's rain coming, and I want my car undercover." She put her hand on her hip. "Isn't that why we hired him, dear?"

Alicia and Elias stood toe to toe for a moment in silence.

No one moved for a long moment when Flynn finally cleared his voice.

"Jasmine," Flynn said, "I know a great ice cream parlor down the way. Would you and Bo like to join me?"

Jasmine looked between Ryan, Elias, and Alicia. She gave Flynn a wary smile. "Sure, we'd love to." She motioned for Bo to come with them.

Ryan watched as Bo swiped a piece of bread from the table and followed his mom outside. The door closed as the stare-down between Elias and Alicia heightened.

"Don't ever do that again, Alicia," Elias said coldly.

"And how do you want me to treat him in public, Elias? Didn't you claim we hired him? Why can't I play along?" She glared at Ryan and then back to Elias.

Elias stepped closer to her, rage infusing his features. "You know what, Alicia? I'm done." He gave her an unwavering stare. "We're done. The sham is over."

"What the hell?" she said, twisting the diamond on her finger. "After everything I've done for you? You'd give it all up for your little boy toy?"

"Don't talk about him like that, Alicia. Don't ever." He drew in a ragged breath. "You should leave Alicia. The charade is over."

Alicia's face reddened. "Oh, you think so? Do you think this won't go all over the press? I promise you, Elias. You're going to pay."

They continued to argue, oblivious to their surroundings. Setting the coat and keys down quietly, Ryan backed out of the room. He found the bathroom and entered, shutting the door behind him. He could still make out Alicia's shrill voice. "You promised me, and I believed you!"

He turned the faucet on to drown out their voices. Splashing water on his face, he gazed up at himself in the mirror. What was he doing here? He didn't belong in this world. It would be so easy to get on his Harley and ride away.

But then he thought about Elias and his dark, sincere eyes. His touch. He continued to look in the mirror. Why did everything have to be so complicated? And now, Jasmine has made everything that much more complex. The thought of her and Flynn made his stomach tighten. How could he tell Jasmine about Elias? Would she kick him out of her and Bo's life?

But above all the noise and confusion, there was Elias. Not seeing him again was too painful to contemplate. He splashed more warm water on his face.

The knob on the bathroom door turned. "Elias?" he asked softly.

The door opened a crack. Alicia Sandstone stood in the doorway, her eyes moist with tears. "Aren't you clever?" she spat, taking a step forward. "Worming your way into Elias's life."

"What do you want, Alicia?" he asked, backing away towards the wall. She came toe to toe with him, her perfume overpowering his senses.

She gave him a mirthless smile. "I want you to know something." She bent in and whispered in his ear, breath hot against his skin. "I know who you are," she said. "And Elias will, too." Scorn filled her eyes as she turned and left, slamming the door behind her.

Ryan stared at the closed door, heart thudding in his chest. What the hell did she mean? He leaned heavily against the sink, trying to compose himself. Ryan had the sinking feeling that everything was about to fall apart.

CHAPTER 32

The night was still. Too still. Elias couldn't sleep and propped himself on an elbow, watching Ryan sleep. Clouds parted as the half-moon shone through the curtains, illuminating Ryan's bare chest.

He was stunning, absolutely stunning, from his blue, expressive eyes to the tips of his toes and everything in between. It took all his willpower not to wake Ryan up for round two. Elias just couldn't do it. He looked so peaceful and content.

That hadn't been the case last night when dinner ended in disaster. Elias caught Ryan outside just in time. He was on his bike, engine running, and ready to ride away. Who could blame Ryan?

By some miracle, Elias had convinced him to come back upstairs. As he watched Ryan undress, he knew there was something special between them. Something neither of them could deny. They lay in each other's arms for a long time, watching the flames of the fireplace lap and flicker.

Elias let out a sigh. Sleep still eluded him. His mind wandered to Alicia and the way they had ended things. Flynn had taken Elias aside days ago and warned him something was wrong. Alicia started drinking heavily, and Flynn feared she wanted more than friendship.

He couldn't think of Alicia now.

Sliding under the covers, he eased his body against Ryan's side. The warmth radiating from him caused Elias's eyes to grow heavy. He was almost asleep when the phone buzzed on the nightstand.

Elias's eyes snapped open. It could be his London team calling about the high-end property he was trying to acquire. He rolled away from Ryan and grabbed the phone.

The caller ID lit up in his hand: Caesar Gretsky.

What was he doing calling him in the middle of the night? Ryan stirred briefly but did not awaken.

Elias grabbed the phone and stumbled into the bathroom. "Hello?" Adrenaline surged through his body.

"I'm outside." There was a brief silence on the other line. "The debt has come due."

Elias suppressed a groan. "Do you have any idea what time it is?" He looked in the mirror, smoothing down his matted hair.

"I'm still a night owl, Elias. And this is your debt. There's nothing you need to do, actually. I plan to give you something."

Elias straightened and found some pants to slip on. "Give me?" he repeated.

That was damn strange. Elias felt a shudder go down his spine. A debt always needs to be repaid, no matter what. That was what his father taught him. And this debt was to protect Ryan. "All right," he whispered. "I'm coming down. But after this, it's over."

"It will be over. Completely."

Elias hung up, swearing quietly as he gathered his clothes and slid his gun into his shoulder holster. He took one last guilty look at Ryan before heading out.

Outside, Elias wrapped his warm coat tighter around him as he watched the headlights at the end of the drive. Moving closer, he could see Caesar smoking a cigarette, leaning against a black BMW.

The words of his father echoed in his mind. Never put any one person above the company. Ever, Flynn had reiterated. And yet, here he was, doing just that. He had dreaded this call. What would Caesar want him to give up ensuring Ryan's safety?

"Hello, Elias," Caesar said, smothering the cigarette on the ground with his heel. He opened the back door of the BMW and motioned Elias inside.

Elias stopped, looking back at his mansion before he ducked into the back seat. An older driver in a formal black cap sat in the front, his eyes riveted straight ahead. The opposite door opened, and Caesar slid in beside him.

"Poor Alicia," Caesar said with a chuckle, shutting the door and activating the lock. "What did you do to that poor girl?"

"You've been watching me?" Elias looked straight ahead as the car drove off into the night.

Caesar said nothing, motioning for the driver to go.

"Where are we going?" Elias felt reassurance in the gun close to his chest.

"I have a surprise for you."

"I don't like surprises." Elias shook his head. Typical Caesar. "You couldn't give it to me here?"

Caesar gave him a mysterious smile. "No."

This was more manipulation. Manipulation on top of manipulation. Where was Caesar taking him? Fatigue threatened to overcome him. This was too much. Catching him tired was likely part of the plan.

Elias's thoughts turned to Ryan. Secrets were terrible for relationships, and nothing could jeopardize what they had. Ryan was so different from Caesar and anyone he'd been with. The contrast was stark. Being with Ryan was both sensual and loving.

Back with Caesar, it had never been loving. Sex was rough and a bit desperate. At times, Caesar would make him beg. He had introduced Elias to some bondage and discipline. It was fun until it wasn't. It all devolved into something dark and ugly.

Embarrassing memories. Elias had been young and naïve back then. The car slowed, and Elias looked out the front window. The headlights illuminated a harbor entrance. Caesar's driver tapped in a code on the keypad, opening the massive gate. Multiple expensive-looking yachts were ready to be taken out on the water.

Not long ago, Elias had wanted to purchase one. What had kept him? He'd been too damn busy with his work. Then, he remembered confiding to Caesar over a luxurious dinner in Venice. "I want to sail the world someday," he told him wistfully, looking out at the water.

Back then, Caesar had promised a weekend cruise on the Mediterranean. Was this his plan? Use memories to keep Elias off his game?

Outside in the night air, waves lapped gently against the shore, and the low bell of a buoy rocked on the waves. A few gulls called out overhead, hoping for some scraps.

"That's my boat, Victory, on the left." Caesar pointed to one of the luxury yachts. As he did so, his arm came too close for comfort.

Illuminated by the dock lights, the Victory was over 30 feet long, with a large inner cabin and plenty of sitting room on the deck. High above at the helm, the views would be breathtaking.

Elias felt envy wash over him as he took it all in. "Everything is inside." Caesar smiled and motioned towards his boat. Climbing aboard the deck, he extended a hand for Elias.

Elias hesitated, refused Caesar's hand, and climbed up the ladder. Caesar didn't look back as he headed into the cabin. Following him, Elias glanced back at the BMW waiting for them in the parking lot.

Caesar poured himself a scotch in the large galley and offered Elias a glass. Shaking his head, Elias sat at the dinette and glanced out the window. The open waters beckoned him. If only Ryan were here with him instead.

He was brought out of his reverie when he realized Caesar was watching him. "Get it over with," Elias snapped.

"Certainly," Caesar said and ducked into the bedroom. He came out with a large, plain manila envelope. Elias gazed at it, and Caesar threw it on the table.

Elias glanced warily at Caesar and back at the envelope. It was light, with barely anything in it.

This was his debt? He fingered the tab, deep in thought. Caesar watched him with anticipation. Slowly, half expecting something to jump at him, Elias tore open the top. He scanned the first page skeptically. Then, taking a closer look, his heart raced. What he saw on the page couldn't be true. It just couldn't.

Chapter 33

Ryan sat outside his Sergeant's office, impatient to know why she had called him in. Fellow officers passed him, averting their eyes and speaking in hushed tones. He sipped the last of his coffee, hoping the dark brew would energize his mind.

Last night, he walked out on Elias and almost rode off on his bike. That dinner was a disaster. Alicia's warning seemed like a threat, and he needed time to process it all.

When Elias came after him, his heart melted, and he relented. Sex had been good last night. All his worries faded away as he held Elias in his arms. Ryan didn't want to lose him. Couldn't imagine life without him.

Elias was gone when he woke up this morning. His hand came down on cold, empty sheets. Where was he? He had searched the entire mansion, and no one was there. Taking his phone from his pocket, he frowned. The screen was empty. Still no return call.

Through the glass window, Sergeant Collins talked on the phone. Her eyes were closed, and she rubbed her temples.

What was this about? Could they have implicated him in the man's death on the rooftop? No, it couldn't be, he assured himself. He would be formally questioned and detained. Ryan wanted answers and wanted them fast.

The door opened behind him. "Officer Ward, come in." Sergeant Collins regarded him with a doubtful gaze. She was an impressive, middle-aged woman with a distinguished military background. Calm and steady self-assurance borne of her 20 years on the force emanated from her. "Have a seat." She motioned to the chair in front of her desk. The Sergeant put on reading glasses and flipped through a file on her desk.

Different scenarios flooded Ryan's mind. What was in that file? He watched her closely, but her face remained impassive as she read.

"Honorable Discharge from the military. Near the top of your class at the Academy." She pursed her lips. "All impressive, Ward."

"Thank you, ma'am," he said, his chest tightening as his sergeant took off her glasses and frowned.

"So," she said, drawing in a breath, "we got an unusual request yesterday. Straight from the goddamn state congressman. He requested you by name to provide security for one of the wealthy business owners in the area." She looked straight at Ryan, eyes narrowed. "And I had to ask myself. Why you?"

It took all of Ryan's training not to react. His mouth felt dry. "A security detail?"

"Yes, for one, Caesar Gretsky." She flipped Ryan's personnel folder closed.

"I'm going to say yes. I have to. But can you shed any light on this Ward?"

"I don't have a clue," Ryan said, pushing down a nagging fear. This was wrong. He frowned. "Very strange."

"Good," she said, sighing softly, "that's what I thought too. Does Gretsky know you from the army? Or school?" Again, she eyed him suspiciously.

Ryan shook his head. "No, I don't think so. I'd remember that name."

She frowned again and folded her hands on the desk. "All right. I've spoken to your partner. I'm pairing him with another rookie. He's not too happy about that." She sighed. "You are to check in today for the security detail. Gretsky will fill you in on what he needs." She gave him a piece of paper with printed instructions. "Keep me updated, please."

Ryan stood, taking the paper in hand. As he left, she called out, "And be careful." He gave a quick nod and left the room.

He closed the door behind him and felt sweat on his brow, his chest tightening with each step. Gretsky. What was he playing at?

Heading back to his desk, Ryan stopped cold. Detective Chavez was seated on Ryan's desk, flipping through a stack of papers. Chavez, he thought, a bitter taste coming to his mouth as memories came crashing back.

The Detective looked up and smiled at Ryan. "Hello, Officer Ward. Good to see you again."

Ryan's partner, Fritz, typed away on his computer nearby, avoiding his gaze. "What can I do for you, Detective?" Ryan asked, his pulse quickening.

Detective Chavez slid off the desk and motioned for Ryan to follow.

"Come with me. We need to talk."

Ryan hesitated, gazing at his fellow officers. They were all pretending not to listen. What did they know? Or suspect?

He followed Chavez as they stopped in front of the interview room. He gave Ryan a smug smile as he opened the door. A metal table and four chairs awaited them. The musty smell of sweat and fear overwhelmed Ryan's senses. Murderers, rapists, and cons entered this room. Not him.

"Have a seat, Officer Ward," Detective Chavez said, closing the door behind him.

Ryan took a seat facing the door. As soon as Chavez closed the door, the air turned stale. A fluorescent light hummed and cast a greenish glow onto the table. Above their heads, a camera pointed right at them.

Chavez followed Ryan's gaze to the camera. "This isn't being recorded. It's just you and me." He sat across from Ryan. "There's a buzz in the air. Caesar Gretsky pulled some strings to get you over to him? Is this true?"

He applauded Ryan with his hardened gray eyes, assessing for weakness and telling. Ryan willed himself to relax. He wouldn't give him anything. In Afghanistan, he had faced much worse. "I just heard," Ryan said, regulating his voice. "I'm as shocked as anyone."

"I think you're lying." Chavez locked his eyes on Ryan's face. "If you help me, I can make your troubles disappear." He paused. "Do you understand me?"

Ryan remained silent.

"I've spent 25 years trying to bring Canyon Crest down. Caesar Gretsky has been very slippery. If I had an insider," his voice trailed off. He now looked hopefully at Ryan. "I could finally get this S.O.B." He had a distant look on his face as he scowled. Then he turned back to Ryan. "My number," Detective Chavez said, flipping his card on the table. "Call me."

Ryan nodded, and with that, the Detective stood and opened the door. A wave of fresh air entered the room. Chavez nodded to his card. "These men are dangerous. Gretsky is dangerous. Make no mistake." He pointed to Ryan. "You are in danger."

Ryan watched him leave, then took out his cell phone. "Where are you, Elias? Dammit," he whispered to the phone.

He looked at the paper his sergeant had given him. 'Check-In 1400. Front Desk. Canyon Crest.'

Did Gretsky do something to Elias? Ryan stuffed the instructions into his uniform pocket and vowed to make the man pay. If Gretsky wanted to underestimate him, so be it.

He checked his phone once more. Empty. "All right, Gretsky," he said quietly, drawing in a long breath. "Let's see what you've got." Even as he said the words, the fear washed over him. What if he was too late?

Ryan wouldn't contemplate that. He leaned heavily against the wall, eyes closed. The answers lay with Caesar Gretsky. As he braced to leave, a gnawing feeling clawed at his insides. Gretsky was leading him into an iron-clad trap.

CHAPTER 34

Ryan loosened the black tie on his police uniform. The sun was beating down, making him sweat as he crossed the street. It was not unusually hot in the late afternoon, but his undershirt was sticky and uncomfortable. Elias had not returned any of his calls. The time was coming close to meet Caesar Gretsky.

He took out his cell phone and dialed Elias once again. One ring and right to voicemail. As if Elias had blocked his number. Ryan frowned. "Where are you, Elias?" He said softly to his phone. "I need you."

The whole morning had been unreal. Ryan kept expecting to wake up from a bad dream. Why had Caesar Gretsky summoned him? If Gretsky wanted him dead, there were much easier ways to accomplish that goal.

He slid his phone back into his pocket. Something was wrong. Very wrong. And soon, all would be clear. He just had to walk in and meet with Gretsky. He glanced up at the building on 54 Lakeview Drive, the office of Caesar Gretsky.

Canyon Crest was 20 stories high, made of white granite at the base, and nestled between brick buildings in an older neighborhood. Ryan stepped into the soothing shade of a blossoming cherry tree, light pink petals just coming forth. A late afternoon rush of people came and went from the main building.

Ryan slipped alongside business executives, entering with briefcases and computer bags. He ignored their wary looks as they glanced sidelong at his uniform.

The foyer reflected the building's age. Detailed woodwork from the 1930s covered the walls. High above, suspended from the vaulted ceiling, a large clock hung, Roman numerals showing a few minutes before two.

Security was everywhere, complete with a walk-through metal detector. Three guards were herding the people in, scrutinizing bags and identifications. Odd, for a business, Ryan thought as he watched security take one of the businessmen aside.

As Ryan watched them make the man empty his briefcase on a table, his gaze wandered up to a picture hanging prominently on the wall. The man with white hair and high cheekbones smiled benevolently at everyone below. Ryan squinted his eyes at the caption below. Alexis Gretsky.

A hand came down on his shoulder, and Ryan jumped, instinctively reaching for his gun. "Officer Ward?" a guttural voice inquired.

Ryan turned as a stocky man, a head taller than himself, greeted him. The bulge of a gun was visible just above his belt. "I have an appointment," Ryan said, stepping back.

The man gave a brief, courteous grin. "Yeah, I know who you are. I need your gun. House rules." He extended an oversized hand.

Ryan considered this a moment. He didn't want to part with it. He eyed the man, then took out his gun butt first, unloaded the magazine, and slipped it into his pocket. The man nodded appreciatively and tucked it into his belt. He motioned for the other security guards to let them through.

"Follow me," he said. A musty smell exuded from the paneled walls as Ryan passed. People in spacious windowed offices talked on their phones, intent on their computers.

They stopped before a large door with an opaque window at the top. Affixed to the center was the name Caesar Gretsky, CEO.

The guard knocked and opened the door, peering in. He opened the door wider and motioned for Ryan to enter. A man stood gazing out the window, only his upper back visible behind a large mahogany desk. Beyond him, passing cars raced by on the outside street. "Hello, Officer Ward," he said without turning, "Welcome to Canyon Crest."

He turned to face Ryan and gave him a wickedly handsome smile. It was, Ryan thought, the celebratory smile of a conqueror—a cat that had finally caught its prey.

Caesar Gretsky raised his chin as the sun revealed an afternoon shadow, accentuating his dimples. Brown hair showed wisps of gray at the edges and keen, intelligent eyes that appraised Ryan from head to foot. Very easy on the eyes, Ryan thought. Of course, that fact made Gretsky all the more dangerous.

"Caesar Gretsky," he said, extending his hand. "It's good to meet you at last."

Ryan reluctantly took Gretsky's hand. Gretsky's grip was firm and lingered for a moment. "I called in many favors to get you here." He motioned for Ryan to take a seat.

"Why?" Ryan asked, refusing the offer. The guard closed the door with a thud, and they were alone. "What are we doing here?"

Caesar nodded and gave him a half-smile. He pursed his lips as if chuckling at a private joke. "Security, of course. I know you have some questions. And they will all be answered." He took a large manila envelope from a drawer and flopped it on the desk. "We leave for Vegas tomorrow for an important international conference. And you are now my bodyguard." He leaned back in his chair with a satisfied grin.

Ryan glared at him. He was not leaving with this man. "I came," Ryan started slowly, "because my Sergeant asked me to. This was never part of the deal."

Caesar said nothing but pressed his fingertips together. He reached into a drawer and dropped a large envelope on the desktop. "Everything you need is in there. I've included the information you will find very relevant." He pointed behind the door to new clothes hanging inside a plastic bag. "I've taken the liberty of purchasing some acceptable clothes for you." He looked distastefully down at Ryan's shirt and slacks. "No uniform."

Ryan paused, turning to examine the new clothes. A $1000 price tag dangled from the coat. He shook his head emphatically. "No, forget this." This had been a mistake—a huge mistake.

"Cole Miller," Caesar said, emphasizing each syllable and fastened an intent gaze on Ryan. "I have information on his murder and proof of who is responsible."

Ryan's chest tightened as he sucked in a deep breath. The man who had tried to kill him and Elias. The one who died at his hands in self-defense. Ryan turned to face Caesar, eyes narrowed. "I have no idea what you're talking about."

Caesar waved his hand dismissively. "All actions have consequences, Officer. As you well know. Refuse to come, and all my information comes to light." The older man stood, extending the envelope to Ryan.

"At 0600, we leave and head to the airport. You will be here on time, wearing the suit." He lifted his chin and gave

Ryan a smug grin. "Take the envelope. You will find it very informative. Trust me on this."

Ryan kept a stony silence, staring at Caesar.

"One job and information on Cole Miller never sees the light of day," Gretsky continued. "You have my word."

Ryan snatched the envelope from Caesar's grip and felt his sharp gaze follow his every move. He tucked the envelope under his arm, ignored the pricey suit, and walked out. He shut the door behind him, letting out a slow, deep breath, relieved to escape Gretsky's intense stare.

Ryan stood for a moment outside in the hall, glancing back at the closed door. There's no way Gretsky had intel on him, he assured himself. It was a bluff. And yet, as he remained still, cold sweat beaded up under his collar.

He shook his head, trying to clear his mind. First things first. Ryan had to find Elias.

CHAPTER 35

It was evening, and the headlights on Ryan's bike illuminated the curved iron gate affixed to two towering brick posts on either side.

Elias's mansion was so close. Just get through the gate. The Harley idled under him as Ryan typed the security code into Elias's gate. *1550.* Ryan frowned. The gate didn't open, and he tried it again, pressing hard as he typed each number. Nothing happened.

Ryan turned the key on his bike, and the engine stopped as he swung his leg over. He grasped the cold iron bars and peered through at the mansion. A single light shone on the second floor where Elias had his study.

A red light flashed on the security camera aimed at Ryan's face. No doubt Elias knew he was there and watched him right now. Ryan mouthed up to the camera. "Elias, please."

He heard a motor coming from the house, and he stopped. It was a silver-colored rag top. It wasn't Elias driving. Flynn pulled up and slammed the door shut on his convertible. His hand rested on the butt of his gun.

"You've got a lot of nerve coming back here," Flynn said,

"Please," Ryan said, pointing up to the mansion. "This is important. I need to speak to Elias."

Flynn pulled himself up to his full height. "How dare you come back here. You betrayed Elias and all of us. He's hurting in there if you've come to gloat. Well, I've got news for you. Elias never wants to see you again." He spat on the ground. "And if I see your face again, I'll kill you myself."

The words pierced Ryan like a dagger, and he shook his head. "There's been a mistake. I would never betray Elias. Not ever."

Flynn glowered at him and took his gun out, pointing the barrel through the bars. "Don't make me use this, Ward or whoever you are," he muttered. "I knew you were trouble the moment I laid eyes on you."

Ryan raised his hands and stepped back. "Please tell Elias there's been a mistake."

"He doesn't want to see you. He never wants to see you." Flynn motioned to Ryan's bike. "Get out of here before I call the cops."

Ryan shook his head, chest tightening. There was nothing left to say. Not until he got more information. He had to figure this out. Ryan put his helmet back on, fastening the chin strap tight.

His mind spun as he sped off down the street, not caring where he ended up. How could this be the end? He couldn't accept it. Ryan would see Elias again, somehow. This couldn't be the end. What had happened? Caesar was behind this—that much he knew for certain.

Moisture stung his eyes as he rode his bike through the tree-lined boulevard. He blinked them away under his helmet.

His father told him many times crying was inexcusable. A weakness that others could exploit. The night his father died, Ryan curled up in the strange bathroom, pressing his cheek to the cold tile floor. He dried his tears with his coat sleeve and vowed never to cry again.

Ryan got on the freeway and took a familiar exit. He had traveled this path a thousand times, only to head back home. The bar Rumors flashed in front of him with its red neon light. He pulled his bike into the parking lot and kicked the stand down.

His mind was numb. Before Elias, he would sit outside, watching the door, only to head home. There was no hesitation tonight as he parked the bike and hung his helmet on the bars. He wanted a stiff drink to numb the pain.

Inside, a beautiful drag queen was on stage, with long red hair and a sequined dress, microphone in hand, playing to the crowd.

Back-up singers dressed in matching slinky black dresses danced behind her. Baby, I Was Born This Way, thumped through the loudspeakers as Ryan took a seat at a corner table and motioned for the bartender.

Nearby, two men necked in the shadows. A young bartender dressed in leather came up to him. "Whiskey, neat," Ryan yelled over the music. He looked in his wallet and handed him a $50 bill. He was going to get smashed tonight.

He took the envelope Caesar had given him out of his coat pocket. His pulse sped up as he tore it open. Several papers fell out onto the table. Ryan downed the whiskey and motioned to the bartender for more. The first paper on the table was a birth certificate.

He realized it was his birth certificate. Ryan glanced around the room. This stuff was supposed to be buried long ago. How the hell had Caesar gotten it?

The birth certificate read Ryan Sterling Blake, born to Stephen Blake Jr. and Frieda Blake.

"Forget your name," the social worker had said. "We have to change it to keep you safe. It's what your father would want." So he had kept it locked deep inside. Forgotten it, really.

He touched his mother's signature on the birth certificate. His memories of her were cloudy, with just touches, cuddles, and her calling out to him for dinner. Ryan held his father's hand at the gravesite when he was five. "The pain will make you vulnerable, son. You have to keep it locked deep inside. Do you understand?"

Ryan fiddled with his whiskey glass. He longed for another shot as he pushed the certificate aside. Everything from the past lay exposed on the table. A matchbook with the Rumors logo lay in the corner. One spark of the match, and he could burn it all away. But he couldn't stop. Not now.

He picked up the following handwritten letter, squinting in the low light to see the faded words. It was yellowed with time, its edges bent, and Ryan knew it was his father's handwriting. The signature below was Stephen Blake. Ryan's father. He moved it towards the little light on the table, trying to still his trembling hand.

My dear boy, if you are reading this, something terrible has happened. I have faith whatever the circumstances, it will only make you stronger. Our family rose from the ashes. I was nobody, shining shoes and taking out the trash until I came up with the answers.

I promised your mother I would give you the best, and I intend to keep that promise. And that answer is Canyon Crest, the company and legacy I created for you, and the promise I made to your mother on her deathbed. Canyon Crest is built from our family's blood, sweat, and tears.

If fate takes me from you, Alexis Gretsky has promised to care for you. He is your godfather, Ryan, and I trust him with my life. One day, Canyon Crest will be yours. Please know I am watching over you and protecting you from above. I love you with all my heart.

Ryan sat for a moment, holding it in his hand. The bartender brought him another whiskey, and he downed it, feeling it burn his throat. The last paper was a will. A highlighted section stated Ryan Sterling Blake was heir to Canyon Crest.

Forget the past. That was what Ryan held on to. Was this why Elias wouldn't speak to him? Something out of his control? He glanced at the surrounding tables.

The bartender came back with another whiskey. The room started to spin.

"This one is from the man in the other corner," he said with a smile. "The rest of your drinks are on him tonight."

Ryan peered over into the shadows. There, toasting him with a glass, was Caesar Gretsky.

CHAPTER 36

An elegant singer dressed in a sparkly gown caressed the microphone seductively and mouthed the last few lines of "The Way We Were." The music quieted as she took a bow and blew a kiss to the crowd as the stage lights dimmed.

A few couples slowly danced on the floor. Men had paired off at tables or stayed in groups playing pool, beer mugs in hand. It was a weekday, and some customers had already quietly exited.

Caesar Gretsky watched Ryan expectantly, swirling his glass. Ryan stuffed the envelope in his leather jacket and took another swig of whiskey for courage.

Their eyes locked across the room as Caesar gave him a wry smile. The information now in Ryan's pocket was supposed to be buried ages ago. How the hell had Caesar gotten his hands on it?

Warning bells went off in his mind. Get as far from Gretsky as possible. Curiosity was also in play and kept him from bolting. This man likely knew his father.

All these thoughts flickered through his mind, and Caesar remained stone still. He had looked away now, seeming to respect the weight suddenly dumped on Ryan's shoulders.

Was there a connection? Was this something he wanted to explore? There was only one way to find out. Ryan's feet decided. He planted his whiskey glass on the table across from Caesar.

"Have a seat," Caesar said, beckoning Ryan into the chair across from him. "Please," he said with a flourish of his hand.

Ryan looked behind him. The hairs on the back of his neck prickled. Two burly men stuck out like a sore thumb. They huddled in the corner, eyes wide, trying hard to ignore the two men holding hands at a table nearby.

Caesar followed his gaze. "Security," he explained with a smile. "You can't be too careful."

Ryan took the envelope out of the inner pocket and flopped it on the table between them. "Where did you get this?" He looked into Caesar's eyes but couldn't hold his stare for more than a moment. Ryan had the distinct feeling he was being dissected from head to toe.

"I have many resources and deep pockets," Caesar replied, giving Ryan a sly grin. "I get whatever I want."

Ryan sat back in his chair and folded his arms, looking down at the envelope between them.

Caesar sipped his drink and followed Ryan's eyes to the envelope. "My father always thought we'd find you someday. I was 18 when your father died. He was a good man."

"You tried to have me killed." Ryan scooted his chair back and glanced at the exit.

Caesar gazed up at him with a pained expression. "My employees get a bit," he paused, dabbing his lip with a napkin, "overenthusiastic. I did not order the hit." He motioned with his hand over to his bodyguards. "You killed one of their own, and they wanted revenge."

Ryan winced, turning his head towards the bodyguards. He caught a glimpse of a gun pointed under the table. This could get ugly fast. He swallowed. "And they still want revenge?"

Caesar chuckled. "Don't worry, Ryan. You're under my protection now. They won't touch you." He glanced out at the dance floor. "I never would have found you if it weren't for Elias." He motioned for the bartender for another round of drinks. "Elias used you. He knew of your connection to Canyon Crest, and he was going to use that fact to his full advantage." He pointed markedly at Ryan. "Elias Hastings doesn't care about anyone but himself. Best you understand that now."

The young bartender grinned flirtatiously at Ryan as he set the fresh glasses before them. "Last call, gentlemen."

"Elias would never do anything to hurt me." Ryan shook his head, taking the glass and staring at it. He took one last sip before pushing it away.

Caesar slapped his hand on the table hard, drawing glances from the surrounding patrons and causing his bodyguards to stand. Ryan almost spilled his drink.

Motioning for the bodyguards to sit down, Caesar took a deep, cleansing breath and regarded Ryan. "All that bastard cares about is his company and his next fuck; excuse my language." He smiled at some private joke. "As soon as you are no longer useful to him, he'll discard you like yesterday's trash. Mark my words." Caesar took a long drink from his glass and set it down. "I knew you'd have questions, and I plan to answer them all. When I heard you came to Rumors," his voice trailed off.

"You followed me," Ryan said, completing the sentence.

"You fault me for protecting you?" Caesar shook his head. "Come to Vegas with me tomorrow. It'll be harmless, I promise. I'll show you some of the things you've been missing and fill in the gaps. Two nights, and you'll be free from me forever. I promise."

Standing, Ryan slipped a twenty on the table and took one last sip of the whiskey. "And if I refuse?"

Caesar pursed his lips and shook his head. "As we've spoken before, there will be consequences if you choose that route."

Ryan stared down at him and pulled his jacket together. The sudden motion caused the bodyguards to move their hands on the butts of their guns.

"Think about it," Caesar said, motioning to his bodyguards to stand down.

Freezing in place, Ryan raised his empty hands to the guards. He glared at Caesar and then turned to exit, realizing he had made a fatal error.

Ryan had far surpassed his drink limit. The world was tilting at strange angles, the lights brighter than he remembered. He clung to the wall momentarily, trying to gain equilibrium. Had Caesar slipped him something?

He needed a taxi. "Shit," he said softly as the world swayed beneath him. He staggered to the exit, relishing the cold night air as it hit his face. Ryan chided himself. Always be in control, never vulnerable, especially not with Caesar Gretsky.

His fingers fumbled with the phone, his thumbs not cooperating as he searched for a number on his tenuous internet connection. The streetlights swam before him, and the sidewalk buckled as he swayed to a stop.

Footsteps came quickly behind him, and Ryan turned, drawing his gun. Caesar had followed him outside, and a large black limo followed beside them on the road.

"You're in no condition to walk," Caesar said. "Come on, I'll take you home." A hand came down on Ryan's shoulder, and he pushed it away.

"I'm fine. I'm fine. I'll get home myself," Ryan slurred.

The two bodyguards came up beside him and grabbed his arms, the one taking his gun from his grip.

Caesar opened a door, and they herded Ryan unceremoniously into the back seat. The door slammed shut, and Caesar got in beside him, murmuring something unintelligible to the driver.

Moments later, he sank into the back seat as the Limo accelerated. A hand fell on his shoulder. "Your father wouldn't forgive me if I didn't care for you right now."

Streetlights blurred into each other, and the smooth rumble of the engine made his eyelids feel weighted down. He fought it, but soon gravity won out, and he closed his eyes.

Only for a moment, he promised himself. Ryan thought of his father as his mind drifted into a deep, steady sleep.

Elias gripped the steering wheel, his knuckles turning white, as he watched Ryan get in the Limo with Caesar. Could he have been this gullible? Had Ryan lied the whole time they were together?

This was why he never got involved. He hit the steering wheel with his fist. Stupid, stupid, ridiculous, he chided himself. He watched the Limo pull out into traffic and disappear down the road. Did he even bother following? They were going in the opposite direction of Ryan's dingy apartment. Could Caesar be taking him home?

A flood of deep jealousy invaded Elias, threatening to drown him. When he saw Ryan stumble out into the street, he wanted to run to him and take him in his arms.

Had Ryan tried to infiltrate his company? Learn its secrets from within? How had he fallen for it hook, line, and sinker?

Caesar had given him the information about Ryan. Knew it would hurt him. Show Elias that he could do anything, win anything. And Elias could do nothing. Get his ass handed to him time and again. Caesar had won, clear and plain and without a doubt. "I'll always win, Elias," Caesar told him, with a chuckle, after showing him the papers. "I always hold the cards. Never forget it."

He hated them. Ryan and Caesar. To hell with both of them. He imagined them laughing at what a sucker he'd been.

This time, Caesar hurt him more than he cared to admit.

It was best to move on and forget that Ryan had ever existed. He was with Caesar now—gone and forgotten, and good riddance, as Flynn would say. Elias gazed at the point where the taillights had disappeared. One thing was crystal clear in his mind: Elias wasn't sure he could ever let Ryan go.

CHAPTER 37

Sun streamed through the sheer curtains and directly into Ryan's face. The light was painful, and he groaned, sliding farther under the covers for respite. The inside of his mouth felt like dry cotton, and his temples pulsed with a deep ache.

His bare legs stretched out on the red silken sheets. A brief fantasy of Elias sliding under the sheets beside him entered his mind, being wrapped safely in his arms. Then he realized that he wasn't wearing anything. Only underwear. The dream of Elias disappeared in an instant.

Ryan sat up straight, his stomach protesting the sudden move. His clothes were nowhere to be seen. A Van Gogh painting stared down at him with its swirls of deep blues and yellows. And right above it, a camera lens aimed straight down, red light glowing and indicating a live feed.

Bad memories flooded back, including his night at Rumors and the papers from his father and Caesar. Ryan's eyes locked on the camera as he pulled the sheet up and wrapped it around himself as his feet hit the stone tile floor.

His legs felt stiff as he made his way to the bathroom. The suit Caesar had bought for him hung on a hook encased in plastic. Above the sink, the wooden-framed mirror reflected bloodshot eyes, matted hair, and the ugly scar on his chest. Ryan looked away. He didn't want to see it anymore.

The bedroom door opened, and Ryan glanced up at the mirror. Caesar's reflection smiled back. Already clean and crisp in his lavish suite, Caesar's eyes roved downward appreciatively. "Good morning, Ryan," he said, "I trust you slept well?"

Ryan exited the bathroom, wrapping the red sheet tighter around himself. "Where are my clothes?" Ryan asked, eyes searching Caesar's. "Did you drug me?"

Caesar shook his head, now frowning. "You don't handle your liquor very well, do you, Ryan? I was only trying to keep you safe. As for your clothes," he pursed his lips, "they are being cleaned." He nodded to the hook in the bathroom. "There is a perfect suit right here."

Controlling his breathing, Ryan resisted the urge to punch him. He flexed his fingers and let the anger wash away. It wouldn't do any good here.

An infuriating grin spread over Caesar's face. "Wash up, get in the suit," he said, glancing at his Rolex. "We leave in an hour." With one last glance down Ryan's body, he left, latching the door firmly behind him. The unmistakable click of a lock turned with finality.

Cursing under his breath, Ryan turned the shower on and stepped into the warm, soothing stream of water.

O'Hare airport was usually a madhouse of lines, crowds, endless walking, and waiting. Large passenger airliners taxied, and their engines roared as they took off. Ryan was hustled to a private jet, idling its engines on the tarmac.

The suit fit him perfectly. Caesar looked him over from head to toe, nodding his approval as they boarded. Per Caesar's instructions, Ryan checked in with his sergeant and told her everything was fine and that he'd be back soon.

Ryan was shown to the rear of Caesar's private jet, with a single door separating the back from the main cabin. Four plush leather chairs adorned the back, with plenty of reclining room, and a large screen silently scrolled through the news headlines. A small kitchen and bar stood behind them, partially covered with a curtain. The intercom crackled as the pilot's voice boomed overhead, "Fasten your seatbelts. We have clear skies ahead."

Outside his small window, Ryan watched as they took off. The last remnants of Chicago faded away to suburbs and multi-colored fields.

A young man shared the space with Ryan. In his mid-twenties, he sat on the other side, eyes closed, white earbuds stuffed in. He wore a suit similar to Ryan's, expensive and well-fitting. Jet black hair swept back from his face, and he had a trim beard. He looked like a younger version of Elias, maybe five years younger, with a shorter, slight build.

As if feeling Ryan's stare, the man opened his eyes and glanced over.

Their eyes met briefly before Ryan looked away.

The young man removed his earbuds, eyeing the closed door. He leaned closer to Ryan. "Listen," he confided, his voice just audible over the engine's roar, "people disappear." He snapped his fingers and looked again at the closed door. "Just like that. Do as he says. It makes everything easier." With that, he stuffed the earbuds back in his ears, his eyes closing as he leaned his head back.

Ryan continued to stare, trying to digest his words.

The door hinge creaked in front of him. Caesar entered with a martini in hand. Behind him, men in his entourage were seated around a conference table. Caesar closed the door and glanced out Ryan's window. "What the hell?" he said. "I told them to clean these." Caesar frowned and collapsed in the chair beside Ryan.

He ran a hand down the smooth white leather. "It's beautiful, isn't it? Our fathers made this possible." His hand fell briefly on Ryan's leg. "The world is your oyster now, Ryan. I promise you."

Caesar turned abruptly to regard the young man. "Philip, join me in the back." Caesar stood, his eyes narrowed, as the young man slowly took his earbuds out.

Philip gave Ryan a wary look, then followed Caesar and disappeared.

Ryan watched the closed curtains for a moment, frowning. He gazed out his window as snow-covered peaks loomed up at him.

He thought about his father. There was so much he didn't know and didn't want to know. Forgetting the past was sage advice. But he had to know. And the key was now behind a curtain doing god knows what with Philip. A few moments passed, and Philip emerged, suit slightly crumpled, followed closely by Caesar.

Caesar took a satisfied breath and sat beside Ryan. He smiled to himself as he adjusted his tie. "Philip," he called out, "get a martini for our friend."

"Yes, sir," Philip said. Caesar watched Philip's back appreciatively as he went down the aisle. "I have so much to show you once we land."

Ryan shook his head. "Show me?"

"I think it's time you understood your family's history. Our fathers sacrificed much for the both of us."

Philip returned, handing Ryan the long-stemmed glass. "Philip," Caesar reprimanded, grabbing the glass, "take a sip and prove we don't drug people." He shook his head as he gazed disapprovingly at Ryan.

Philip locked Caesar with a seductive gaze and put his mouth on the little straw, sucking in the fluid. Then he handed Ryan back the drink.

"Good," Caesar said, nodding his approval to Philip. His attention returned to Ryan as his eyes roamed down Ryan's suit. "It looks good on you."

Shifting uncomfortably in his chair, Ryan looked at Philip and back to Caesar. "Two days," Ryan said, "and I'm back in Chicago."

Caesar gave him a bemused smile. "Of course. That's what we agreed on." He stood and stretched. "I have a business to attend to, but I look forward to our time together once we land."

He gave Ryan one last smile as he opened the door to the main cabin.

Caesar spoke, his hand on the door handle. "Your father wanted this, Ryan. I promise to open your eyes to a whole new world."

With that, Caesar disappeared behind the door. All noise disappeared except the rumble of the engines and his own jumbled thoughts.

Ryan gazed out the window, feeling truly alone. What the hell had he gotten himself into?

CHAPTER 38

The late morning sun beat down on the veranda at Hasting's mansion, illuminating the front carved door complete with a lion's head knocker. Elias had changed the locks. Alicia Sandstone stood alone on the porch, feeling like an intruder.

She looked out at the manicured estate, admiring the crocuses blossoming along the front path. Alicia smiled, remembering when Flynn planted those bulbs, ecstatic at finding his wife's favorite shade of purple.

She drew in a deep breath. A bird flittered into a weeping willow, holding a twig in its beak. Summer fast approached, and Alicia thought she'd be married long before this. And she was so close to having everything: half the Hastings fortune, and she thought wistfully of Elias's love. How had everything gone so wrong?

Flynn's call this morning had given her a glimmer of hope. A chance to make this right. As she went to Elias's front door, her feet were killing her from yesterday's runway gig. The new Versace dress had wowed everyone. Nearing 30, she wasn't recovering as fast from these all-day stints.

She knocked on the front door and hoped she wouldn't have to stand long in her sandals. Leaning against the brick wall, she shifted her weight uncomfortably from foot to foot.

Staring at the front door, memories of Elias's last words stung her again. *We're* done. The sham is over. Nasty words. How had it come to this? The past few weeks, she endured the pitying looks of her girlfriends, irritating calls from gossip rags, and Caesar's nagging insistence that she get back together with Elias.

Caesar Gretsky. Seemed like ages ago she was locked up in that filthy prison in Rome. The guards watched her through the bars with lascivious grins. She was barely 20, in jail, and unsure how to tell Daddy. It had been just a little trinket swiped from a shelf. Daddy's money could have easily paid for it. But the occasional shoplift was so much more exhilarating.

She never had to tell Daddy. Caesar Gretsky, the suiter she met at a fashion shoot, bailed her out and swept her off her feet. Alicia felt like a princess, and Caesar was her knight in shining armor. The places he had taken her, the plays, operas, and fancy restaurants. He even bought her that bracelet; she remembered it with a guilty smile.

Just slip a few inconsequential papers to Caesar. That was all he asked. She glanced behind her and knocked more insistently on the door.

Caesar had been in close contact recently. Previously, it had been once or twice a year. Now, she was getting calls from him almost daily. He asked her to do something big this last week. She had resisted at first, but he had wined, dined, and somehow talked her into it. Planting evidence at the cop's apartment was risky.

But, she reminded herself, it was all for the greater good. How could Elias have been so foolish? Falling for a cop, of all things?

She shifted her weight again and knocked more insistently. The last try, she told herself. Finally, she heard footsteps and movement behind the door.

Sig Flynn opened the door, looking older and frailer than the last time she saw him. His tired eyes took in her red miniskirt and matching tank top and then up to her perfectly contoured face. Slowly, his eyes lit up.

"I'm sorry, Alicia. I was on the phone." He stepped back and motioned her inside. "Come in. It's good to see you again." He kissed her cheek and smiled at her. "Seeing you is indeed a breath of fresh air." He looked down, his eyes narrowed, and shook his head. "We have a big meeting with our foreign investors this week," he glanced up the stairs. "He has to be there."

"I'm glad you called Sig," she said, following his gaze. "I'll talk to him."

Flynn grimaced. "Elias isn't doing well, Alicia. He barely eats and keeps the room dark. He won't talk to me." Flynn shook his head. "You two are good friends. I hope you can talk some sense into him."

Alicia nodded, looking up the staircase. "I'll talk to him, Sig. I'll make things right." She straightened her shoulders, conjuring up some confidence she didn't feel. The cop was no good for him—that was clear from the start. His affairs rarely lasted more than one night. Now it was up to her and Sig to set him straight.

She stood for a moment outside the master suite and rattled the knob. It was locked. "Elias?" she called out. She winced as something crashed, and a loud curse came from inside.

"Go away, Sig," Elias called out, voice thick and slurred.

"Elias, it's me, Alicia. Can I come in?"

She heard slow footsteps, and the doorknob turned. Elias stood in the doorway, unshaven, with matted hair, wearing nothing but a dirty white T-shirt and boxers. Alicia sniffed and made a face. Clearly, bathing was not high on his agenda. "Elias, can I come in?"

"I don't want to see anyone," he said. But he didn't leave the doorway. She peered around him at the empty vodka bottles on the dresser and fast-food wrappers strewn across the floor.

Alicia ducked past him, shoved some dirty laundry out of the way, and sat on the bed. A whiskey bottle lay on its side, soaked into the sheets. Hopefully, it was whiskey, she told herself, nose wrinkling. "Elias, don't you think you've had enough?"

He shook his head and poured the whiskey into a glass. "I haven't had enough of anything," he said, his words slurring together as he took a sip.

Alicia shook her head, biting her lip. "He wasn't good for you," Alicia said. "You deserve so much better."

"I can't get him out of my mind." Elias began pacing. "How could I not see he was working for Caesar?" With an abrupt motion, Elias hurled the glass towards the fireplace. It smashed against the brick, glass shards scattering across the tile.

Elias collapsed on the bed, moaning. He hit his forehead repeatedly with both hands. "Nothing makes sense. Nothing." He pointed to the papers scattered on his desk. "I found those in Ryan's apartment." He let out a dry chuckle. "All this time, he was stealing my information for Caesar. All this time. It makes no sense."

"Caesar never makes sense," she reminded him. Alicia stood and moved closer to him. "Come on, Elias. Let me give you a back rub."

Elias eyed her for a moment, then nodded. Alicia crawled on her knees behind him and touched his tight shoulder muscles. His undershirt was sweaty, and it took all her willpower to keep her hands in place. "Relax," she whispered in his ear. "Let it go, Elias. Let it all go."

Elias drew in a deep breath and let it out. His muscles started melting under her touch. "I thought he was the one," Elias muttered. "I thought...."

Alisha knelt over and put a finger to his mouth.

"It's in the past now, Elias." She took him in her arms. "We'll get through this together." He relaxed into her embrace, and she rocked him and ran her fingers through his matted hair.

"You've always been there for me, Alicia. Even when everyone else was against me." He wrapped his hands around her arm. "I'm sorry I said those hurtful things. I was wrong to send you away." His hand caressed her face.

These were the words she longed to hear. She allowed herself a small smile and rocked Elias gently. "Come on," Alicia said, facing him. "Let's get you cleaned up. You'll feel so much better." She frowned at the dirty wrappers on the floor. "We'll get you some real food."

Elias nodded and got up unsteadily as he headed for the bathroom. "I love you, Alicia," he said, turning to her, the words slurred.

"I love you too, Elias," she said as he shut the door firmly behind him. Retching sounds came from the bathroom, and Alicia cringed. This was for Elias's good, she reminded herself. The cop would have broken his heart eventually, but better now than later.

Ryan would soon be a distant memory. She held up her engagement ring, letting the small amount of light from the closed curtains reflect off the perfect diamonds. Alicia allowed herself a smile. Soon, everything would go back to normal.

Chapter 39

Memories flooded back as Ryan sat in the back seat of the black Mercedes. The blustery Nevada landscape stretched out as they drove farther from the bustle of Las Vegas.

The turquoise waters of Lake Mead rippled with white caps from the cold northern wind. Ryan remembered dipping his toes in those waters as a young boy.

Caesar Gretsky spoke quietly on his phone while Ryan watched a few die-hard boaters forged through the wind, trolling slowly with fishing poles cast over the stern. Caesar returned Ryan's cell phone this morning, and that, at least, gave him hope. He clutched it in his hand like a lifeline.

The landscape near Lake Mead was so eerily familiar. Caesar was taking him to what was once his father's house. You must know your father's humble beginnings to understand how far he came. And appreciate it. Caesar had spoken those words in the luxurious hotel and casino founded by Ryan's father.

The endless low brush stretched out towards the red-hued cliffs. Ryan's chest tightened as a memory flickered into his mind. As a young boy, he had run through these very grounds, terrified and tripping on the low brush.

Ryan overheard part of Caesar's conversation, and the memory evaporated. "Good," Caesar said quietly, "Give Philip his compensation."

Two men had led Philip away that morning. The young man's haunted eyes briefly met Ryan's. "What compensation?" Ryan interrupted. What are you talking about?"

Caesar shrugged, narrowing his eyes at Ryan as he hung up. "Focus on yourself," he snapped. As if catching himself, he spoke more gently. "That's what happens when you break the rules. We had to let him go."

Turning his attention out the window, Caesar slipped the phone into his pocket. "But that is the past, and now, we have to look to the future." He faced Ryan squarely. "Our future." Ryan glimpsed the gun under Caesar's jacket. "You have many important decisions to make."

Those gray eyes were unwavering and cold, and Ryan felt himself flinch.

More than anything, Ryan wished he had his 9MM close at hand. He'd stick it right in that smug face. But that had disappeared along with all his clothes. So Ryan sat and waited, thankful that he at least had his cell phone. For now, he reminded himself.

"Tomorrow, you prove yourself," Caesar continued, looking out the window. "Loyalty is everything. Remember that." He tapped the side of his head. "Philip couldn't grasp that."

Ryan frowned. Had they overheard Philip's warning to him on the plane?

He drew in a deep breath. "I'm headed back to Chicago tomorrow," Ryan said, then stopped when he noticed a scowl cross Caesar's face.

"Of course, you can go back," Caesar said with a forced smile. "But, understand everything has changed. If you return without the blessing of our company, there will be consequences."

Silence fell between them.

Caesar gazed at him with his unreadable gray eyes. "I will never lie to you, Ryan. Not ever. You are family."

When Ryan said nothing, Caesar continued. A hand came down and patted Ryan's leg. "Tomorrow is the big day. Our partners overseas are here. I want you at the meeting." He paused, "I will need a favor."

"What favor?" Ryan repeated slowly.

The car came to an abrupt stop, and Caesar ignored him. "Ah, here we are—your mother and father's humble beginnings."

A forlorn two-story house stood facing them. Peeling white paint and scattered roofing material had fallen victim to the high winds. Overgrown grass and shrubs took over the front walkway.

Ryan gripped the seat under him as everything vanished from his mind except the house in front of him. Ryan had been here as a very young boy—he knew it in his bones. The memories came back fresh and raw.

"Go ahead," Caesar said with an amused smile.

Ryan got out, the cold wind whipping his face. Caesar had not given him a coat, and the gray clouds threatened rain.

The windows were boarded up and smashed in places. As he ascended the stairs, the wood creaked under his shoes.

He stood with his hand on the doorknob. One last glance back, and he opened the door to the house.

White sheets covered a couch and two recliner chairs. A musty smell emanated from the worn carpet, and cobwebs lined the corners high above. A picture frame lay face down on a coffee table. Ryan hesitated before turning it over. Forget the past. They were wise words.

Hand trembling, he picked up the picture frame and turned it over. He let out a sudden breath, feeling a gut punch. His father and mother stared back at him. Both smiled on a beach, his father holding up a fish and his mother in a hood and coat, enveloping him in her arms.

Ryan didn't have any pictures of his mother. This was the first time he'd seen her since he'd been whisked away. He glanced out the window through the tattered lace curtains. Caesar was waiting for him in the car. "I'm going to make this right," he said aloud. The words echoed back into the empty house. He fingered the two happy figures in the frame. "What happened to you?" He took the picture from the frame and tucked it into his jacket.

The house had the sad, abandoned feel of a life interrupted and changed. His gaze turned to a hole in the wall to the right of the fireplace—a perfectly circular hole the size of a bullet. Around it, the wallpaper had begun to peel. He ran a finger over the rough edge of the hole.

His phone vibrated in his pocket. Ryan took it out: Jasmine. She had called him seven times in the last few days. "Jasmine, I can't speak right now," he said.

"Where are you, Ryan?" Jasmine's voice was tense. "Why haven't you answered your phone?"

"I'm on assignment." He grimaced at the half-truth.

"We missed you at the game," Jasmine continued. "I asked Sig where you were, and he didn't know."

Ryan's chest tightened at the mention of Flynn. "Jazz, I warned you about him."

She let out a light laugh. "Sig is so good with Bo, Ryan. You have to get to know him. It's all good, I promise you."

Caesar opened the car door and stepped out, stretching. Ryan had to make this short. "Be careful, Jazz. I'll see you soon. I have to go."

"All right, but call me tomorrow. You promise?"

"I promise," Ryan said, but he wasn't sure of anything. Whatever this favor Caesar wanted, it would not end well. *People disappear.* Philip's words still haunted him.

Caesar stood behind him with an inquisitive look on his face. "Who were you talking to?"

Ryan shook his head, tucking the phone away quickly.

"I know about your life in Chicago, Ryan. The widow and her son. Your friends are my friends, and all their needs will be taken care of."

Ryan glared at him, fingernails digging into his palms. "Don't you dare go near them, Caesar. I'm warning you."

Caesar raised his hands in surrender. "Of course, of course," he said, swiping some dust on the marble mantel. He turned to face Ryan. "Do right by me, and everything will be fine. Do we understand each other?"

Crystal clear, Ryan thought as he turned away from Caesar. He felt like a caged animal, trapped and muzzled.

"It will get better, Ryan. I promise. Just like your father wanted." Caesar let those words hang. "For now," his eyes narrowed, "you do as I say." He ran his hand across the table where the picture frame had made a clean spot in the thick dust. "This will be yours, you know." He glanced around with an appraising eye. "We can fix it up nicely."

After the favor, Ryan thought dryly, watching Caesar appraise the room. He had to figure something out, and fast. Whatever this favor was, clearly, it would seal his fate forever.

CHAPTER 40

Outside the Canyon Crest Hotel and Casino, a marble fountain provided a constant stream of water into a stone-lined pool.

The Greek Titan Oceanus, complete with pitchfork, stared down imperiously at the gamblers strolling through the main entrance.

Silver coins lined the pool bottom, the last entreaty for a bit of luck. Outside on the Las Vegas strip, the activity never seemed to die down.

Ryan gazed at the main entrance from his top-floor suite. More like a prison, he thought. The door only opened from outside, which meant he could go nowhere. Meals were served like clockwork. A breakfast cart stood untouched by the doorway.

Nerves were getting to him locked up like this. The favor came due today. Whatever that was. Not having a weapon only heightened his unease.

The steak dinner last night included a knife. Ryan had slid it into his belt, hoping no one would notice. Ryan imagined Caesar's well-armed security would have a good laugh if they found it. To make matters worse, the dull blade took forever to saw through the meat.

Far below his window, the Canyon Crest entrance was a bustle of activity. Endless streams of gamblers and lovers came and went. A stretch limousine piqued his interest as it pulled up to the front drive. Five men exited from the rear doors.

They appeared of mid-eastern descent, wearing neatly pressed suits and wing-tip shoes. The stench of old money oozed from them. One man clutched a briefcase under his arm and appeared to be the leader as he pointed and barked out orders.

Ryan squinted his eyes, trying to garner every detail, every movement, when the door rattled behind him. Instinctively, he reached for the hilt of his gun and came down on empty air. The door opened, and Caesar stepped inside regarding the uneaten food.

"Why aren't you eating?" Caesar asked, pushing the cart away with amusement. "Don't you like our food?"

As Caesar joined him at the window, Ryan shook his head and said nothing.

"Beautiful, isn't it?" the older man said, following Ryan's gaze to the Vegas strip. "Amazing what our fathers created," he said with a sigh. "We owe them everything."

Those words died in silence.

"It was only recently that we captured the market here in Vegas. Vegas was always your father's dream. Unfortunate circumstances made us start in Chicago. But now," he pointed towards the strip and an endless glow of flickering signs, "the skies the limit."

He leaned against the window to face Ryan. "Today is a formality with our new business partners, the final contract signing and celebration." Those gray eyes regarded Ryan warmly. "I want you to be there."

Ryan fidgeted under his gaze as Caesar continued, voice lowered. "You killed one of my best men, Ryan. I can't forget that. You must atone for your past. You understand that, don't you?" Crossing his arms, Ryan took a step back.

"I know you're uncertain," Caesar said. "I know this is a big step for you. Can I count on you?"

Words once again failed Ryan. His mind wandered to the picture tucked under his pillow. Ryan had spent the night holding it, looking deep into his mother's eyes, trying to grasp some memory or image of her—anything to hang on to. Nothing came to him—only emptiness and profound loss.

Caesar smiled, taking Ryan's silence for consent, and took Ryan into a deep embrace. "I look forward to having you in the family," he whispered into Ryan's ear. "How long has it been since you've had a family?"

Ryan didn't pull away. The sincerity of the embrace seemed to clear his mind. A dangerous man, Ryan reminded himself. At that moment, he wanted to be part of a family. Longed for it. A part of his father's legacy. Caesar let go, and Ryan stood still, unable to move.

"I want you with me," Caesar said, touching Ryan's shoulders. Tonight, everything opens up for you." He gave Ryan a hearty pat on the back and glanced at his watch, motioning to the bodyguards positioned outside the hall.

Now dismissed, Ryan watched him leave, his mind an un-settled mess. He stared at the locked door with a growing sense of dread.

∾

The sky outside turned cloudy, and the sun gave its last gasp before setting. As dusk fell, the lights of Las Vegas came to life. Neon lights and flashing ads lit the strip as cars pushed toward their favorite watering and gambling holes.

Canyon Crest Casino was bustling with activity, not that Ryan could tell, holed up in his suite. Only gazing below could he see the heavy traffic flow into the adjoining park-ing garage, and the valets were hopping as women and men dressed in their best came to party.

The knock came sooner than he expected. Greeted by two of Caesar's bodyguards, they escorted him down the ele-vator and into a spacious hotel conference room.

Recessed lighting above shone on an oak table that stretched the room's length. A large screen lit up with the Canyon Crest insignia stretched above the head of the table.

Men surrounded the conference table, conversing in hushed tones. At the head of the table, Caesar welcomed his guests warmly in their native tongue.

Bodyguards stood in strategic positions around the room. Ryan was certain he was the only one not carrying a gun.

The hotel wait staff hustled about the room, passing out glasses to each man at the table and popping the cork of fine champagne.

Caesar stood, raised his glass to the man beside him, and spoke in English and then in the man's native tongue, "To my good friend Samir. To a long, fruitful partnership."

Glasses were raised and toasted towards the two men.

Caesar set his drink down, uncapped a pen, and signed a paper before him. Caesar embraced his new business partner, and they shook warmly.

A standing ovation ensued as Samir slipped the paper into his briefcase. "To a lasting and fruitful partnership," Samir said, gazing around the room.

Ceasar leaned in and whispered something to Samir, who nodded his approval.

In an instant, Ryan was in Caesar's clutches. His hand squeezed Ryan's arm as he spoke in his ear. "This is it. Make sure Samir has everything he needs. They will depart shortly, and he will need your assistance." When he noticed Ryan hesitating, he added. "Do this, and all will be forgiven."

Caesar winked at Ryan and then sat down, leaning back with satisfaction.

Samir raised his chin, eyes inspecting Ryan slowly from head to foot. He motioned with his head to follow. He had a heavy girth contained by a tailored striped suit. A thick mustache and a full head of meticulously groomed black hair accented his angular features. Ryan could picture him in his headdress and robes, leading his company back in the Middle East.

The bodyguards stood still as Ryan followed Samir out of the conference room. The older man opened a door adjacent to the room and flipped on the light switch.

Fluorescent bulbs came to life and hummed, casting everything with a greenish hue. Chairs stacked five high, and folded tables lay stored against the walls. "Close the door," Samir ordered as he set his briefcase down.

Ryan shut the door, uncomfortable with the penetrating gaze now directed his way.

"I hope," Samir said, stepping towards Ryan, "you're as good as Philip." He adjusted his pants. "I've been assured you are better." He motioned to Ryan impatiently, "Get on your knees, and we'll seal the deal."

Ryan balked, not sure he heard right. He was in shock and stood senseless in front of the man. Rage settled on the older man's features, lips turning to a snarl. "You dare defy Caesar?" He took a menacing step closer. "Defy *me*?"

Adrenaline surged as Ryan leaned down and pretended to go down on his knees. The man visibly relaxed, and at the last minute, Ryan pulled the knife out of his belt and pushed Samir hard against the tables behind them. Samir grunted as his head recoiled, and his eyes grew wide with surprise.

The older man recovered his bearings and reached for his gun. Ryan grabbed an arm and twisted it forcefully against his back. Now, behind Samir, Ryan plunged the tip of the knife into his shoulder. He felt it penetrate the skin.

The man let out a painful scream as blood oozed down his white shirt. Ryan reached under Samir's jacket, grabbing the gun out of the holster. A Beretta. That'll work just fine.

Ryan backed away, the gun aimed at Samir's head. "You'll pay with your life," the older man said, clutching his shoulder. "Caesar will pay for this."

Snatching the briefcase on the table, Ryan backed towards the door, the gun held so tightly his fingers turned white. He then turned and fled.

Samir's screams and curses echoed down the hallway. There was nothing to do but run. Ryan clutched the briefcase to his chest. This was a mistake, he knew. As he sped blindly down the hall, it was possibly the last mistake he'd ever make.

CHAPTER 41

The states ran together the last 24 hours, and the truck stops all looked identical. Missouri was no different. Hitchhiking out of Nevada was the easy part. Samir had money in his briefcase, and Ryan now had a bus ticket to Chicago. An early morning bus would get him there by evening.

The bus depot was in view, lit by a few streetlights. It was open, with a metal roof and clear plastic siding providing minimal cover from the elements. The war against graffiti was lost a long time ago. Inside, a homeless man camped out beside the vending machines, sound asleep.

Ryan couldn't afford to be out in the open. The shadows were now his home, and he crouched in an alley. He snugged his new knit cap farther over his ears. The surplus army jacket was still wet from the drenching rains in Kansas.

The industrial district in Springfield had rows of warehouses, all silent and dark in the early morning fog. Streetlights illuminated sections of the sidewalk, and an old payphone was just feet away from Ryan's hiding spot.

More than anything, Ryan wished for a shower and shave. He was ripe, to say the least. *Elias, if you could see me now,* he thought with a grimace.

When Ryan returned to Chicago, he would find Elias and speak to him face to face. And, Ryan thought, he wasn't giving up without a fight.

Cash was growing thin in his wallet, and he'd long ago switched his phone for a burner. But Ryan's real treasures lay in the papers and Beretta he took from Caesar's business partner. The signed documents were still there, folded and slightly damp in his pocket. If something in those papers were not above board, Caesar Gretsky was going down.

That was the question. Hopefully, Detective Chavez would have some answers. Ryan fingered the coins in his pocket. Making his way out of the shadows, he slipped into the phone booth. Exposed and vulnerable in the open, his eyes roved over the street. He dropped the coins into the slot and dialed the number for the Chicago PD.

One ring, two rings, and a recording came on. He entered Detective Chavez's extension.

A car was approaching, and he could hear the tires rolling on the pavement. His body tensed as headlights swept around the corner.

Cursing, he hung up the payphone and sprinted to the alley. A dark sedan rolled by just as he ducked back into the shadows.

He sat back against the brick wall, letting his pulse slow. Had Caesar tracked him somehow? The bus ticket was too risky. He had to get out of here.

A gunshot rang out from the street, causing Ryan to freeze. One staccato burst and then silence before a nearby warehouse alarm started blaring. He peered around the corner of the alley and saw four shadows moving inside the depot.

Get out of here, Ryan told himself. Don't get involved. Stay, and Caesar has you.

A whimpering cry came from inside the depot, and Ryan cursed. He knew what he had to do. Keeping flush to the sides of the buildings, he moved towards the station, Baretta drawn and ready.

Following the barrel of his gun, he peered around the corner of the station. Four men surrounded the homeless man, who was now on his knees. The attackers were young and wore baggy clothing and expensive high tops. One of them couldn't be out of high school. This was not Caesar's men. Ryan wasn't sure whether to laugh or cry.

"The next shot will be through your fuckin' head," a tall man in a baseball cap said, waving his gun carelessly. "Did you think you could hide from Blaze? Huh? If you don't have the money, we take something else." The men gave themselves a knowing look. The leader held up a knife. "I don't think you need all your fingers, and Blaze will certainly appreciate the gesture."

The homeless man whimpered. "Please, please, I'll get the money for you. I promise."

Ryan shook his head in disgust.

They brought the man up by his collar, forcing his fingers down hard on a counter. The knife blade flashed in the victim's face. Ryan took a deep breath and moved in.

"Police. Freeze!" he yelled, turning his gun on the men. "Drop your weapons."

The men looked up, surprised. "Oh shit, man! Police!" The knife fell to the ground as three men took off. The leader took one look at Ryan's gun and followed.

Ryan kept his gun raised as he watched them flee. He shook his head as he lowered his gun and crouched beside the victim. There was no blood, and his breathing was regular, but he was in shock. Wide, bloodshot eyes regarded him from the floor. "You've got to get out of here," Ryan said, prodding his shoulder.

A blinding light flashed on, illuminating Ryan, the homeless man, and the entire bus depot. Ryan raised his gun, eyes squinting, unable to see a thing.

A bodiless voice shouted out, "Ryan Ward! Drop your weapon. Now!"

Ryan took off running, jumping over the homeless man. Multiple footsteps followed him out the side of the depot. Orders were barked out behind him.

He turned down an alley, and the security alarm grew louder, and a high-powered beam tracked his movements from behind. Out in the open, he was sitting duck, and he spotted a door to his right. Ryan rattled the handle. Locked.

All Ryan could do was turn and stand his ground. He squared himself towards his pursuers, gun raised.

Three men materialized in front of him, stopping at the sight of his gun. Automatic rifles were trained on his head.

"You are outnumbered," an older man in a rumpled suit yelled over the alarm. "Caesar doesn't want you harmed. Put your weapon down."

Multiple police sirens started raging in the distance. One man looked over his shoulder. "Shit, the police are coming, Sal." He threw a sneer at the warehouse. "Damn security alarm."

The man regarded Ryan a moment. "Caesar wants you alive. This is your last chance. Come now, or dig your own grave." He glanced back towards the sirens. "Do you understand me?"

Ryan held his gun steady. He wasn't giving up without taking a few with him.

The sirens grew louder and came to a stop outside the alley. "Come on," one man said with urgency. "Police are almost here."

The man lowered his gun, swearing under his breath. "Very stupid, Ryan You had your chance. Next time, we kill you. That's a promise." More sirens blared in the distance.

As they disappeared out of sight, Ryan turned, running in the opposite direction as fast as he could. He had no desire to deal with the local police, and explaining these events would not end well.

Next time, Ryan knew he wouldn't be as lucky. Caesar's patience would grow thin. All he had were the papers. If he didn't bring Gretsky down soon, he might as well be digging his own grave. He ran for all he was worth, adrenaline taking him far away from the wailing sirens in the distance.

CHAPTER 42

Ryan watched from the bushes, waiting in the darkness. The park was quiet early in the morning except for a few determined joggers. He knew this park like the back of his hand. Being back in Chicago came with many mixed emotions.

He'd hitched a ride with a few truckers and made it back to Chicago in the early morning hours. Memories of Elias were everywhere. It was a chilly morning, and Ryan rubbed his hands together, blowing into his fist.

The army surplus jacket wasn't doing the trick. Behind him, the gentle waves of Lake Michigan lapped onto the shore, and the seagulls called out, looking for food.

Coming in from the cold was all he wanted. Find Detective Chavez and tell him everything. Come clean and bring Gretsky down. He patted the papers in his breast pocket for assurance and maybe some luck. They were his ticket to freedom.

All his plans of finding Elias had to be on hold for now. But soon, he'd find him. Make sure Elias understood. He wanted Elias to yell at him, push him, punch him, anything but the silence.

It had been days now since he showered or had a good night's sleep. He could just hear Jack, his sergeant, kicking his ass for whining. He chuckled at the thought, and then Ryan's eyes grew wide. Jasmine and Bo. He hadn't spoken to them since Nevada.

Ryan cursed himself, and his chest grew tight. No, he assured himself, she and Bo were fine. But he had to check. She should be at work right now.

He opened the little flip phone and punched in Jasmine's number. *"Please be okay,"* he whispered. Jasmine's phone went to voicemail. That was not like her. He tried again. "Come on, Jazz," he said, bouncing on his heels, "answer." Once again, Jasmine's voice came on with a cheery, "Leave a message!"

Panic rose inside him. His hands trembled as he dug for more coins in his pocket. He dialed the number for the

NICU unit at Memorial Hospital. A receptionist with a nasal twang answered, and Ryan asked about Jasmine.

"Right, Jasmine." There was a pause. "She should be here." She called out to her co-workers. "Is Jasmine around?"

Ryan overheard someone in the background say, "She didn't show up yesterday." Ryan gripped the phone tighter and leaned his weight into the phone. His breath left him as the receptionist returned to the line and cleared her throat. "No, she isn't here today. Can I take a message?"

Hanging up, Ryan's mouth turned dry as he gazed down the road. Dread gnawed at him.

He swore under his breath. Detective Chavez would have to wait. If anything happened to—he refused to believe. There had to be an explanation.

Ryan caught a bus towards the outskirts of Chicago and the little Glenview neighborhood.

With his unkempt beard and lack of hygiene, he had the entire back of the bus to himself. The people in front cast nervous glances his way. He couldn't blame them.

Leaning against the window, he watched as traffic jammed up the freeway. Horns honked, and tempers flared. The early morning rush was now in full swing.

Nearby, a man discreetly took a bite of his egg and cheese sandwich. Ryan's stomach grumbled and complained. He pushed the hunger aside, but he could feel his strength waning.

Jasmine's neighborhood was quiet as he got off at his stop. It was a usual morning, with kids laughing and waiting for the school bus.

He walked up to Jasmine's house, and relief washed over him. Her red jeep was parked in the drive, and he allowed himself a smile. Paranoia was not his friend. The worry had been for nothing.

Still being cautious, he went to the back door and turned the knob. It turned easily. The door opened, and he frowned, stepping back. Jasmine always locked her doors.

Ryan drew his gun. As he entered the kitchen, it was dark inside, with no hint of life. He stopped cold when he saw the dirty dishes in the sink.

Jasmine would never leave them like that.

He cleared the bedrooms, bathroom, and living room. There was no sign of a struggle and no sign of Jasmine and Bo. Jack's picture smiled down at him from above the dining room table.

If only Jack was with him now. He tucked the gun back in his belt and whispered up to him, "I'll make this right. I promise."

The home phone sat on a small desk in the living room. He picked it up and dialed his station's main number.

A photograph of Bo sat on the side table next to the phone. A baseball bat swung over his shoulder, and he smiled from ear to ear in his Badger's uniform. The call connected, and a woman's voice chimed, "Chicago P.D., can I help you?"

Before he could answer, a sudden movement from the left made Ryan turn. A hand came down and ended the call.

Ryan reached for his gun when the barrel of a Glock smashed into his cheek. An angry voice admonished him. "Move away from the phone."

Ryan knew that voice and Irish brogue. It was Flynn. Raising his hands, Ryan turned to face him.

Flynn kept his gun raised, a vein pulsing in his neck. "Word on the street," he started, "is that Gretsky has them, and, make no mistake, he *will* kill them." He glared as he waved his hand toward the phone. "So, you'll give Gretsky what he wants. Do you understand?"

"Yes," Ryan said, taking a step back.

Drawing a deep breath, Flynn picked up the phone receiver and handed it back to Ryan. He punched in numbers with his thick finger, each punctuated with a scowl.

The answer came after the first ring. "Hello, Ryan," Caesar answered, his voice relaxed as if he hadn't a care in the world.

"Where are they?" Ryan asked, gritting his teeth. "Where's Bo?"

Ominous silence greeted him on the other end of the line. Caesar inhaled, then answered, "Do you have the papers?"

"Yes," Ryan said, glancing at Flynn, who listened intently.

"That is a start. An excellent start. Bring the papers behind Canyon Crest. Come alone." The dial tone buzzed in Ryan's ear as Caesar hung up the line.

"Papers, huh?" Flynn said, holding out his hands. "Maybe I should kill you and take the papers to him myself."

Ryan stared him down, unmoving. "Shoot me then," he said, straightening. "Do it."

Flynn's gun wavered. "You've got a lot of nerve coming back to Chicago after what you did to Elias." Catching himself, Flynn shoved his gun back into Ryan's face.

"I didn't do *anything*," Ryan said, shaking his head. "I promise you."

"Your word means nothing," he spat. "Elias *knows* who you are."

Ryan collapsed into a dining room chair, defeated as the world tilted on its side. Dizziness washed over him. Lack of sleep, food, and water all crashed down on him.

This was Ryan's fault and his fault alone. I've failed you, Jack, he thought, completely and utterly. He closed his eyes and buried his head in his hands.

Darkness was what he wanted. Maybe Flynn would put him out of his misery. One thing was obvious: Caesar Gretsky had won.

A hand clasped his shoulder, jerking him out of his reverie. Flynn spoke to him, his voice calm. "Caesar doesn't take prisoners. Make no mistake. He'll kill Jasmine and Bo himself."

Ryan nodded, letting each word pierce him. He wanted pain right now. Preferred to be punished.

Flynn's grip on his shoulder tightened. "They need you right now, Ryan. They need you to do the right thing."

Flynn tucked his gun into his belt and moved a chair closer, scraping the linoleum floor.

He sat facing Ryan, leaning down. "Despite what you may think of me, I love them. And damn it, I know Jasmine and Bo love you." Flynn pointed to himself. "I'd do anything for them...."

Ryan studied Flynn. The man he hated almost as much as Caesar. But they had one thing in common. At last, Ryan said, "I'd give my life for them."

Flynn nodded, then extended a hand towards Ryan. "We get them back," he said, "or die trying."

Ryan hesitated, then took Flynn's hand in his own. The grip was firm, and his hands rough. "I'd give everything to get them back." Whatever it took, he would do it.

Standing up from the table, Flynn had a determined look on his face as he drew his gun and checked the magazine. Ryan's mind raced.

The next few hours were crucial. Jasmine and Bo's safety relied on keeping a cool head. Flynn turned to him and offered a hand up. Ryan took it warily. This time, he wouldn't face Caesar alone.

Chapter 43

From his perch on the 4th-floor parking garage, Ryan trained his binoculars on the street below.

Flynn's Jag, with its tinted windows, made the perfect blind. Ryan raised the binoculars to the building before him, emblazoned with the Canyon Crest insignia.

Somewhere inside, Jasmine and Bo were being held captive. What was once his father's company was now firmly in the grasp of Caesar Gretsky.

From his few days with Gretsky, Ryan knew he was both impulsive and prone to violence. A dangerous combination. No telling what he would do if pushed.

All he knew was that Flynn's plan had better work. Jasmine and Bo depended on it. Drawing in a deep breath, Ryan continued his surveillance.

The noon sun reflected against the building, making it impossible to see inside.

On the street level, pedestrians walked towards the little café across the street, unaware of the drama about to unfold.

Movement below caught Ryan's eye, and he focused the binoculars towards the front door. Flynn, wearing a gray jumpsuit and baseball cap with a Mobile Electric logo, tipped his head in Ryan's direction before entering.

Okay, Ryan told himself, Flynn was inside. It was a few minutes before showtime. Ryan lowered the binoculars and checked his gun's magazine.

If this went bad, it would be really bad. No room for mistakes. Flynn had military training, perhaps in the IRA or the British Armed Forces. He didn't want to know. Elias trusted Flynn with his life, and right now, that was good enough for Ryan.

He fished out the papers from his jacket. Folded, crinkled, and now damp, they held the key. Something in them had Caesar worried. Worried enough to keep Jasmine and Bo alive a little longer, Ryan hoped.

The new burner phone buzzed beside him, and Ryan answered it.

Flynn's voice came on in a low whisper. "Basement," he said. "I'm going down. It's time."

Ryan remained silent for a moment. "Flynn, if I don't make it back, tell Elias..."

Flynn interrupted him. "Tell him yourself. When all this is over." The line clicked, and a dial tone followed.

Ryan took one last look at Canyon Crest and got ready. This was the moment. As he stepped out of the parking garage into the bright sun, he squinted his eyes and held his hand up against the sudden barrage of light.

No doubt he was in the sights of long-range rifles. Ryan could feel a prickle on the back of his neck.

Even as he thought of his own death, memories of Elias intruded into his thoughts: his touch, his voice. Ryan shook his head. The chances of making it out alive were very slim.

He had to stay alive long enough for Flynn to rescue Jasmine and Bo. His primary objective, the *only* objective coming back from Afghanistan, was to keep them safe. As with everything else in his life, even that had fallen apart.

Crossing the street, he made his way to the alley. A few people turned their heads, pity in their eyes. They no doubt thought he was another homeless man down on his luck, looking for a spot to drink his liquor in peace.

The alley was empty save for a single rusty door and a dumpster farther down. Ryan kept his hands visible, knowing that any sudden movement could bring it all to an end.

Caesar's instructions were clear: Wait in the alley with the papers. Now he waited, staring up into a security camera, the little red light glowing. Somewhere inside, Caesar Gretsky stared back.

Locks clicked from behind the door, and it opened.

A deep voice rumbled out. "Keep your hands where we can see them. Come through the door, slowly."

Ryan raised his hands and prayed Flynn was quick. He stepped inside, letting his eyes adjust. A single light bulb swung from the ceiling.

Remnants of surveillance equipment lay scattered on the ground, and in the center, a lone wooden chair faced the door.

Ryan's arm was yanked from behind and twisted behind his back. His body shoved hard against the wall, smashing his face on the hard plaster.

Ryan made no move to resist as the two men patted him down and took his gun. *Get them*, Flynn, he thought. *Let this be enough time.*

The man bound his hands tightly behind his back and forced Ryan into the chair. For the first time, he saw his two attackers. One man could have been a linebacker. The graying edges of his hair, balding top, and deep lines betrayed his age. The other was leaner, dressed in a suit, and had dark, intelligent eyes that bore through Ryan. He spoke into his phone. "He's clean, boss. "

The lean man bound his ankles with a zip tie as the linebacker kept a gun trained at Ryan's chest. Ryan watched them, trying to stay calm. Panic was his enemy.

The door opened, and Caesar stepped in. He stood framed in the doorway for a moment, eyes roving from Ryan's bearded face to his tattered sweats. "Papers?" he asked with a sharp tone.

"Inside my jacket," Ryan replied. "They're all there."

Caesar motioned to the lean man, who grabbed Ryan's jacket and reached into his pocket. Holding the papers reverently, he handed them to his boss.

Whipping out his reading glasses, Caesar looked them over. "They're all here," he said with a slow smile. "Congratulations, Ryan. The first smart thing you've done."

Caesar handed the papers to the man in the suit with a nod. He stepped closer to Ryan, then backhanded him hard across the face. The pain made Ryan grunt as he struggled to free his hands. Blood trickled onto his tongue.

"That was for Samir," Caesar said, eyes cold.

Ryan shook the cobwebs out of his head and stared defiantly forward. Caesar motioned to the two men. "Leave us."

The door closed, and they regarded each other in silence.

Ryan swallowed some of the salty blood. "You've got what you want, Caesar," he said. "Jasmine and Bo are innocent. Let them go."

Caesar smiled as he removed his reading glasses and stuffed them into his shirt pocket. "The widow and her son will be fine." He gazed at Ryan, then added, "As long as you comply."

Ryan gritted his teeth. If only he could break free and slug the bastard.

Caesar let out a mirthless chuckle and shook his head. "Show some respect, Ryan. I've kept your father's business running all these years. Sacrifices you couldn't even understand." Caesar stared at him. "A thank you will suffice." He was quiet, lips pursed, waiting for a reply.

"Thank you," Ryan spat. The words were bitter. Give Flynn time, he told himself.

Caesar stepped closer to him. An unwelcome hand came down and caressed Ryan's cheek. "Was that so hard? Following my orders? It was the first step." He tapped a hand on Ryan's chest. "One day, you'll feel it in your heart. I promise."

An alarm blared from behind them, the noise deafening. "What the hell?" Caesar yelled, covering his ears. Another curse left Caesar's lips as he opened the door. Ryan allowed a tiny bit of hope to enter his mind. Had Flynn activated the alarm?

Shouting out orders in the doorway, Caesar gestured towards his men. As soon as it began, the alarm went quiet. A tense silence followed. The only sound was the ringing in Ryan's ears.

Caesar returned, a triumphant smile on his face. "Looks like we have a guest."

Ryan watched him, and all hope evaporated.

"This couldn't be more perfect," Caesar continued.

Ryan struggled against the binders as the two men re-entered the room.

"Take him upstairs," Caesar ordered. "It's time to prove his loyalty once and for all."

A knife flashed out, and they cut the binders, each taking a side and lifting Ryan by the elbows.

Caesar's eyes bore into him as the men escorted him out. The likely scenarios playing in Ryan's mind all led to disaster.

CHAPTER 44

Ryan felt Caesar's eyes boring into his back as the elevator moved toward the top floor of Canyon Crest.

Two men flanked Ryan on either side, guns visible under their jackets. The zip-tie binding his wrists together became tighter the more he struggled.

Wherever they were taking him, Ryan didn't want to go.

The elevator doors opened, revealing a row of windows facing out towards the cityscape. A painful shove forced Ryan out into the hall. He glanced back at Caesar, who regarded him with smug satisfaction.

Caesar passed by them all and motioned to a door at the end of the hall. "Bring him in," he ordered.

Ryan entered, still flanked by the two men. What he saw inside took his breath away.

Flynn sat bound and gagged in the center of the room. His right eye was swollen shut, and a black bruise formed on his forehead. A tight gag absorbed blood oozing from his lips. One milky blue eye regarded Ryan with a stoic gaze.

Not able to take his eyes off Flynn, Ryan stepped forward. "What the hell did you do to him?" His eyes fell on Caesar. What he wouldn't give to have a gun in his hand right now.

Caesar moved closer and whispered in Ryan's ear. "He was the one who broke in."

Walking over to Flynn, Caesar slid a hand under his chin, jerking it upward. "Do you want to tell Ryan, or should I?" Caesar untied the gag and let it fall to the floor.

Flynn spat at him, hitting the mark on his white dress shirt. Swearing, Caesar threw a punch square in the gut.

"Pitiful," Caesar said, wiping the blood off his shirt as Flynn tried to catch his breath. "Cowardly." He turned his attention back to Ryan and gestured around the room. "This was your father's office at one time." He motioned to a portrait framed behind them.

Ryan turned and instantly knew that rugged face. His father smiled down at him, posed in a dark blue suit, arms crossed over his chest.

"The day your father died," Caesar continued, "Canyon Crest lost its most valuable leader. Stephen Blake gave everything, sacrificed everything so we could have this." He turned to Ryan. Blake is your true name—the name they wanted you to forget." His voice softened. "Did you forget it, Ryan?"

Countless memories came to life as Ryan gazed at his father's portrait. *Never speak that name.* The words echoed in his mind. We can only protect you if you forget everything.

But Ryan never forgot. He kept the pictures hidden and carefully protected. "I'll never forget him," Ryan said, almost to himself.

"That's right," Caesar replied, now eyeing Flynn. "Sigmund Anthony Flynn," Caesar said with relish, "you will now pay for your crimes."

Flynn glared back at Caesar defiantly.

"Leave him alone," Ryan said, stepping forward. "Flynn has nothing to do with this."

Caesar turned his gaze to Ryan with a tight expression. "He has everything to do with it, Ryan. Everything to do with you." He bent down close to Flynn. "Once more, do you want to tell him, or should I?"

Flynn sat stoic and quiet, not moving. His one eye fixed on Caesar.

"It's high time you learned the truth, Ryan." Caesar motioned to the portrait. "Seventeen years ago, Flynn shot your father in the back, like the coward he is." he prodded Flynn. "Tell him."

Flynn shook his head, gaze drawn to the floor.

Caesar's hand squeezed Flynn's shoulder tightly. "Tell Ryan what you did."

"No," Flynn said, wincing. "Just get it over with. Shoot me and get it over with."

"Tell Ryan, or the boy and his mother will suffer."

Flynn coughed, and a vein began to pulse in his neck. "It's true, Ryan. All true. I pulled the trigger. Shot him in the back."

Ryan gazed at him, unable to speak. He shook his head. No, this wasn't possible. Not Flynn. It had been some drunk thugs bent on revenge.

They were faceless, nameless boogeymen that haunted his dreams.

There had never been a name attached to his father's murderer. And now, as he gazed at Flynn, his chest tightened.

Caesar patted Flynn affectionately on the shoulder. "Was that so hard? So difficult?"

Pulling a revolver out from under his jacket, Caesar opened the chamber and let the bullets clatter to the floor.

He held up a single bullet towards Flynn. "This bullet will end your life. But I think it's only fitting that we savor the moment. A little game of Russian roulette will give you time to think about your crimes."

He placed the bullet in the chamber and spun it. Slowly, he raised the weapon at Flynn's head.

Flynn locked eyes with Caesar. "Do it," Flynn said, scowling. "Finish it."

Caesar pulled back the hammer and raised the gun, aiming between Flynn's eyes.

"No!" Ryan screamed and charged forward. Both guards grabbed him by the shoulders and restrained him.

Gretsky pushed the barrel into Flynn's temple. Ryan struggled with the guards as Caesar pulled back on the trigger. Flynn's eyes widened as a loud *CLICK* filled the room.

The Russian roulette had begun. Chuckling, Caesar turned towards Ryan. "One down, 5 to go. Ryan, get ready. You're up next."

Ryan stepped backward, shaking his head. "There's no way in hell I'm shooting him."

Caesar motioned to his men. "Free his hands."

The guards cut the ties and let them drop to the floor. Rubbing his sore wrists, Ryan shook his head. "Not like this. He'll confess, and I'll bring him to justice."

Caesar let out a mirthless laugh. "Do you really believe that Ryan? He'll be out in a heartbeat. Just ask Elias. We are the only ones who can bring him to justice."

In that instant, Ryan's entire life flashed before his eyes. Every step he had taken led to failure. Failed his platoon, failed Jack. Even failed Elias. And now, his father's killer sat in front of him. A chance to make right what went so very wrong.

"Do it, Ryan," Flynn said. "It's okay. Don't let this son of a bitch win. Do it for Jasmine and Bo."

The mention of Jasmine and Bo shook Ryan out of his racing thoughts.

His mouth was dry, and he turned to Caesar. "I need to know that Jasmine and Bo are safe."

Caesar thoughtfully nodded and motioned to his guards. "Get her on the phone, " one of the guards mumbled, then held the phone out to Caesar. Caesar pressed the speaker button and said, "I have Ryan here. Tell him you're okay."

"Ryan!" he heard Jasmine's panicked voice. "We're okay. I have Bo with me. We're okay." Hearing her voice gave Ryan a new resolve.

"Point the gun," Caesar said, "pull the trigger, and Jasmine and Bo go free." He took several steps towards Ryan, the gun lying in his hands, ready to be picked up and aimed. "Take it," he ordered.

The words swirled around Ryan's mind. He couldn't breathe, couldn't think. He took the gun from Caesar and felt the heft and smooth wood handle in his hands.

Caesar's voice was silky smooth. "Pull the trigger, and Jasmine and Bo will go free. You have my word."

Ryan's voice wavered. "Is it true, Flynn?" He swallowed, wanting more time to think.

Flynn's voice brought him back. "It's true, Ryan. I'm sorry." His eye was cloudy and locked onto Ryan's. "It was so many years ago."

Aiming the barrel at Flynn, he pulled back the hammer and fingered the trigger. This would never end. Another death, and he'd be forever in Caesar's debt and firmly under his control. "No, I won't do it," he said, taking a long breath. "Forget it, Caesar."

Caesar yanked the gun out of his grasp. "You coward," he sneered as he raised the gun, cocked the hammer, and pulled the trigger. Again, an empty CLICK.

Ryan rushed him and wrestled Caesar for the gun. As he fought Caesar, a heavy blow landed on his head. Stars exploded as Ryan fell to his knees.

Landing hard on his stomach, Ryan heard Caesar from above. "You will prove your loyalty. I promise."

Sprawled on the floor, Ryan glimpsed a familiar pair of eyes, staring at him through the cracked door. He locked eyes with Alicia Sandstone. What was she doing here? The thought rattled in his brain momentarily, and everything went dark.

CHAPTER 45

Alicia Sandstone slumped against the stairwell wall as shock threatened to overcome her. Any moment, a gun would fire, ending Sig Flynn's life. If I try to stop him, I'll be dead too, she thought, hands trembling.

Caesar took his smoke breaks in this stairwell. She hoped today would be no different. He'd made love to her in this very spot. It sickened her. She glanced up at the window, wanting to forget the image of him coming down on her.

Caesar assured her that the weekly meetings were optional. But the dark undercurrents were always there.

Refusing meant consequences. Caesar always wanted to know about one person: Elias Hastings.

Elias was Caesar's true obsession. Tears stung her eyes. Self-pity was not something she could afford to do.

Wiping her tears, she drew in a steadying breath. Caesar promised he wouldn't hurt Sig Flynn or Elias. Promised her.

Sitting in that room, her heart ached for Sig, clinging to his life. He had been the father she never had: both attentive and loving. He treated her like a goddess. She couldn't imagine her life without him.

Sometimes she needed to remind Caesar of his place like the night he ordered the attack on Elias.

Today, she would do it again. Caesar needed her to keep his little fantasy in place. A fantasy that would never become reality. Elias would never willingly come to him and be his.

She heard a voice and the creak of rusty hinges. Caesar entered the landing and whipped a cigarette case out of his suit. "Caesar," she whispered.

He turned, reaching for the gun in his belt. "Alicia, what the hell?" He took out a cigarette and reached for a lighter. His eyes roved down her low-cut dress as he lit up and took a long drag.

"You forgot our luncheon," she said, voice wavering. Her resolve was fading fast.

Caesar raised a brow. "You know very well my business can be unpredictable." He took a drag, blowing the smoke up towards the window as he ogled her cleavage. "But I'll make it up to you," he grinned. "I promise."

Alicia shook her head. "You promised not to hurt Flynn."

Caesar leaned against the wall, regarding her. "How much did you see?"

"Enough." She straightened and took a step forward. "You broke your promise, Caesar. This changes everything."

He chuckled as he blew smoke at her. "What are you going to do, Alicia? You want me to tell Elias everything?" He took a step closer and whispered in her ear. "Is that what you want me to do?"

She shook her head, glancing down, hoping he didn't see the fear in her eyes.

He continued, voice mocking. "Sweet little Alicia," he gave her a scornful smile, "spying on Elias this whole time. What would he think?" He let out a laugh and regarded her with steel-gray eyes. "You are nothing without me. I want to make that very clear."

Alicia turned towards the steps when Caesar grabbed her by the arm, fingers tightening. "You tell Elias anything, and he'll find out the truth. You're just another slutty piece of trash."

Gasping, she reached up to slap him with her other hand. He grabbed her wrist and twisted it painfully. No cry came out of her throat as she looked into those dangerous eyes.

She yanked herself away from him, almost tumbling down the stairs. His grip loosened, and she fled, not daring to look back. Once outside, she pulled a scarf over her head and fumbled for her dark glasses.

Alicia took one last glance up at the top floor of Canyon Crest. Sig needed her help.

She straightened her dress, then broke into a run for her car. Caesar was going to pay.

Elias's mansion seemed lonely now, shaded by trees and with no hint of life. The dark windows loomed down on her, and Alicia gazed up at it from her convertible.

Without Flynn, it was a horrible place indeed. Everything would fall apart without him. Sig had taken up the slack since Elias's permanent dark mood overshadowed every-thing.

Last week, she tried in vain to snap him out of it. $1000 for a male escort. He was gorgeous and took Alicia's breath away. Elias just kicked him out. She shook her head.

This was not the Elias she knew. And it couldn't just be about Ryan. That guy wasn't worth Elias's time of day. Alicia made her way up the steps, uncertain what she would find.

The entryway was piling up with empty liquor bottles and half-opened delivery packages. Elias was now officially a shut-in. "Elias?" she called out. There was no answer.

Taking up drinking was no way to solve his problems, and Elias knew it. If only she could show him how perfect his life was. Perfect with her by his side.

She found him lying in bed, the sheets over his head like a corpse. She let out a sigh of relief when his chest gently rose. He was alive. She nudged him. "Elias," she whispered, "wake up."

The breathing became deeper, and he rustled. "Ryan?" he slurred.

She bit her lip and shook her head. "Elias, please wake up. Sig is in danger." As soon as she said the words, his eyes snapped open.

"Flynn?" Bloodshot eyes met hers. His voice was raspy. "What happened to Flynn?"

Elias got up, wrapping the sheets around his waist. He glanced in the mirror and ran a hand through his hair.

"Flynn's in trouble, Elias," Alicia said, sitting on the edge of the bed. "Caesar has him."

Elias turned towards her. "You're sure?"

She tried to hide her growing impatience. "Don't ask questions, Elias," she snapped. "I know because I know."

"And how do you know?" His eyes narrowed. "What aren't you telling me?"

Shaking her head, Alicia closed her eyes as he came nearer. "The truth, Alicia. I need to know the truth if I'm going to help Flynn."

Memories of Sig's disfigured face came unbidden. The sobs threatened to come again, and she steeled herself.

She had to be strong for Sig. The words flowed from her like a dam that had waited so long to break. "You need to know this, Elias. Please don't hate me. I loved you from the moment I saw you."

Holding back a sob, the tears came unbidden. Elias put a steady hand on her shoulder, a gesture she knew she didn't deserve, but it calmed her. She had to pull herself together. For Sig.

Her eyes went down to the engagement ring on her finger. Don't do this, her mind screamed. Stop now.

Sig was going to die, she knew it in her gut, and it all came out in a rush. "It's all a lie, Elias. The whole thing."

She squeezed her eyes shut. "Caesar arranged our meeting all those years ago. Made me spy on you." The breaths came jagged now as she buried her head in her hands. Elias's hand came off her shoulder.

This was far worse than anything she could imagine. His next words tore her heart in two. "Alicia, how could you?"

She held her head high as she wiped the tears. "Save your hatred for another time. Sig is in danger, and we have to save him."

Elias dressed, opened a drawer, and pulled out a gun. "I'm finishing this once and for all." He slammed it shut and regarded her again.

Hatred filled those eyes. Smoothing out her hair, Alicia met his gaze. With just a few words, her entire universe crumbled around her. A nightmare of her own creation.

"Elias, if you go in there alone, Caesar will kill you. We have to go outside for help. Get your men together. We need the numbers."

He shook his head. "That ensures Flynn's death." He checked the cartridge in his gun. "I know what I'm doing."

"There's more," Alicia said, biting her lip. "He has Ryan prisoner, too. They struck him unconscious when I left."

Those eyes turned icy cold, and a shiver went down her spine as he regarded her. "Ryan," he repeated the name with a reverie she could only dream about.

Alicia swallowed. "Caesar made me frame Ryan." When she saw the pain in his eyes, she said simply, "He made me do it." The words were unconvincing, even to herself.

Elias said nothing but gave her a withering stare as he left the room.

"Elias!" she called out into the hall. She raced after him down the stairs. "Don't go after Caesar alone. Elias Hastings, you listen to me! You're going to get killed."

He never slowed down as the front door slammed shut behind him.

Alicia sunk onto the steps, feeling lost and alone for the first time since her arrest in Rome. She knew one thing for certain. This was the last mistake Caesar would ever make.

She had one last ace up her sleeve. It was the nuclear option, but to save Elias and Flynn, she would do it. Pressing her lips together, she took out her cell phone and dialed.

CHAPTER 46

R yan became aware of the cold floor beneath him. His hand stretched onto the damp cement, and he groaned. The smell of bleach was overpowering, and he turned his face to get away from it.

His eyes adjusted to the dim light, and he focused on the drain beside him. Dark red stains encircled the edges.

Panic rose inside Ryan as he forced himself to sit up. People disappear, echoed in his mind.

"You're awake," a familiar voice called out. Ryan turned towards the voice. Bound to a chair and hands tied behind his back, Flynn looked like a Mack truck had smashed into him. A shiner extended from his eye to his cheek, and dried blood crusted his skin.

Sig Flynn. Ryan grimaced. The sight of him made Ryan sick. The admission of guilt was still fresh and painful.

His father was shot in the back, helpless. No one ever told Ryan how his father died, and he never asked. It was the bad guys. Nameless and faceless monsters. Right now, the monster sat in front of him.

Out of the corner of his eye, Ryan spotted an object hidden in the shadows. Ryan reached for it and came up with a revolver.

He stared at it in horror. The same gun Caesar used in his horrific game of Russian roulette. What the hell? He flipped open the chamber and saw the single bullet waiting to meet its mark.

Flynn watched him intently from the corner. "The bullet is still there?"

Ryan nodded as he closed the chamber. "It is." A shiver went down his spine. What was Caesar's plan for them?

He tucked the revolver in his jeans and surveyed the room. Stained cement walls surrounded them, and a floor sloped towards the drain. Above their head, pipes fed through the ceiling. The only exit was a single metal door.

Gripping the handle, Ryan tugged and pushed. The door didn't budge. He stepped back and surveyed the room again. "Any idea where we are?"

"Basement, as far as I can tell. Recently occupied by the looks of things." Flynn nodded towards the blood on the floor.

Ryan flexed his fingers. If Caesar hurt Jasmine or Bo, Ryan would rip him apart with his bare hands. He drew in a deep breath to calm his racing thoughts. Think, he prodded himself.

"Let's get your hands freed." Ryan knew that taking the guards by surprise might be their only option. It would take two of them. He knelt behind and worked quickly to remove the tight knots. After a few minutes, the rope fell to the floor.

"This won't work," Flynn said, rubbing his wrists. "There's only one way out."

What do you mean by 'one way out?'" Ryan asked, stopping. "What aren't you telling me?"

Flynn scoffed. "You think either of us gets out of here alive? Wake up, Ryan. If Caesar doesn't get his way, we all die." He shook his head. "It's very simple. Prove your loyalty, and he frees Jasmine and Bo."

Nothing was ever that easy. Ryan shook his head as he slumped against the wall. His failures were stacking up, one after another.

Jasmine and Bo may already be dead. For an instant, he saw Jack's accusing eyes staring down at him through the smoke. Ryan failed then and failed now. His head pounded as he tried to form a coherent thought.

"Ryan," Flynn whispered. "Put the bullet right here." He tapped a finger on his forehead right between the eyes. "Quick and easy. The only way to save Jasmine and Bo."

Shaking his head, Ryan glared at Flynn. Playing Caesar's twisted games was the last thing he wanted. "I won't let Caesar win."

"Do it for Jasmine, then." Flynn stood unsteady on his feet and braced himself against the back of the chair. He glanced up at Ryan. "Do it for your father."

Ryan watched him for a moment. Sig Flynn looked so frail and helpless.

"What you said before...was it true?"

Flynn gazed at Ryan, bracing himself now against the wall. "That was a dark time."

His eyes glossed over for a moment, and he shook his head. "Elias's father, William Hastings, helped me out of the gutter when I wasn't much older than you. I owed him my life and loyalty and gave it without question."

"And my father?"

Glancing down at the floor, Flynn continued. "Your father, Stephen Blake, came on the scene like a wrecking ball, sparing nothing in his wake. No one even knew what hit them."

Flynn let out a wry chuckle. "Charisma and street smarts made your father climb to the top in record time. So much so that he threatened our operation." He gave his head a wistful shake. "We were only supposed to give a warning that day."

Ryan was held in rapt silence as Flynn continued. "It all went so very wrong." He grimaced. "Your mother had a terrible accident when we chased her. And that day, her death changed everything."

Flynn glanced away. Memories of running across the brush crashed back into Ryan's mind. He remembered screaming into the wind for his mom. Over and over again. She never answered, and she never would.

A pained expression came over Flynn's face. "A full-blown war broke out in the streets of Chicago. I swore to protect Elias's father with my life, and I failed the moment your father put that bullet through his brain."

Flynn's hands flexed. "I watched him die, helpless, and I raised my gun as your father fled."

Silence ensued. Ryan couldn't find any words as he stared at Flynn. They had taken everything. So senseless and depraved. A stupid vendetta. Flynn would pay someday. He would make sure of it.

"You have your father's eyes, you know." Flynn regarded him as he tilted his head to the side. "Keen, intelligent, and, oh, so haunted. Elias has that same haunted look. Perhaps that's what drew him to you...."

Elias. His heart ached at the thought of never seeing him again. Wished he could have said goodbye.

"If by some miracle you get out," Flynn said, "promise me you'll watch out for him. Elias doesn't have anyone. Not really."

Straightening, Ryan shook his head. "We're both getting out of here, and we're sure as hell not playing Caesar's games." Ryan stepped back and aimed the revolver towards the lock.

Before Ryan set his feet, a forceful blow came down on his arm, and the gun went clattering to the floor.

Ryan had no time to react as Flynn swept up the gun and backed away. No longer looking frail or injured, Flynn stood upright, the barrel pointed directly at Ryan. "Stay back," Flynn warned.

Ryan raised his hands and stood stone still. "What are you doing, Flynn? Give me the gun." Ryan held out his hand and took a step forward.

Flynn shook his head and squeezed his eyes shut. He pointed the barrel of the gun at his temple, finger itching on the trigger.

"Flynn, no!" Ryan ran forward but was stopped cold when Flynn drew back the hammer with his thumb. "You're not doing this, Flynn. Think of Elias. Think of Jasmine."

Repositioning the gun against his temple, Flynn said, "This is the only way."

Before Flynn finished speaking, Ryan lunged forward, grabbing Flynn by the wrists. They wrestled for control.

Flynn's finger held the trigger and gave a sudden downward jerk that took Ryan off balance.

The gunshot was instant and deafening, exploding into Flynn's chest. He collapsed to the floor, eyes wide in terror.

Ryan wrestled his jacket off and applied pressure to the wound. "Stay with me, Flynn. Don't you dare leave me."

"Tell Caesar you shot me. Promise me," Flynn whispered, one eye still focused on Ryan. "Save Jasmine and Bo."

"You're not going to die. I won't let you." Outside in the hall, Ryan heard footsteps getting closer.

Flynn reached a hand up, and Ryan grasped it. "For Jasmine," Flynn said as his fingers lost their grip and fell limp to the floor.

"Hold on, hold on, hold on!" Ryan yelled.

Echoes of Afghanistan invaded his senses. Sand clung to his nose and mouth as he held on to Jack. The staccato fire of bullets sounded in the distance. Jack whispered that same name as he died in his arms.

Ryan folded the jacket to increase pressure. He glanced back at the door, through which he heard loud voices and keys jingling.

He willed Flynn to keep breathing as the door creaked open. The next few moments meant life or death. And whatever happened, Ryan was ready.

Chapter 47

As he crossed the busy street, Elias dodged between angry commuters, deadlocked and honking. Wearing a courier uniform, Elias clutched the legal envelopes under his arm. He hoped the illegally acquired visitor badge was still valid.

Behind him, a man cursed and laid on the horn. Elias barely glanced at him. His mind was far away and focused on one man: Caesar Gretsky.

The amount of deceit and manipulation was beyond comprehension. One thing was now clear. Alicia Sandstone was the mole. The traitor he always suspected was there.

He had trusted her with his life and secrets, and her duplicity certainly caused death. Silently, he thanked the loyal men who gave their lives for intel on Gretsky's organization, but even now, it could be outdated.

His step quickened at the thought of Flynn. He couldn't comprehend life without him right now. He was a father, confidante, and advisor.

He had raised him since childhood, and now, one man had taken it all away. He might be too late, but not too late to exact revenge. Tonight was a long time coming.

A mere block away, the hairs on his neck prickled. Elias glanced behind him. Several people waiting for the bus stared down at their cell phones.

Above him, the rooftops were barren. A plane thundered overhead.

Nothing out of the ordinary. Trust your instincts, Flynn taught him. Always. Something wasn't right. A lingering glance here, a car driving slowly there. Nothing he could put a finger on. Every fiber of his being was on high alert.

Canyon Crest soon loomed before him, its white marble and mirrored windows reflecting the sunset's purplish hues.

He stopped across the street, glancing at the top floor. Was Caesar expecting him?

The master puppeteer, Elias thought. Caesar guided all of their lives with suffocating control. That's what Caesar liked. Absolute control. The man craved it. It was what had broken them up so long ago in Rome.

Caesar took everything and demanded more and more. And in the end, Caesar had obtained it. The ultimate control over Elias's life.

Alicia Sandstone had been the key, offering support to Elias while handing valuable information to Caesar behind his back. He hated them both.

Elias paused at the entrance to Canyon Crest. Caesar's words echoed in his mind: One day, you'll come, and I'll welcome you with open arms. Tensing his shoulders, Elias willed himself forward and opened the door.

A young security guard at the front desk glanced up when he entered. "We close in just a few minutes, sir," he said, pointing to the clock on the wall. "I'm afraid I can't let you enter."

"I just need to drop this off at accounting. They said it was urgent. It will only take a few minutes."

The guard sighed, eyeing the envelopes and glancing at his watch. "Be back in ten minutes sharp. The elevators and doors will all be locking soon."

Elias saluted him with two fingers and headed to the elevators. At the last minute, he veered to the stairwell. He punched in the code at the door. Nothing.

His pulse quickened as he glanced over his shoulder. He tried another 5764, and relief washed over him as the door handle twisted.

Sprinting up the stairs, Elias didn't pause as his lungs burned. The ten flights winded him, and he took a moment to catch his breath.

As he entered the hallway, only one guard stood sentry, and Elias smiled and held up the envelopes.

The middle-aged man's eyes narrowed. "Stop right there."

Elias held up the envelopes further. "I've got an important message for Mr. Gretsky. I have orders to give these directly to him."

The man glanced at him warily, then motioned Elias forward. When he was inches away, Elias grabbed his gun and struck the guard hard on the side of the head.

The guard slumped to the floor, unconscious. Elias drew in a deep breath and cracked open the door.

Seated behind an oak desk, a phone in his hand, was Caesar Gretsky. Elias raised his gun and approached.

Caesar was oblivious as he spoke into his cell phone. "No. There's no reason to worry. The papers are safe now." His eyes locked onto Elias, and he faltered for a fraction of a second. He recovered immediately and reached down under his desk.

"Hands where I can see them," Elias warned as he moved closer.

Caesar complied, and a slow smile spread over his face. "Elias Hastings. How good of you to come."

Elias drew closer, gun ready. "This ends tonight, Caesar."

Caesar steepled his fingers on the desk and continued to smile. "You won't make it out of here alive, Elias. You know that, don't you?"

Elias released the safety and aimed for Caesar's face, his finger caressing the trigger.

The smile on Caesar's face vanished, and he leaned back in his chair, crossing his arms over his chest. "If you want to see Flynn again, you will lower your gun."

The mention of Flynn made Elias hesitate, and his gun wavered. "Take me to Flynn. Now," Elias ordered, motioning for Caesar to stand.

Caesar did as instructed, a scowl on his face. "As for his life, you'll have to talk to Ryan. Flynn killed his father. He is the one you'll need to stop. Not me."

"For everything you've done," Elias said, "I should kill you right here and now." There was silence between them as Elias placed the gun at the back of his head, motioning him to the door.

Caesar let out a mirthless chuckle. "You need me, Elias," Caesar said. "You'll be under my protection, as I always promised."

Elias gripped the gun tighter. "Shut up."

"We could have been great together," Caesar continued. "And we still could be."

"Don't say another word," Elias warned as he motioned Caesar into the hall. A flash of irritation crossed Caesar's face when he regarded the unconscious bodyguard, then stepped over him to the elevators.

Caesar punched the down button as Elias stood behind him, gun at the ready. There was silence between them as the elevator began its descent.

Once it stopped, the doors opened with a chime, and Elias motioned for Caesar to exit in front of him.

The instant Caesar stepped out, a loud BANG resonated from the hall. Elias ran toward the sound as Caesar's guards rushed to unlock a door and enter.

Elias gasped at the sight in front of him. Flynn lay covered in blood, with Ryan over him, holding pressure. A revolver lay on the floor nearby. Elias rushed to Flynn's side.

"Sig," Elias said, grasping his hand. "Stay with us." His gaze traveled up to Ryan

"Elias," Ryan said, fear in his eyes as he pressed on Flynn's wound. "Call the medics. He won't last."

Grabbing his cell phone, Elias cursed when he saw no signal.

Caesar hovered over both of them, the guards with guns trained. He gave them a slow clap. "You've done well,

Ryan," Caesar said, gazing down at Flynn's lifeless body. "Your father would be proud."

There was a smile on Caesar's face. A smugness that infuriated Elias as he watched his life crumble around him.

Knowing it would mean his death, Elias raised his gun toward Caesar. A door slammed in the distance, and voices shouted. "What the hell?" Caesar asked, turning. It was too late.

Police officers rushed into the room, full body armor and automatic weapons at the ready. Within seconds, Caesar's guards surrendered. "Chicago PD," a familiar voice said. "On your knees. Hands where I can see them." Elias knew that voice and rugged face anywhere. It was Detective Lorenzo Chavez.

Elias threw his weapon down and got on his knees as rifles aimed at him. "We need medics!" Chavez shouted. "We need them now!"

Two officers rushed to Flynn's side as the detective turned to Caesar. His hands were now cuffed behind his back, kneeling. "I've waited a long time for this," the detective said with a smile. "Caesar Gretsky, you are under arrest for trafficking in weapons, money laundering, and drugs."

"That's outrageous," Caesar said indignantly, shaking his head. "You'll pay for this. I promise," he motioned over to Flynn. "Ryan Ward and Elias Hastings are the guilty ones, and I can prove it."

"Oh?" Chavez said with a smile. "Alicia Sandstone gives you her regards. She's collected an impressive amount of evidence against you. You're going to jail for a very long time."

Elias saw the shock cross Caesar's face. "She'll pay for this," he said under his breath. "She'll pay dearly."

She's under our protection now, Caesar." The detective motioned to his men. "Get him out of my sight."

More footsteps came down the hall as Detective Chavez directed the medics into the room. Men and women in white uniforms took over for Ryan. They started an IV and got Flynn on a stretcher.

"We've got a woman and child in this room!" a voice yelled from the hall. "They need medical attention!"

Elias watched Ryan rush out and tightly embrace Jasmine and Bo. Both were filthy and drawn, with parched lips and matted hair.

Then Elias and the detective faced each other. Detective Chavez offered him a hand up. "You get a pass this time, Elias. But I'll be watching you." Elias nodded as he rushed to Flynn's side. Ryan, Jasmine, and Bo soon joined him.

"Will he make it?" Ryan asked, his shirt soaked with Flynn's blood.

"Vitals are dropping," a medic said, spiking another bag of fluids. "He's lost a lot of blood."

Elias met Ryan's eyes, and they stood facing each other. The pain Elias saw there was unbearable. Hesitating, Elias took him into a tight embrace, feeling the trembling in Ryan's shoulders relax as he pressed him close. "Soon," he whispered in Ryan's ear.

Elias let go and sprinted after Flynn down the hall. The elevator doors opened, and the medics rolled him into the lift.

Taking Flynn's icy hand in his, he begged anyone or anything watching over them to intervene. "Stay with me, Sig," he said. There was no response or even a twitch on that pale face.

Tears filled Elias's eyes as they raised the stretcher into the ambulance.

Flynn had always been by his side. His true north amidst all the chaos. "Don't leave me." Flynn's thumb and forefinger gave a gentle squeeze on his palm. As soon as it happened, Flynn's hand fell away, unmoving.

Elias held on to that brief touch as the ambulance drove away.

Chapter 48

Ryan filled a Styrofoam cup with lukewarm coffee. At midnight, Memorial Hospital's cafeteria was a ghost town.

A couple of workers in scrubs grabbed a snack from the vending machine and left. Taking a sip of the bitter coffee, Ryan tried to wake up as he filled two more cups for Elias and Jasmine.

The entire night had been a blur.

Detective Chavez held Ryan for a full hour, extracting a lengthy deposition.

Fortunately, Jasmine found him a shower and fresh surgical scrubs to wear. She pointedly handed him a razor and muttered something about mountain men.

Running his fingers over his clean-shaven chin, he sighed. An unhappy Jasmine wasn't worth it.

He balanced the three cups on a cardboard tray as he walked the abandoned halls.

Hopefully abandoned, he told himself. The reporters smelled a good headline and were everywhere.

The last straw was Elias getting accosted in the bathroom stall. Security contained most of them, but they were determined.

A swarm of them waited outside the hospital, cameras and microphones at the ready.

A bright FLASH went off in Ryan's face. Blinded, Ryan tried not to tip over the tray as he stumbled backward.

A man in a black cap shoved a microphone in his face. "Officer Ward, do you have any comment on the arrest of Caesar Gretsky?"

"No comment," Ryan murmured as he changed course, hurrying back towards the cafeteria.

He took the stairs to the third floor, hoping to avoid more confrontations.

As he entered the surgery waiting room, it was as quiet as a morgue.

Jasmine and Elias glanced up.

Still in dirty jeans and a baseball cap, Elias's unruly black hair stuck out of the edges. He looked more like a street vendor than a wealthy CEO.

Even that disguise wasn't fooling the reporters. The bathroom incident proved that. At least Elias had enough restraint not to pop the guy in the jaw.

Elias's eyes roved down appreciatively to Ryan's surgical scrubs and back up to his newly shaven chin. A wistful smile crossed his lips as Ryan handed him the coffee.

"Any word?" Ryan asked, setting Jasmine's coffee beside her. Elias shook his head, gazing down into the murky coffee. Jasmine ignored the question and read her outdated Home and Garden magazine.

Jasmine refused treatment despite the ER doctor's many entreaties.

Nurses make the worst patients, Ryan heard the staff whisper behind her back. Bo was now safe with his grandparents. The little guy was doing fine despite being scared out of his wits.

Now, they all waited for word on Flynn. Ryan glanced at the clock. It had been over an hour.

A heavy silence fell over the room as nerves continued to fray.

Ryan sipped his coffee, watching the minute hand on the clock tick slowly. The events of the night played repeatedly in his mind. Elias had whispered soon in his ear. What had he meant? There was so much to say, to explain, and to ask. Would it all come to an end? The questions racing through his brain were too much to bear.

Elias set his coffee on the table and leaned in towards Ryan. He whispered, "Can I have a word with you out in the hall?"

Ryan glanced back at Jasmine, who ignored them and was absorbed in her magazine. As he followed Elias outside the waiting room, his stomach churned. What did he want?

Elias motioned him towards a pantry and ushered him inside. A small refrigerator hummed in the corner.

Elias closed the door and then gazed at Ryan. Those mesmerizing eyes penetrated him inside and out. Then he leaned down, a hand caressing Ryan's head as he brought him in for a gentle kiss.

Everything disappeared except Elias in that next moment. The hospital, the last few weeks, all melted in that embrace. Elias came up for air and held Ryan close. "I've wanted to do that since I first saw you tonight," Elias said, bringing Ryan in for a close embrace. "I could have lost you forever."

Ryan grabbed Elias's shoulder and took him in, wanting to savor the moment. It had been so long since he'd felt his touch. "Flynn tried to take his life to save us. You need to know that." Ryan knew the ugly truths of the past would haunt them all forever.

Shaking his head, Elias said, "There's so much to process." He took Ryan's hand. "We'll have time for that. But right now, I only know I want you in my life." He glanced around the small pantry. "If it needs to be hidden, so be it, but I'm tired of living a lie."

Wincing at the thought of Jasmine finding out his secret, Ryan paused. How would she react? How would his work react? There were so many unknowns. "Hidden is fine. I need to think about this. The consequences..." Elias cut him off by coming in for another kiss.

"Take your time," he said with a sly smile. "You're worth the wait." He took Ryan's hand and led him out of the pantry.

They released their hands before entering the waiting room. Jasmine glanced up from her magazine, then back down again, worry creasing her eyes.

Moments later, everyone froze as a young doctor entered the room, clipboard underarm. She smoothed out her white coat as she gazed at each of them. "Mr. Flynn is out of surgery. He's serious but stable."

Elias and Jasmine both let out a deep sigh of relief. "We had to place a chest tube," the doctor continued, "and we'll need to monitor him, but I think he's out of the woods. He's asking to see Elias."

When Elias stood, she said, "Please make it short; he needs to rest." Elias nodded and followed her out.

Jasmine stood and embraced Ryan. "This is good news," she said. "Hopeful news."

It was just Jasmine and him, and Ryan felt his chest tighten. He had to tell her. So many times, he tried, then chickened out. He licked his dry lips. "Jazz, I need to talk to you."

Concern flooded Jasmine's eyes. "What is it, Ryan? What's wrong?"

Ryan drew in a long breath. There was no going back after he started. Chaotic thoughts whirled around in his brain. What if she didn't want to see him anymore?

He didn't think he could handle that. Jazz continued to watch him, her face increasingly worried. "You're scaring me. What is it? Did something else happen to you?"

Ryan closed his eyes and tried to summon up courage. At the moment, he'd rather face enemy fire. Anything else. "Umm," came out of his mouth. He drew in another breath and turned to face her. "Jazz, I need to tell you this."

He watched her a moment and said the words, "I'm gay." His face flushed, and his entire body felt like it would catch fire. He felt himself babbling. "I should have told you first thing. I don't know if this will affect our friendship. I'm sorry I didn't tell you before. I understand if this changes everything."

As Ryan gazed down at his shoes, words spewed out of his mouth. He wasn't even sure what he said next. He looked up when a giggle escaped Jasmine's lips.

"Is that what you wanted to tell me? Oh, honey, I've known." She stifled a smile. "How could I not? That moment, I caught you and Elias in the hall." She shook her head, an amused smile spreading over her face. "That was the clincher."

Hot heat spread across his face. Jasmine chuckled again and embraced him. "I love you just the way you are, Ryan Ward. Never forget it. And Bo will understand, too." She took his hand in hers. "Jack would have felt the same way. I know it."

The entire world disappeared around him as Ryan stood in stunned silence, his mouth open as he regarded Jasmine.

"There's a problem, though." Her eyes tightened as she moved away. Ryan knew everything would fall apart now. The reality of the situation would hit her hard. He knew it in his gut.

Ryan gazed into her unreadable brown eyes, waiting. Finally, Jasmine said, "I've got to find a way to tell my niece." She shook her head. "She'll be heartbroken."

Ryan punched her in the arm, trying not to laugh as a smile broke out on Jasmine's face.

Voices came from the hall, and they both turned towards the door. "Go get your man," Jasmine prodded, motioning to the doorway.

Ryan smiled at her as she gave him a wink.

Outside, Elias talked to several doctors. He acknowledged Ryan out of the corner of his eye.

"How is he?" Ryan asked, walking up to him.

Elias shrugged. "He's stable but very weak." His voice caught, and he continued, "I talked to the surgeon, and I think he will be okay. I will stay here tonight and make a brief statement to the press outside." His eyes turned cold. "Our investors are getting itchy."

"I'll come with you," Ryan said.

Elias raised his brows regarding him. "Ryan, I'd love to have you with me, but," he paused, "it'll cause more questions. I have to warn you."

"I don't care," Ryan said, not looking away from Elias's eyes.

A slight smile crossed Elias's lips as he nodded, leading him out of the surgery center and into the hall.

Outside the hospital, reporters were bundled up in their coats, waiting. When the front doors opened, they all shoved forward, shouting questions in unison.

Elias cleared his throat as he stood on the steps above them. A hush fell over the crowd. "Caesar Gretsky is behind bars," he told them, as camera lights flashed, "and those he took are now safe. Sig Flynn is stable and out of surgery." He paused for a moment. "The events tonight are not related to Hastings Enterprise. I want to make that very clear." Ryan stood by his side, watching reporters take notes and more cameras flashed.

A man shouted out. "What about the Chicago PD?" He pointed a pen at Ryan. "What's Officer Ward's involvement?"

Elias smiled and turned his gaze to Ryan, who nodded. In one motion, he took Ryan into a deep embrace and kissed him right there on the steps. Lights flashed as the kiss lingered between them. Ryan gazed up at Elias, smiling. At that moment, there was no place he'd rather be.

CHAPTER 49: EPILOGUE

Six months passed in a heartbeat, and Ryan gazed in the mirror, fumbling with his bow tie. Elias insisted on not having a clip-on for the wedding; this was his third attempt to tie it.

He squinted in the darkness of the church vestry. The little stained-glass window far above wasn't helping.

The bow tie wouldn't defeat him. Not today. Years ago, he'd learned to make the perfect bow, but his fingers weren't cooperating. After a couple of folds, it crumpled in a mess around his neck.

Jasmine tried twice before throwing her hands up in the air. As Ryan's best man, Bo was still indignant about Elias's ring. "I won't lose it. I promise!" he grumbled as they left.

"I'll give it back," his mom said with a wink. "Just a little longer."

Already, the church was packed. They chose the same place where Jack's memorial was held. Ryan felt closer to him here and hoped he somehow knew how much he was missed, especially today.

The old stone church harkened back to the late 1800s, complete with a bell tower and a beautiful stained-glass window overlooking the altar.

Elias wasn't sure about the old church at first. He was all in when he heard about Jack, sparing no expense. If there was ever a definition of bridezilla, Elias fit the bill.

Everything had to be perfect: from the flowers to the reception to folding the napkins correctly. Ryan smiled as light violin music floated up from downstairs. Voices rose and fell with laughter.

Detective Chavez offered Ryan a job in the White-Collar Crimes Unit a few months ago. It was fascinating work that kept Ryan on his toes, with the benefit of better hours.

Ryan's high-profile relationship didn't cause much of a stir at work. This was thanks to Sergeant Collins, who suddenly introduced everyone to her wife. She also put together Ryan's bachelor party at Rumors.

The bachelor party was memorable. Ryan smiled. His former partner Fritz had come a long way, even dancing with Esmerelda to "I Will Always Love You." Now, that was a sight Ryan would never forget.

Ryan took the bow tie in his hands for another attempt when a knock came from the door. "Come in."

Sig Flynn stood in the doorway, dressed in his suit coat, looking debonair and trim. He walked with a slight limp but grew stronger each day.

After his discharge, Jasmine made it her mission to get him better. "She's worse than any drill sergeant," Ryan heard him complain, but always with a twinkle in his eye.

As for Ryan, Flynn mostly avoided him since the incident with Caesar. They were cordial, yet distant, more so once Elias proposed.

"I heard you needed some help," Flynn said gruffly, eyeing Ryan's bow tie.

"I got it." Once again, Ryan started the process—left over right and up through the top. The resulting tangle was cringe-worthy.

"Let me see that." Flynn grabbed onto the tie. With a few deft moves, he finished the perfect bow. Turning Ryan towards the mirror, Flynn admired his handiwork.

"Thanks. I appreciate it," Ryan said, smoothing out his jacket.

Flynn stepped away from him, pointing to the door. "Well, I better get over to Elias. If he changes one more thing, I swear I'll punch the living daylights out of him."

Ryan nodded with a knowing smile. The changes had been non-stop since they first started planning.

Flynn stopped at the door before leaving as an uneasy silence enveloped the room. "Something I've been meaning to say," he said, eyes cast down on the stone floor.

Clasping his hands behind his back, Flynn's eyes rested warily on Ryan.

"Elias has been so happy," he began, "since you came into our lives."

He looked down at his shiny black shoes. "I can't make up for the past." His voice trailed off as he drew in a ragged breath. "Your father would be proud today." He came forward and placed a hand on Ryan's shoulder. "I promise I'll do all I can to protect you and Elias. You have my word."

Those few words meant so much to Ryan as he gazed at Flynn. The past was too painful and too complicated for all of them. "That means a lot, and I hope in time," Ryan said, glancing down, "we can put the past behind us."

Flynn gathered him into an enormous bear hug. So tight he couldn't breathe. "I'm so proud to have you in the family," he whispered in Ryan's ear. With those words, he released his grip and left, closing the door behind him.

Ryan watched the door as Flynn's words echoed back into his mind. He adjusted his cuffs and smoothed down his hair.

If only he could see Elias once more before the ceremony. Flynn said it wasn't proper, and as the best man, he forbade it. "You'll have plenty of time after the ceremony," he chided, rolling his eyes. Still, Ryan longed to see him one last time.

Another knock came from the door, and Ryan smiled to himself. It had to be Elias.

Upon opening it, Ryan's eyes widened as he took in a delivery man holding 24 red roses and a lavender envelope.

"Who's this from?" Ryan asked as the man pushed the flowers into his arms.

"No return address. Sorry," the man said, shrugging. "Congratulations on the wedding, sir." With that, he turned on his foot and scurried away.

Ryan set the flowers down on the side table. An icy sensation went down his spine when he gazed at the envelope.

In flowery print were the words Ryan Blake. His father's name. There was only one person who would send that: Caesar Gretsky.

His hands trembled as he tore open the envelope and brought out the lavender-scented paper.

Dear Ryan,

I'm going to beat these bogus charges. That's a promise. Someday we will fulfill your father's dream at last.

Fondly,

CG

Caesar's trial was coming soon, and Alicia Sandstone was the primary witness. He looked at 20 years to life, and with the amount of evidence. Detective Chavez was confident he'd be put away for a long, long time.

Ryan was staring at the flowers when he heard footsteps behind him. An arm came around his chest and took him into a tight embrace.

Ryan knew those hands anywhere. He turned and looked up into Elias's sparkling eyes. "I got away from my jailer," Elias said, grinning. "I wanted just another moment with you." He glanced back at the door. "Are you ready?"

Elias straightened Ryan's bow tie and took in every inch of him, from his head down to his toes. "You look amazing. Better than amazing." He smiled as he drew Ryan into a soft kiss.

"Who are the flowers from?" Elias asked as he gazed at the table.

When Ryan remained silent, Elias's eyes narrowed, and he picked up the letter.

"Just like Caesar," Elias said, grimacing as he read. He crumpled up the paper and threw it in the trash. "That's the last gasp of a drowning man," he said, eyes cold. "I won't let him ruin this day."

He took Ryan's hands in his own as his gaze softened. "I love you. I don't deserve you, but I love you." Elias glanced again at the roses. "Your life will never be boring." He traced a finger down Ryan's cheek. "That, I can promise."

Ryan smiled at him. "I wouldn't have it any other way."

Elias leaned in and took Ryan into a deep kiss. Ryan closed his eyes and savored the moment. "Are you ready for this?" Elias asked with a shy smile. "They're waiting for us."

Sunlight streamed through the upper windows as they stepped out of the vestry. Gazing into Elias's eyes, Ryan felt his love erase all those years of darkness and searching. He grabbed Elias's arm as they walked together into the light.

AFTERWORD

Thank you for reading! Though my journey with coming out was much different from this book, I'd love to see the day where coming out isn't fraught with so many difficulties including the heartbreak of losing family. A part of the proceeds from this book will go to the Trevor Project, protecting LGBTQ youth, a subject near and dear to my family's heart.

Stay in touch for new releases and updates:

Sign Up For The Newsletter! or go to SLDieruf.com

Please consider a review of this book. Reviews are a great way to support authors, and the feedback is invaluable.

www.ingramcontent.com/pod-product-compliance
Lightning Source LLC
Chambersburg PA
CBHW071147100726
47908CB00002B/276